The Recollections of Sherlock Holmes

Arthur Hall

Edited by David Marcum

Paperback ISBN 978-1-80424-182-0
ePub ISBN 978-1-80424-183-7
PDF ISBN 978-1-80424-184-4

MX Publishing
335 Princess Park Manor, Royal Drive,
London, N11 3GX
www.mxpublishing.com
Cover design by Brian Belanger

Arthur Hall was born in Aston, Birmingham, UK, in 1944. His interest in writing began during his schooldays and served as a growing ambition to become an author.

Years later, his first novel 'Sole Contact' was an espionage story about an ultra-secret government department known as 'Sector Three' and has been followed, to date, by five sequels.

Other works include seven 'rediscovered' cases from the files of Sherlock Holmes, three collections of short stories featuring The Great Detective, two collections of bizarre tales and two novels about an adventurer called 'Bernard Kramer', as well as several contributions to the ongoing anthology, 'The MX Book of New Sherlock Holmes Stories'.

His only ambition, apart from being published more widely, is to attend the premier of a film based on one of his novels, ideally at The Odeon, Leicester Square.

He lives in the West Midlands, United Kingdom, where he often walks other people's dogs as he attempts to formulate new plots.

His work can be seen at: arthurhallsbooksite.blogspot.com, and the author can be contacted at: arthurhall7777@aol.co.uk

By the same author:

Contents:

The Adventure of the Christmas Threat

In the years of my association with my friend, Mr Sherlock Holmes, I was privileged to witness many demonstrations of his remarkable abilities. By means of his skill in deductive reasoning he solved many an intriguing puzzle, and brought villains to book who would otherwise have escaped justice. Murderers, blackmailers and perpetrators of the vilest crimes found themselves in the hands of the official force as a result of my friend's investigations, far too few of which were ever accredited to him. There were also occasional cases laid before him which turned out in a most surprising manner, where Holmes' enquiries revealed that where wrongdoing was suspected there was none, where it was thought that a criminal was at work there was only circumstance.

As I reflect in particular upon these, the example which comes immediately to mind is that of Mr Clarke Jefferson, who presented himself at our lodgings unexpectedly late on a Christmas Eve which had seen Holmes conclude no less than three cases without leaving our sitting room.

My friend stretched his thin body, and sighed with satisfaction.

I lowered my newspaper, glancing towards the window and the thickening dusk. "I take it that everything has transpired as you predicted, Holmes? Can we now allow some Christmas spirit to enter our lives before you embark upon another investigation? As your doctor, I advise rest and relaxation for the next few days at least. I have observed your recent behaviour, and your increasingly nervous demeanour has not escaped me."

"Do not concern yourself, old fellow." He sat up straight in his chair and folded his arms across his chest. "I have no work, other than four cases which I expect to see the end of early in the New Year, to occupy me. What else then, can I do but spend my time idly, as you suggest? As for my behaviour, I admit that the Yardworth scandal has taken its toll of my resources, but I expect the effects to be much lessened before the month is out." He glanced at me and I felt, not for the first time, that he could see into my thoughts. "Oh, do not worry, Watson, I have no intentions towards the cocaine bottle."

I gave him a critical glance, before rising to pour us both a glass of port. We wished each other compliments of the season, and reminisced for a while about his activities since this time last year. Presently Mrs Hudson, our good landlady, brought us a fine dinner of roast pork, and I was glad to see Holmes attack it with unaccustomed relish.

When the remains of our food had been cleared away, we again repaired to our armchairs. I saw that my friend had paused to peer from the window, his attitude suddenly becoming wary.

"Has the snow ceased yet?" I asked.

"It has, and frozen hard. There is not a cab to be seen, but my attention was drawn to a fellow slipping and sliding about the pavement in a comical fashion. It was only as I saw him scrutinize the doors as he passed that I realised that he is bound for here."

I put down my unlit pipe. "Oh no, Holmes, not on Christmas Eve."

"It is possible, Watson, that it is *your* assistance that he seeks."

"But unlikely. I ensured that my practice displayed a notice advising that I am unavailable until after the holiday, together with the address of the nearest hospital. Must you really undertake this now?"

"I have never stated that I consult only within certain hours." He smiled rather slyly, I thought. "But take heart, Watson, we do not yet know what this gentleman seeks. It may be something which I can settle here and now. At the very least, it will give me something to consider over Christmas."

I sighed and scowled as the door-bell rang, and after a short exchange Mrs Hudson announced a man of about thirty years, and of average height. As she withdrew, looking rather surprised at the hour, he removed his hat and faced us cautiously.

His glance flitted from Holmes to me and back again. "Gentlemen, am I addressing Mr Sherlock Holmes?"

"You are indeed, and this is my friend and colleague, Doctor John Watson. Tell me Mr Clarke Jefferson, what is it that brings you to us on a freezing Christmas Eve? But first, remove your muffler and greatcoat and come to sit near the fire, for I see that the cold has affected you."

Our guest complied, his face red from the icy wind. I poured a brandy from the decanter which he drank gratefully, before I took my seat. Holmes leaned forward in his chair, with the air of a hound awaiting the signal to begin a pursuit.

"My first thought, sirs, was to take this matter to Scotland Yard, but then I realised that I have no actual crime to report. I confided in a passing constable who confirmed this, before I recalled seeing mention of you in the newspapers."

"That occurs more often than I would like. But please, begin your story at the beginning, leaving out not the smallest detail. You are far from the first to consult me while undecided as to whether there has been criminal activity. As for Doctor Watson, I assure you that you can trust him as you would me. He has been invaluable in many of my investigations, and is the soul of discretion."

Mr Jefferson nodded. "Thank you, gentlemen. I will try to put my thoughts in order."

"Pray do so," said Holmes. "There is no need to hurry. All I know of you thus far is that you are of Scottish descent, that you work in a clerical capacity, possibly an accountant, and that you have at some time in your life barely escaped with your life from the ravages of a fire."

Our client's face went suddenly blank. "But how could you know those things, Mr Holmes? Your landlady announced me by name, but I have revealed nothing more."

"Surely there is no mystery about it. Your accent betrays your birthplace, or where you have resided until recently, the ink stains upon your fingers and cuffs force me to an obvious conclusion regarding your employment and the scars upon the back of your neck appear to be from burns, though not sustained recently. Is it these that begin your story?"

"Why no, sir." He shook his head slowly, looking confused. "I have no memory of anything of the kind. I always thought of the blemishes as birthmarks."

"Then perhaps they are. I have seen similar, before now."

"No, the matter that I am here about has its beginnings five years ago, when I lived in Edinburgh. I received a letter on

Christmas Eve bearing the message 'I am coming for you', which I could make neither head nor tail of, so I discarded it. I thought nothing more of it, but it came to mind again the following year on the same day, that is to say Christmas Eve, when another message arrived containing exactly the same words. Since then, although I have moved to the capital, a similar such letter has arrived every year at the same time. Finally, I received another in this morning's post."

"But it was different on this occasion," Holmes ventured, "or there was something added."

"Why do you say that, sir?" Mr Jefferson gave my friend a curious look.

"Why else would you choose to act upon this now, after the incident has been repeated for several years?"

"Of course. Yes, you are quite right, Mr Holmes. The additional message was 'Today you will remember Miranda'."

"Is that a name familiar to you?"

Our visitor shook his head. "Not at all. I should tell you that I have no memory of my past before the days when the first letter came to me. I can recollect only that a priest, Father Amos Wilton, and his good wife took care of me after I was found wandering the streets of Edinburgh by one of his parishioners. I have been told that I was raving like a madman and in some distress. The good fellow took me to Father Wilton's home, where I was taken in. Apparently it was feared that I would end my days in an asylum, but the priest resolved to attempt to restore me to health."

"Evidently he was successful," Holmes observed. "You have said that you have no previous memory?"

5

"None whatsoever."

"Except your name?"

"Ah yes, only that."

"We have established that you occupy a clerical position. How then, in the circumstances that you describe, did that come about?"

"For that my gratitude to Father Wilton's wife is endless. Recognising that I would need to earn a living, she instructed me daily until I attained a level of proficiency. She herself had been taught by her father, years before. After two years, having fully recovered, I moved to London where I joined the firm of Cutler & Maybright. I have audited the books of many of their clients ever since."

"I know of them," Holmes murmured, "near Westminster."

"These letters then," I interjected. "Could they not be some sort of jest, by someone from your unremembered past?"

"That is possible, I suppose but, as I have said, I have no recollection of either persons or events before Father Wilton appeared in my life. He often expressed hope that my memory would return one day, but that has yet to happen."

"You are certain that the words in the letters mean nothing to you?" Holmes asked then. "I perceive that they have caused you to fear, nevertheless."

Our visitor nodded. "I understood the message to be a threat, from an unknown source. As it has persisted for so long, it has begun to cause me anxiety. This the more so and, forgive me, I should have mentioned this, because on each occasion the postmark revealed that the sender has drawn nearer. The first letter was posted in

Edinburgh, as I have already stated, then Newcastle, Sheffield and Birmingham."

"And the arrival of this morning?"

He withdrew an envelope from his coat and handed it to my friend. "It was posted in Surrey."

"So it would seem," Holmes concluded, after examining the envelope and the single sheet that he withdrew from it. "The paper and envelope are quite ordinary and, apart from the fact that the writer uses cheap ink and holds his pen in a trembling hand, I can deduce nothing. It appears that the threat, whatever it may be, is now imminent."

"That, sir, is why I have consulted you at such a late hour. I have been going about my business cautiously until now, until there are but a few hours remaining. I know of no other place to turn."

"I take it that you live alone."

"That is so. My maid calls daily, otherwise I am rarely visited."

"You employ no cook?"

"None. I often eat in hotels or restaurants, save when I prepare a simple meal at home."

"Why, I wonder, has it taken the writer so long to arrive at a point where you are within his reach," I mused. "He has known of your whereabouts for three years, or he could not have sent the letters."

"Quite so, Watson." Holmes got to his feet and walked over to the curtained window. "Doubtlessly this will become clear as we progress."

He stood in silence for a few minutes, during which I knew his mind was racing. The crunching of a carriage along the snow-laden street reached us faintly and I saw our client shiver, although whether this was in anticipation of his forthcoming return to his residence in freezing conditions or of what might await him there, I could not tell.

"Could it be," Mr Jefferson proposed, breaking the silence, "that I have been mistaken for another? Perhaps I am being persecuted for deeds that I have not committed."

Holmes glance settled upon him, and for an instant I thought that he was angered by the interruption of his thoughts, but his expression was one of mild concern as he spoke:

"Mr Jefferson, I am unable at the moment to form any definite conclusions. I advise you, therefore, to first furnish Doctor Watson with the address of your place of residence and that of Father Wilton, and then to return to your home. It will not be easy to procure a hansom, but there are bound to be several abroad despite the inclement weather. I suggest extreme care during the journey – ensure that you are not followed – and that you examine the snow near your front door to ascertain whether your premises have been entered in your absence. Once inside, you must bolt your door and answer it to no one save Doctor Watson and myself."

"I am most grateful to you both," our visitor stammered, a little taken aback by my friend's instructions. "I cannot tell you the relief you have brought to me."

"Good evening to you then," Holmes said dismissively, and I took this as a signal to show our client out into the freezing darkness.

I returned to find Holmes leaning to peer through a gap in the curtains, remaining in that position for some little time.

"Mr Jefferson has secured a cab," he informed me at last, letting the curtain fall back into place. "Where is he bound for. Watson?"

I lowered myself into an armchair and consulted the notes I had made from our client's dictation. "He lives in Highgate, not far from Hampstead Heath."

Holmes nodded his head. "I regret I must leave you for a while, old fellow. The poor weather aside, I cannot exclude the possibility that our client's mysterious correspondent might seek to do him some harm, this night. I intend to prevent that, if I can." He reached for his ulster and ear-flapped travelling cap as I rose from my chair. "No, do not allow me to disturb you. I would not presume upon your good nature, at such a time."

"Holmes, I insist."

He smiled warmly, handing me my greatcoat and hat. "I thought I knew my Watson."

We stood shivering, outside our lodgings. I anticipated a long and possibly futile wait, but Holmes seemed little surprised when a hansom appeared after less than five minutes had passed. I watched as the cabby kept his horse at a slow pace, treading carefully upon the icy surface. He acknowledged my friend's instruction with a muffled sound, from behind a thick scarf that he had wound around his face.

The journey to Highgate seemed interminable, because of our necessarily slow rate of progression. Holmes said little, but looked out onto the icy scene from time to time with, I thought, some impatience. I could tell, from his frequent shiftings in his seat, that he was anxious for the welfare of our client and I was glad that I had brought along my service revolver although he had not requested me to do so.

Albermarle Street, and particularly number fourteen where Mr Jefferson resided, was unremarkable. The heavy snow could not conceal the monotonous regularity of the dwellings, each with identical doors and darkened windows in a solid square structure. As the hansom, the driver having received an extra half-sovereign, retreated slowly from our sight, we turned our attention to our surroundings.

"There are two sets of footprints, approaching the house," I observed, "and one leaving."

"Indeed," Holmes replied. "As you see from their shape, those which both arrive and leave are of a woman, which will be the maid. There has been a fresh snowfall since early this morning, so our client's departure is obscured. Not so his recent return."

"We can be certain then, that no intruder awaited Mr Jefferson tonight."

"Unless he gained entry elsewhere. This is unlikely however, since the snow is undisturbed around the passage at the side of the house, and I can see no other means of ingress."

"If our adversary is to arrive tonight then, it must be soon."

Holmes smiled thinly. "And we shall be here to greet him. There is no need for us to seek a place of concealment for, as you see, our client's house has a deep doorway. If we stand within the alcove we will be quite invisible, if uncomfortably cold."

Our vigil was indeed devoid of comfort, since we could not stamp our feet or otherwise move to maintain our circulations against the bitter cold for fear of alerting our unknown adversary.

We had stood, still and silent, for no more than ten minutes when a figure appeared from around a nearby corner, losing his balance frequently and barely recovering it while making his way towards us. As he approached I saw in the light from a nearby street-lamp that his movements were that of a young man but was able to discern little else, since his long coat almost touched the ice beneath him and his muffler effectively concealed his face. He carried, with some difficulty, a large square parcel which was covered in thick paper and secured with string.

"Good evening," Holmes said as the parcel was placed near the doorstep.

The effect on the young man was electrifying. For an instant he became absolutely still, before turning and retracing his steps at a run. Three times he fell headlong, and Holmes and I almost laid our hands upon him, but the treacherous surface defeated us and we were obliged to strive to remain upright. When he had disappeared around the corner from which he came, Holmes put his hand upon my arm.

"He may have fallen as he entered the next street. Come, Watson, we shall see."

We made our way carefully and almost disastrously to the other side of the street and around the corner. We were met by another deserted scene, with the only movement a cart diminishing unsteadily and already some distance off.

"He had his escape well planned," Holmes commented. "But I fear for the horse if he maintains such a speed."

We made our way back to our client's home and Holmes retrieved the parcel.

"I am sure that Mr Jefferson will soon display the contents for us," I anticipated. "Let us see if we can rouse him."

I raised my stick to beat upon his door, but Holmes at once prevented me.

"No, I think we will return to Baker Street with this. I do not propose to alarm our client further. If he remains inside with the entrances secured, as I advised, he should be safe enough for now."

It was fortunate that a passing police coach saw us and came to a halt as we trudged through Highgate. We had endured the appalling conditions as far as the High Street, when the familiar voice of Inspector Gregson offered to share the conveyance.

"I am much obliged to you, Gregson," Holmes said gratefully as we took our seats. I concurred and saw that the inspector glanced more than once at the parcel my friend carried, although he did not refer to it. We arrived back at our lodgings with little conversation and without further incident, and wished our companion and his driver the compliments of the season before they left us.

I knew that Holmes would be eager to open the parcel before retiring, and my own curiosity compelled me to witness this, so it was with glasses of brandy in our hands that we sat with the flat object on the floor between us. After a single sip, he picked it up and ran his hands over its surface.

"About three feet by eighteen inches, wouldn't you say, Watson? No more than three inches in depth. The surrounding paper is firm at the edges but tightly stretched towards the centre, where the depth is approximately less by at least an inch."

He produced his pocket knife and severed the string, then carefully stripped away the paper to reveal a portrait of a strikingly beautiful woman.

"Mr Jefferson's forgotten wife, perhaps," I ventured. "If there was one."

"Possibly, but in any event I think we have made the acquaintance of Miranda."

He examined the frame which was new, as was the portrait.

"Is there any indication as to the artist," I enquired.

"I should be very surprised if there were none. Here, you see, is his signature, which appears to tell us that his name is J. Brunt, and this tiny metal plaque affixed to the back of the frame gives his address as 9, Mundell Court, Hammersmith, where we shall certainly call upon him in the morning."

Our Christmas breakfast was, not for the first time, more appreciated by me than by my friend. We then set out upon a walk until we eventually procured a hansom, which on Christmas Day was not without its difficulties. We arrived at Mundell Court to find the premises, between a saddler's and a maker of walking canes, locked and empty.

"He realised, perhaps, that we would be calling," I said as we stood before the tiny studio.

"Possibly, but it is more likely, I think, that he is at home celebrating. This address is clearly where he plies his trade, rather than his accommodation. Our adversary has made a serious error though, in neglecting to tell Mr Brunt to refrain from leaving any indication of his name or whereabouts on his work. We shall see if he resumes his attendance here tomorrow, let us hope that he has sufficient commissions on hand to make that necessary."

The remainder of Christmas Day was spent contentedly in our lodgings. I have seldom tasted the equal of the superlative luncheon that Mrs Hudson produced a little after mid-day, and was glad to see my friend in such fine spirits as to do justice to the roast goose and plum pudding. Holmes had put aside a fine wine to accompany our meal, and an excellent cognac which we shared with our good landlady when she appeared to remove our plates.

Afterwards, he stood staring from our window as I took my seat near the fireplace. The joyful strains of carol singers reached us faintly from the frozen street.

"Extraordinary, don't you think, Watson, how men suspend their grievances during the festive season. I have just seen no less than three examples of this, men who I know to be not on good terms now acknowledging each other cheerfully though they are usually rivals or enemies."

I looked up from my copy of the latest edition of *The Standard*. "It is, after all, the season of goodwill."

"True, but can you imagine some of the vicious criminals that we have encountered on occasion, changing their ways temporarily in acknowledgement of it?"

"I must confess…" But my response was cut short, for Holmes' posture had altered and I saw that something had arrested his attention.

"I wonder," he said after a moment, "if that young woman is connected with our present enquiry, or if she represents something new. She has evidently decided not to disturb us on Christmas Day, but I suspect she will return before long."

I put aside my reading. "What has happened out there?"

"A hansom discharged its passenger directly opposite, and the woman alighted. That she was enduring an agony of indecision was obvious from her movements, side to side and thrice starting to cross towards us. She looked up finally, and saw that I was observing her, before returning to the waiting hansom and departing."

"If her need for your assistance is sufficient, then you may see her again."

"I consider that highly likely. But for now, Watson, let us enjoy an afternoon of pleasant conversation and perhaps another glass of this cognac. In the morning we will once more seek out Mr Brunt."

And so it transpired. As Holmes seemed in such a jovial mood, I seized the opportunity to secure his permission to send my accounts of more of our adventures to my publisher. From the glitter in his grey eyes I knew that he had at once realised my use of the occasion, and felt a measure of relief when he agreed. The afternoon swiftly became evening, and I had little appetite for the cold meat and pickles that Mrs Hudson served at our usual dinner-time, while he had none. We retired early, each pleasantly satisfied by a day spent, for the most part, in quiet companionship.

The following morning, the second day of Christmas, saw us dispense with breakfast quickly. Holmes was anxious to return to Mundell Court early, so as to encounter Mr Brunt on his arrival. The scene was unchanged until the artist arrived on foot, carefully avoiding the snowdrifts and patches of ice which had not yet begun to thaw.

From our concealment in an entry passage further along the street, we observed him remove the lock from the door and enter. Slowly, so as not to disregard the slippery surface, we crossed to the premises and stepped into a room piled with empty picture frames and smelling strongly of chemicals.

Mr Brunt laid down the palette he was preparing, and I saw that he had recognised us.

"What do you want?" he asked rudely.

"Ah, I see that you remember us from our recent encounter," Holmes replied. "My name is Sherlock Holmes, and my companion is Doctor John Watson. What I want, as you put it, is to understand your involvement in the continuing persecution of my client, Mr Clarke Jefferson."

"Your client?" The young man wiped a grimy hand down the front of his well-worn shirt. "Then you are not from Scotland Yard?"

"No, I am a consulting detective."

"Then I am not obliged to tell you anything."

Holmes frowned. "That is of course your entitlement, as least until enough time has passed for me to summon an inspector to participate in our discussion. It is, I assure you, in your own interests to co-operate with us now."

"What do you want of me?" But I had seen the quick flicker of fear that had crossed his unshaven face, as he wondered how much we knew about this and heaven knew what other unlawful activities. Clearly, the suggestion that the Yard could be brought in had not been received well. "I painted a picture for him, that's all."

"How did that come to be?" Holmes saw the artist's reluctance, and I heard faint impatience in his voice as he continued. "Come, man, I am concerned only with my client. Anything else you may be concealing is a matter for the official force, if they are sufficiently astute to have detected it. If you tell us all, they will learn nothing from us."

Mr Brunt shrugged his shoulders, and a lock of unkempt hair fell across his brow. "I had a letter, a few months ago. It surprised me, because I don't get many letters. With the instructions was a cheque, for more than I usually charge, and a photograph to paint from. The subject was a woman, a lady by the look of her, and I was told to deliver the finished portrait on Christmas Eve to the address where you saw me. I should have known there was something strange about this."

"Did you, by any chance, retain the envelope?"

"I had no reason to."

"But you have never met the sender?" I enquired.

"Not that I can remember. I can't explain how he knew of me, either. The letter was unsigned."

"It is possible," Holmes stated, "that he is someone whose acquaintance you have made in the past, but cannot now identify. Were you given directions as to your acceptance of the commission?"

"I had to send a telegram to a Post Office, to be held as *poste restante.*"

"Can you recall the destination?"

Mr Brunt considered for a moment. "I think, no, I am certain. It was Birmingham."

I saw an expression of satisfaction cross my friend's face. "Excellent. I have but one more question. Why did you run last night? According to your account, you have committed no crime."

"I was instructed to make the delivery unobserved. This was written in bold capitals and underlined in the letter, but it was not explained. Also," he avoided our eyes, staring down at the stained floor, "I have other reasons."

"Already, I have stated that they are of no concern to us," Holmes reminded him.

"Then I will not be troubled by Scotland Yard?"

"If you are, for whatever reason, it will not be because of anything they have learned from us. My thanks to you. Good-day, Mr Brunt."

"I wonder why else he fears the law," I mused as we searched the streets for a cab.

"That is irrelevant now, I think." Holmes' gaze swept up and down the High Street. "Ah, but I see that the Post Office next to the church is open for business. Be so good as to look for a hansom, Watson, while I despatch a telegram. I do feel that the pieces of this puzzle are beginning to fall into place."

By the time he emerged, I was waiting in a conveyance nearby. As the horse broke into a trot Holmes was about to enter into one of his silent reveries, but my curiosity was aroused and so I sought to prevent this.

"The telegram, Holmes, was it to Lestrade?"

After adjusting his position in the hard seat he turned from the window, smiling faintly. "Why should I be seeking to communicate with the good inspector, Watson? He is not concerned here. I have despatched a message to Barker, the private enquiry agent who I have used from time to time. I have requested that he take the morning train to Edinburgh, tomorrow. I must have confirmation of our client's version of the events in his life of five years ago."

"He is to enquire of Father Amos Wilton?"

"Precisely. As for us, I fear that another evening, or perhaps more, at Albermarle Street is indicated."

Both luncheon and dinner were hurried affairs that held little interest for Holmes that day. He had adopted that restless demeanour that I knew of old. It indicated with certainty that our enquiries had come to a temporary standstill while my friend's mind, racing engine that it was, refused to slow down.

Our landlady had scarcely cleared away the dinner things when he leapt from his chair eagerly.

"Our hours of enforced idleness are at an end, Watson. Let us retrieve our hats and coats and return to our client's home. It should be easier to procure transport now that the festivities are all but over, and I have a strong suspicion that our unknown letter writer will pay him an unwelcome visit soon."

Finding a hansom was indeed less of a problem for us. No sooner had we stepped out onto the icy surface of Baker Street, than we were confronted with a conveyance delivering two jovial young fellows in evening dress a short distance ahead. We promptly boarded it and my friend gave the cabby our intended destination.

The horse had just got into its stride with my gaze flittering among the pavement, when something in the gas-lit scene arrested my attention.

"Holmes, I saw a young woman back there, who I would swear was observing our lodgings. She turned away as we passed, and vanished into the crowd."

"I hope she will not find the increasing cold too uncomfortable. You will recall that I noticed such a woman yesterday, almost certainly the same. I have no way of knowing her intentions but it has become obvious that she waits for someone, or perhaps for something to happen, before approaching us. I believe that we will make her acquaintance soon."

Albermarle Street was as deserted and dismal as before. A light shone in an upper room of Mr Jefferson's house, and we concealed ourselves again in the deep doorway.

"Why are you so certain that our client's tormentor will appear tonight?" was my whispered question to my friend.

"You will recall that every letter was received on Christmas Eve," he replied in a voice so low that I could hardly hear, "and the latest one was different to the effect that it is the last and that the matter will somehow come to its fulfilment now. This time of year therefore, holds some significance here, although our presence may be necessary on several more occasions if our adversary's actions are not strictly accurate as to their timing. A little patience, I think, Watson, is required, but I do not expect that it will be long before we see some sort of development."

As always, Holmes was correct. My pocket-watch showed the hour to be eleven o'clock precisely, which I discerned with difficulty in the meagre light, when a hansom appeared at the end of the street and moved slowly towards us. It came to a halt, the horse slipping but regaining its balance, directly outside our client's house. A thick-set man, no longer young by his movements, alighted carefully and picked his way across the snow.

"Holmes, he carries a picture, as Mr Brunt did," I whispered.

"Quiet, Watson. Let him approach."

This man ventured nearer than his predecessor, laying down his burden against the door. Holmes' hand shot out and grasped his shoulder, startling him.

"Good heavens, sir. I didn't see you there."

"We are acting for the owner of this house. Kindly open the parcel."

"I was instructed to deliver it here, exactly at this time."

Holmes nodded and took out his dark lantern, which he lit with a vesper. "Pray enlighten us, as to how this came to be. You are, I presume, an artist?"

"I am indeed," the man's grey head moved into the glow, "though I was for many years an engraver of tombstones, and after that a soldier. My name is James Pickman. To whom am I speaking, sir?"

"I am Sherlock Holmes, and this is my friend and colleague, Doctor John Watson."

Mr Pickman's face brightened, as I stepped out of the shadows. "Why, I have read of you. Very exciting tales they are, too."

"I am glad that you think so," I said, noting Holmes' glance of disapproval at my interruption.

Mr Pickman's account had much in common with that of Mr Brunt, given previously, except that he had actually met the man who commissioned the portrait."

"His face was hidden from me by a high collar and muffler, but I did see him again. I knew him by his walk. People rarely realise how significant that can be. We all move differently, but few know it."

"I have long been aware of it," Holmes said. "Such knowledge can be instrumental, in my profession. But tell us, where did you see this man subsequently?"

"It was in the Four Keys, a tavern where I often spend my evenings, in Chelsea. I noticed that he sat alone, night after night, and that he seemed to be troubled with his breathing since he coughed a lot."

"But you did not converse with him?"

"Not at all, sir. In fact I began to feel sorry for him, sitting there with a sort of confused and despairing look about him. He showed no sign that he had recognised me. Once or twice I almost took it upon myself to approach him, but he looked as if such an intrusion would not be welcome. If anyone sat near to him, he would suddenly rise to his feet and trudge up the stairs away from everyone."

"Did you gain the impression then, that he had hired a room at the Four Keys?"

"That struck me as very likely, Mr Holmes. At any rate he did not return, for I was there for long after."

Holmes nodded. "You have been most helpful, Mr Pickman, for which I thank you. Can we now see the picture? I assure you that its intended recipient, Mr Clarke Jefferson, has allowed us full permission."

"Very well, sir." He proceeded to unwrap the parcel as a brougham appeared travelling at a fast pace. I had a glimpse of a single occupant wearing a top hat as it passed beneath a street lamp, before it vanished into the darkness. I saw from my pocket-watch that it was now exactly midnight.

Mr Pickman held up the portrait proudly. "It was an unusual request, but I did my best to follow the gentleman's instructions. I hope this sufficiently resembles the photograph."

"I am certain of it," Holmes confirmed.

Before us, in the light from my friend's dark lantern and the meagre glow from the street lamp, was a scene of a young woman surrounded by flames. Her arms were raised as if to protect herself, and her expression was one of absolute terror.

"I must confess," said Mr Pickman, "that I have never received such a commission before now. I ventured to ask the customer the meaning of such a scene. He seemed reluctant to answer, but after a short silence he murmured '*in memoriam*' and left."

This seemed to have some significance for Holmes.

"My thanks to you, Mr Pickman," he said again. "But now I see that your driver is getting cold, since he is beating his arms across his chest. I am sure that he will be driving his hansom home as soon as he has delivered you to yours. Good night to you, sir."

Holmes seemed in good spirits as we returned to Baker Street, despite the lengthy walk we were obliged to take before we discovered a hansom with its driver encased in a thick travelling rug, fast asleep. We retired soon after our arrival, but not before he had held the two pictures together and compared them.

"Both men are adept at their craft," he observed as he noted the resemblance between the painted figures. "We will probably see the conclusion of this affair soon after tomorrow. As I suspected, our adversary had intended to call upon Mr Clarke Jefferson at midnight, one hour after the delivery of the second picture and as close to Christmas as could be arranged. You did not fail to observe the passing brougham, of course? We rather thwarted his intentions then, I think." He smiled as I stifled a yawn. "Well, I believe us both to be weary, and there is more to be done tomorrow. Good night to you, Watson."

Soon after breakfast Holmes began to consult his index and add to it, though I am uncertain as to whether this activity had any connection with our current case. I had a prior appointment at my surgery which occupied me until almost mid-day, when an urgent call summoned me to an address near Charing Cross. Consequently, dusk was closing in as I entered our sitting-room to find my friend brandishing a telegram which, judging by the torn envelope discarded upon the carpet, had not long been delivered.

"At last!" he cried. "I have been awaiting this for most of the day, Watson."

"The reply from Barker, I presume."

"Indeed, and it confirms much that I had suspected." He became silent abruptly, and I saw that he peered past me through our window, where he had neglected to draw the curtains. "The woman has returned, the one that both you and I have seen watching our lodgings before. Be so good as to go out and speak to her, and bring her in out of the cold."

I put down my bag and, remembering her hasty withdrawals of before, went out and walked along Baker Street for a short distance. I then crossed to the other side and approached her unseen, noticing her apparent anxiety from some way off. I confronted her and raised my hat.

"Good evening to you. Forgive my forwardness, but I see that you are again watching our premises. Mr Sherlock Holmes and I would be most pleased if you would consent to accompany me to our rooms, where whatever is troubling you may well be put to rest."

She was startled by my intrusion, her face full of alarm. But after a moment she seemed to collect herself, and spoke to me in a subdued voice:

"Yes, I suppose you are right, sir. There has to be an end to this. I will come with you."

Holmes had already called for tea as we settled ourselves around a blazing fire. The young woman clearly found the warming liquid most welcome, and she ceased to shiver after a short while.

I sat in my usual armchair across from him, as he filled his clay pipe from the Persian slipper and regarded our visitor with interest.

"Please begin your account when you are ready, Mrs Sarah Hall, there is no need to hurry and we will do all that we can to assist you with your difficulty. We have not yet made the acquaintance of your brother, but we will doubtlessly do so very soon."

Her expression was one of complete amazement. "How do you know these things, sir? I have not yet disclosed either my name or that I am searching for my brother."

"As a consulting detective, it is my business to know such things. Forgive me, but I found it unnecessary to introduce either

Doctor Watson or myself, since you were evidently already aware of us."

"That is true," her eyes fell momentarily to the carpet, "for I followed Mr Clarke Jefferson here on Christmas Eve, recognising your address and hoping that my brother would eventually arrive here also, since he is still seeking him."

"Does he intend to do him harm?"

"On my life, I do not know, sir. I have not seen Gabriel for some years, although he has sometimes communicated by letter. I have prayed that he has not changed, for he was never a violent man."

"Let us hope that he has not become so. As far as I can tell, he has as yet committed no crime." Holmes blew a cloud of fragrant smoke into the air. "I must apologise again," he said hastily, "for I neglected to ascertain whether you have any objection to strong tobacco."

She shook her head. "None at all."

"Excellent. I take it that you knew of your brother's intentions from his letters, and when his travels took him so close to where Mr Jefferson now lives you perceived that a confrontation was imminent and resolved to travel here from Edinburgh in the hope of persuading him to abandon his quest."

"Indeed, sir. If I find him, I am sure that I can convince him. I have lost my husband and my sister already, and cannot bear the thought of being deprived also of my only remaining kin. The law would surely find him and he would be hanged." I noted that her Scottish accent became more noticeable as her excitement grew and reflected, since Holmes was now aware of the situation, that Barker had done his work well.

"We will do our utmost to prevent this. If you would care to attend here at, say, three o'clock the day after tomorrow, I would expect to be able to set your mind at rest. Until then, Madam, I will bid you good evening. Doctor Watson will be pleased to show you out and procure for you a hansom."

When this was accomplished I returned to our sitting-room to find that Holmes had put on his hat and coat.

"I must send a telegram, Watson, if I can reach the Post Office before it closes."

"To Mr Clarke Jefferson, no doubt?"

"You presume correctly, old fellow. I would be obliged if he would present himself here at the same time as Mrs Hall."

He returned soon and Mrs Hudson served a fine dinner of roast chicken and vegetables. After a dessert of stewed apples and custard which he barely sampled, we repaired to our usual seats for brandy and cigars. We smoked and drank in companionable silence for a while, and I waited with enforced patience until our glasses were empty and the remains of our tobacco consigned to a crystal ash-tray.

"Holmes, I am uncertain as to how this affair has developed. Do you intend to enlighten me?"

He leaned back in his chair, a look of contentment upon his face. "Providing our adversary, Mr Gabriel Newman, is still in temporary residence at The Four Keys, I see no reason why the situation should not be quickly cleared up to our client's satisfaction."

27

"Is Mr Clarke Jefferson a criminal, since he is being sought so relentlessly by Mrs Hall's brother?" I persisted.

"He is, in fact, completely innocent of any crime, as is his pursuer until now. We will attempt to cause Mr Gabriel Newman to realise this before any regrettable action takes place, if we can find him at The Four Keys tomorrow evening. In my telegram to our client, I strongly advised him to remain at home until his attendance here."

"Barker seems to have been extraordinarily successful in his enquiries in Edinburgh."

"Very much so, although he discovered, regrettably, that Father Wilton has now passed away. His widow however, was most forthcoming, and has, since our client left them, pursued her own enquiries as to his previous life out of curiosity." He smiled as a thought occurred to him. "If there should ever be a requirement for female consulting detectives, she appears to be well qualified."

"Do we now know then, *why* Mr Jefferson is being so pursued?"

"We do. He is thought to be responsible for the death of Miranda, who was Mr Newman's and Mrs Sarah Hall's sister."

"But, as you implied, he is innocent?"

"Absolutely. Mr Clarke Jefferson was engaged to be married to Miss Miranda Newman and they, together with a female chaperone whose identity has not been discovered, were dining in an Edinburgh restaurant. A fire broke out and spread quickly from the kitchen through the building, and in the panic that followed both Miss Newman and the chaperone lost their lives. Mr Clarke Jefferson was injured, probably by a falling beam, resulting in a permanent loss of memory up until the time when he found himself in Father Wilton's care."

"The scars upon his neck," I remembered. "Your original understanding was correct. They were the results of burns."

Holmes nodded. "Although he remembers nothing of the incident. It seems that he simply wandered away from the scene. As I have stated, Mr Gabriel Newman believes otherwise."

"Why is he so convinced that our client was responsible for his sister's death?"

"According to Barker's investigation, Mr Newman believes that Mr Jefferson committed an act of great cowardice in abandoning his fiancée in order to save himself. He considers Mr Jefferson's immediate disappearance to be proof of this, that it was effected to avoid facing his fiancee's family."

"But there is no substance to this?"

"None whatsoever. Both Barker and Mrs Wilton were meticulous in discovering the truth."

"So, since then Mr Newman has been engaged upon a needless and mistaken quest."

"He has." Holmes took on a thoughtful expression. "But I cannot ascertain why he has waited so long to exact his revenge. Why this travelling from city to city? Why the letter on the anniversary of his sister's death every year until now? Why the different pictures? What are his intentions, now that he has found his quarry, bearing in mind that Mrs Hall is adamant that he is not, or was not, a violent man? Doubtless we will discover the answers when we confront him."

The remainder of the evening passed quickly. The following morning brought Holmes a new client, Mr Corey Whitehouse, who spent several hours with my friend while I ventured out for a much-needed walk. I was glad to see that the sun was shining and the thaw had begun. The pavements were wet, but the danger that the ice had brought to the streets had all but disappeared. Traffic had increased, with horses once again trotting confidently before hansoms or private carriages. I recalled that I had arranged a further appointment at my surgery, which I kept and concluded within a short time.

I returned to our lodgings in time for luncheon. As we ate I enquired of Holmes regarding his client of the morning, to which he responded dismissively.

"Pah! It was a simple matter. I could have resolved it in half the time, had not Mr Whitehouse obscured the true problem beneath layers of irrelevant and unconnected facts."

I discerned that he was possessed of a reminiscent mood, and so we spent the afternoon in pleasant conversation concerning some of our past adventures. As the hour for dinner approached however, I noticed a change in him that I concluded was brought about by the increasing nearness of our time for action. This was confirmed by the rapidity with which he dealt with his food. Refusing dessert, he drank two cups of strong coffee and stood up from the table.

"As soon as you have finished your cherry pie, Watson, we will set off. We have no knowledge of Mr Gabriel Newman's evening habits, so I would prefer to be at the Four Keys early."

I hurriedly ate the last of my food and gulped down the remaining coffee. I had hardly regained my feet before Holmes handed me my hat and coat and was ushering me down the stairs. Baker Street twinkled with tiny patches of ice and snow, more so as the temperature had once again plummeted. A hansom was easily found and we were quickly on our way to Chelsea through streets that were mostly deserted.

The Four Keys was an unimposing little tavern in an out-of-the-way backstreet that I had not previously known existed. Holmes, however, dismissed the hansom some distance from it and led us there unerringly. Not for the first time, my friend's seemingly unbounded knowledge of the capital was a source of some astonishment to me.

We entered the establishment to find it crowded, despite the evening being still young. The smoke-filled bar-room had few empty tables, but we settled upon a newly-vacated position in a corner from where it was possible to constantly keep both the entrance and the stairs leading to the upper floor in view.

"I cannot see our friend Mr Pickman, Watson." Holmes explored the room with his eyes, moving his head but a little. "He did not claim to spend his every evening here, however."

I nodded. "If, as he surmised, Mr Newman is resident here, he will enter by descending the stairs, rather than from the street."

"Quite so."

No waiter appeared, so Holmes approached the bar and prevailed upon the landlord for two pints of his best beer. We sat for about an hour, drinking and saying little as we observed the circus that surrounded us. A young man sitting at a table near the door blew enormous smoke rings and apparently accompanied these by humorous stories, since his companions erupted often into laughter. Several others, invariably the worse for drink, stood up to sing. The landlord had just left his post to eject a troublesome roughneck from the premises, when someone proposed a toast to his friends and two obvious drunkards began to argue. My friend put a hand on my arm.

"There, I think, is the man we seek."

A tall, elderly man who, from his movements and frequent coughing fits, did not appear to be in the best of health, had descended the stairs. His hair, rather long, was so grey to be almost white and his skin seemed tightly stretched across his face. As we watched, he walked clumsily to where the landlord, in anticipation, held a whisky bottle at the ready.

"He has been here for some little time, or has consumed much drink regularly," I perceived.

"Excellent, Watson." Holmes smiled faintly. "But of course both alternatives could be valid. As Mr Newman has found himself an unoccupied bench near the wall, I think we should now make his acquaintance. The necessity is unlikely, but keep your hand near your service revolver for the present."

We rose and made our way between the scattered tables, the noise becoming intolerable until we reached the other side of the room. We sat upon the bench beside Mr Newman, earning ourselves a surprised and disapproving glare.

"Good evening, Mr Gabriel Newman," Holmes began.

"Do I know you, sir?" The response was as unfriendly as I had expected, yet it surprised me to discover that the man had clear and kindly eyes.

"Only from last night. You will recall that you passed the house of Mr Clarke Jefferson rather quickly, in a brougham."

"You prevented me from visiting the scoundrel."

"Pray tell me," Holmes requested, "what your intentions were. It is futile to deny that you meant harm to Mr Jefferson. All is known to us concerning this matter."

Mr Newman appeared astounded. "How could you possibly be aware of the situation? Who are you, sir?"

"My name is Sherlock Holmes. I am a consulting detective. My companion is my friend, Doctor John Watson."

"And what have you to do with my business concerning Clarke Jefferson. Is he your client? Has he paid you to warn me off, or to kill me?"

Holmes smiled grimly. "I am not an assassin, sir. Mr Clarke Jefferson *is* my client however, but my purpose is to ascertain the origin and reason for the letters you have sent to him over the past few Christmases. We mean you no harm, but we are bound to prevent any from befalling him. I perceive from the protuberance in the pocket of your evening-coat, that you are armed."

Mr Newman peered around us until he was satisfied that we were unobserved, then slowly drew a revolver from his coat. My hand tightened on my own weapon, but I saw that it was unnecessary.

"Take it," he said, handing it to Holmes, who quickly concealed it, "for I have discovered that I have no use for it. You will see that it is unloaded. If you know as much as you have stated, then you will be aware of the reason for my pursuit of the man who so nearly became my brother-in-law. Miranda was my younger sister, and no man ever loved a sibling more. I was happy beyond measure, when she became engaged to a man who I quickly befriended, and who seemed to me to be of a most sensible and reliable disposition." He paused to stifle a racking cough, and in that instant a possible reason for the different points of origin of the yearly letters came to me. "When that terrible blaze took Miranda and her companion from us my heart was broken, yet anger such as I had never before known burned within me. There was much talk among the survivors of that blaze, and more than one of them told me with certainty that Clarke Jefferson had been seen, leaving that smouldering wreck of a building without a backward glance."

"I must tell you," Holmes interrupted quietly, "that I have discovered that not to be quite the case."

Mr Newman looked at us with a haunted expression. "But how can it be otherwise, sir? Why did he not come back to us and share our grief? Instead he fled, as I quickly discovered from paid agents who I employed, to the capital after first hiding somewhere in Edinburgh. Why would anyone but a coward leave ladies under his protection in such danger, except to preserve himself? To this day the memory of Miranda's funeral is clear in my mind, as is that of the many who enquired after her intended husband's absence."

"My sympathies are with you, sir." I said then, disregarding Holmes' sharp glance. "For I see that you suffer extensively from consumption to add to your difficulties. Is it not true that you despatched the letters to Mr Jefferson from wherever you happened to be at Christmastime, from the cities containing the various medical institutions where you had continually sought a cure for your condition?"

"It is. Those places were chosen so as to bring me ever closer to where I believed him to be. Several times I was pronounced to be at death's door, but always I recovered. My hatred for that man has, I am sure, kept me alive."

Holmes frowned. "What is the significance of the pictures, pray?"

"My intention was to remind him, first of Miranda's beauty and then of the appalling fate to which he abandoned her, and to cause him to understand that vengeance was at last at hand."

"Yet the weapon you carry was unloaded."

"In truth," Mr Newman bowed his head, and succumbed to more coughing, "I have never been a cruel man. The weapon was purchased years ago as the instrument of my revenge but, as time has passed, my feelings have changed to wanting merely to confront Mr Jefferson for an explanation. I carried the gun as a reminder of what I must not do, of what I almost became. I am not long for this Earth, sirs, and I would not like to leave it by means of the gallows. The letters, the pictures, became no more than a warning to him of a meeting that must inevitably take place."

"And take place it shall," my friend confirmed in a quiet and kindly voice. "If you would care to call on us at 221b, Baker Street, at three o'clock tomorrow afternoon, I have every expectation that this matter can be put to rest. I will say no more to you now, save to give you an assurance that all is not as you have believed, and that you will leave our premises without the hate and resentment that you have nurtured over the years." He rose and I did likewise. "For now, sir, we bid you good-night."

We made our way through the smoke and the boisterous crowd to the street. As we reached the entrance I looked back, to see Mr Newman staring after us with a puzzled expression and trying in vain to restrain a coughing fit that shook him cruelly.

"That man has not long to live, Holmes," I remarked as we emerged from the shadows of the narrow streets into a main thoroughfare. "The treatment he has received has doubtlessly extended his life for a limited time, but I fear that time is near its end."

He raised his arm to attract a passing hansom. "I know it. All the more reason therefore, to settle his differences with our client. I have every hope that tomorrow afternoon will see the conclusion of this case and of their sad estrangement."

I confess to falling asleep during the journey back to our lodgings. Holmes woke me as we arrived and, by mutual agreement, we retired on regaining our sitting-room.

He spent longer than usual over breakfast the following morning, alternating mouthfuls of food with opening his substantial post for long after my coffee cup was emptied. I gathered from his expression that several letters contained items of interest to him.

"I have to attend my surgery this morning, Holmes, but I anticipate that I will have returned in time for luncheon."

"Kindly be here no later than two-thirty," he replied without looking up from his perusal of a crumpled sheet of notepaper.

The day was unusual inasmuch as my procession of patients all suffered from minor ailments which were easily dealt with, and so it was that I closed my practice early and returned to Baker Street before two o'clock. We were served generous portions of steak pie, of which only I consumed all, with Holmes making no reference to either what lay before us or to anything that had arrived in the post.

"We will not have to wait long, I think, before the first of our visitors arrive," he said as we took to our armchairs.

"Mr Gabriel Newman will be surprised by the proceedings."

Holmes placed a lump of coal on the fire and replaced the tongs. "He has been labouring under a misapprehension for a considerable time, so nothing but good can come of his enlightenment. Ah, but Mrs Hudson has answered the door-bell, and

I perceive from the footfalls upon the stairs that Mrs Sarah Hall is here."

"I apologise, gentlemen, for arriving a little early," our visitor began when greetings had been exchanged and our landlady had withdrawn.

"That is of no consequence," Holmes said as he indicated that she should take the basket chair.

"Mr Holmes, have you discovered my brother's whereabouts?" she asked anxiously.

"I have." He peered from the window. "He is in fact crossing Baker Street at this very moment, approaching our front door."

The door-bell rang for a second time, and Mrs Hudson showed in Mr Gabriel Newman.

"I do not fully understand the purpose of this meeting, gentlemen!" He exclaimed rather loudly as he entered, before coming to a sudden halt as he saw his sister.

"Sarah! What in the world are you doing here?"

Her expression was a mixture of relief and apprehension. "Do not be angry with me, Gabriel, I beg of you. I came to London because I knew you were searching for Clarke. I pray that you have not found him."

"I had discovered where he is living," his glance took in Holmes and myself, "but these gentlemen prevented my approaching the scoundrel." He paused and his face became clouded by indecision. "Perhaps that is just as well."

"You are no murderer, despite what you have said before now."

"That is true, but I can never forgive his cowardice."

"You may not have to," my friend intervened, "if you can be convinced that there is none to forgive."

"Again you say this. You insisted as much when you approached me last night, but you have yet to explain."

"Be so good as to settle yourself in this chair, Mr Newman, and I will elaborate with the assistance of Mr Clarke Jefferson himself, for it is certainly he who is ringing our door-bell at this moment."

Anger reappeared on the elderly gentleman's face, and he stifled a harsh coughing fit. I was about to pour a glass of water to assist him when Mr Jefferson was announced and the door closed behind him.

"Good afternoon Mr Holmes and Doctor Watson," our client began, before glancing without expression at the others.

"Clarke!" Mrs Hall half-rose from her chair, looking somewhat relieved.

"I would much like words with you, sir!" Mr Newman growled.

I vacated my chair for Mr Jefferson, who appeared to be in understandable confusion.

"Pray tell me, who are these people?" he asked Holmes after a few moments of confused silence.

"You do not recognise them?"

"How can I? I have never before laid my eyes upon them."

"Is this some manner of deceit, sir? A cheap party trick to escape your guilt?" Mr Newsome's hands were white upon the walking-cane he held.

"Not at all," I answered on Mr Jefferson's behalf. "Although I am not fully conversant with illnesses of the mind, I am very experienced in recognising the deceit of those who, for various reasons, seek to feign them. During our original meeting with Mr Jefferson I observed him closely, from the moment he claimed to have no recollection of his past beyond those events subsequent to the tragedy of five years ago. I am convinced he speaks the truth."

"What then, is his claim?"

Mr Jefferson glanced at each of us in turn, looking increasingly puzzled. "I am all at sea with this. I confess to being totally confused."

"You abandoned the girl you were to marry. You left my sister, and also her companion, to the flames," Mr Newman said harshly.

The shock that filled our client's face was absolute. For the next few moments he was speechless.

"I assure you, sir," he said to Mr Newman, "that I am guilty of none of this. I can only assume that you have mistaken me for another."

"What then, can you recall of your life prior to your time with Father Wilton and his wife?" Holmes asked.

His outraged expression was replaced by one of horror, as he realised the implication. "Oh no! Oh, dear God."

Mr Newman then surprised us all for, after scrutinizing our client intently, his anger subsided. "Have you truly, no recollection?" He said in a calmer, almost considerate tone.

"None." Mr Jefferson raised his hands in despair, shaking his head. "Throughout the past five years I have repeatedly attempted to recover what I have come to regard as my previous life, but to no avail. Before Father Wilton, I may as well have not been born."

"You are either telling the truth, or are the most accomplished actor that ever was." Mr Newman turned to me. "Do you swear, Doctor, that this is possible?"

I looked at him coldly. "I am not accustomed to having my word doubted, sir. I have already said as much. It has long been known that a blow to the head can produce such an effect, either temporarily or, as is the unfortunate case here, permanently. I repeat, I am convinced of this man's truthfulness and our investigation has confirmed it."

The elderly gentleman turned his head away to submit to another fit of coughing. Afterwards, his gaze avoided our eyes. Silence settled upon the room for some moments, but from outside I could hear faintly the cries of barrow-boys and the thud of horses' hooves.

"For all of this time I have hated you," he said to Mr Jefferson. "and now I find that I was in error." He paused, and I saw that his eyes glistened. "I suppose that some part of me never believed that you left Miranda because I knew you, but my grief at losing her consumed my reason. How can I begin to apologise, my boy? How can I make restitution?" He shook his head in an almost frantic manner. "How you must despise me."

40

"I cannot despise you sir, because I do not know you," Mr Jefferson replied. "Neither do I know this good lady. But I have never meant harm to anyone, nor have I ever lacked courage."

Mr Newman nodded. "I can only apologise again, to you and to Doctor Watson. Is it possible that we can, on some future occasion, talk of things as they were before that tragic fire, and perhaps re-establish some of the friendship we once had? There is much that I can tell you of those times, if you wish it."

"I would welcome the chance to reclaim some parts of my earlier life," he said with some dismay, "for I have never expected to have the opportunity. As for friendship sir, it is my way to be, as much as is possible, at peace with all men."

For the first time, a faint smile stole across Mr Newman's face. His expression was now one of concern. All three of our visitors showed some measure of relief.

"And now," said Sherlock Holmes, breaking the short silence, "that all is clear and we are all friends, I suggest we share a bottle of an excellent Spanish wine that I have been saving in anticipation of a special occasion. Watson, kindly be so good as to bring the tray from the table and fill the glasses."

Thus did this adventure come to its conclusion. There was no villain to be seen, no recourse to Scotland Yard nor cause for urgent action. Yet, possibly because of the time of year, both Holmes and I felt a certain satisfaction at its end. It was true that Mr Gabriel Newman had little time left to him to resume his friendship with our client, but doubtlessly they would heal the wound that had given rise to the letters and pictures that had been sent in anger and received in confusion.

Some hours later, when they had all departed and Holmes and I were again settled in our chairs contentedly, we reviewed the affair and I added to my notes which might one day be extended to a story for future publication.

"It ended well, Holmes," I said. "After a while Mr Newman took on the look of a man who has had a great burden lifted from his shoulders. Nevertheless, I confess to experiencing some surprise when he accepted that our client had no memory of his past. He did not strike me as someone who is impressed easily."

"Nor I, old friend, but probably there were other factors. Mrs Hall's apparent reluctance to believe badly of Mr Jefferson, for example, that influenced her brother's change of heart. Or possibly, the spirit that is currently abroad had something to do with it. It is after all, as you were quick to remind me previously, the season of goodwill."

The Adventure of the Disappointed Lover.

From the early days of our association, it had been apparent to me that my friend, Mr Sherlock Holmes, held a great mistrust for the female sex. The initial cause of this was never revealed to me, but it is certain that a case that was put before him not long after we took up our rooms in Baker Street served to convince him of the correctness of his conclusion.

The affair began, at least for my friend and myself, at the instant we heard the startled cries of our landlady. There had hardly been an exchange of words between her and whoever had summoned her to answer the door, before Holmes and I heard her surprised exclamation followed by heavy footfalls upon the stairs. A moment later the door of our sitting-room burst open, to admit a dishevelled young man in a highly nervous state. He came to an instant halt at the sight of us, his hat crooked upon his head and his tie askew.

I lowered my newspaper and turned in my armchair, as did my friend.

"What is the meaning of this, sir" I asked angrily.

He seemed to be quite breathless, as our landlady appeared behind him in the doorway.

"Mr Holmes, I am sorry. I could not prevent this gentleman from entering."

Holmes got to his feet, completely unruffled. "Do not concern yourself, Mrs Hudson. I will attend to this."

Before our visitor could speak, Holmes told the fellow that he had not requested tea or coffee before our landlady withdrew, because it was obvious that something stronger was required. He introduced us to him.

"Do take the basket chair, opposite Doctor Watson. Allow me to pour you a brandy, for I perceive that your nerves are agitated."

"Thank you sir, I am having great difficulty keeping down my anger. I fear that I might do some harm that will bring the law down on me."

Holmes handed him the glass. "Pray drink this, and when you have calmed yourself take a moment to collect your thoughts. Then, when you are ready, you can tell us your name and something of the problem that has brought you to us today. There is no need to hurry."

Our visitor sat, and accepted the glass gratefully. He gulped the harsh liquid down and made a visible effort to get to grips with the fury that possessed him.

"Thank you, gentlemen," he began when he had attained a more settled state. "I cannot apologise sufficiently for my entrance. I am emotional by nature, excessively so, I am told, and I am given to such unfortunate displays."

"An apology to us is unnecessary, but may be better directed to our landlady. I fear that she was rather upset."

"I will indeed express my regrets for my inexcusable conduct as I leave, be assured."

"Very well, then. Kindly state your case. Pray pay special attention to detail."

Holmes lowered his thin form into his armchair and regarded our visitor critically. The young man, I would have said, appeared to be of twenty-six or twenty-seven years with unruly dark hair and eyes which, to my mind, held a surprising look of innocence. His morning suit, although visibly worn and creased, seemed to be of good quality.

"My name is Ebenezer Barlow," he informed us. "I am a junior clerk at the establishment of Berryman's, the well-known manufacturers of artificial hearing appliances. I am here because the woman I love is being cruelly treated, and I am helpless to intervene."

"Who is this lady?" Holmes enquired. "Presumably she is suffering at the hands of her parents, or a sibling?"

Mr Barlow let his ashamed glance fall to the carpet. "No, sir. Her name is Mrs Martha Roper, and she is being mercilessly beaten by her husband."

"Martha Roper?" I repeated. "Are you referring to the former actress?"

Our client nodded. "She left the stage five years ago. There was no further need for her to work, since her husband's sugar importing company has prospered a great deal."

"You must understand," Holmes said then, "that, as a consulting detective, I cannot interfere with what passes between a man and his wife. Depending on the circumstances, the law may even be on his side. Tell me. Mr Barlow, does the lady know of your feelings for her? Have you actually met her face to face, or are your liaisons confined to your imagination only?"

Our visitor's mouth dropped open, and I saw that he was fighting against the rising of renewed anger.

"I am not mad, Mr Holmes! Nor am I an impressionable schoolboy given to romantic daydreams. Mrs Roper and I met at the reception that followed a wedding of a mutual friend, about two months ago. Even then I could see that her husband has little interest in her, since they hardly conversed and he seized the earliest opportunity to leave her to join a circle of local businessmen who were drinking excessively as they discussed their various occupations."

"Did she approach you, or did you seek her out when you perceived that she was neglected?"

Mr Barlow hesitated. "I... I cannot remember. I just recall that I stood alone with a glass of wine in my hand, and the next moment I was in the company of an intelligent and beautiful woman."

"And she proceeded to tell you of her plight?"

"No, not at all. It was weeks, during one of our subsequent meetings, that I enquired as to the extensive bruising which had swollen the side of her face. At first she explained that she had fallen while descending the stairs at their home in Mayfair, but when I pressed her she told me all."

Holmes rested his chin on his interlaced fingers. "Has she reported further injuries since?"

"Indeed she has. On one occasion she was limping noticeably as we met, and on another one of her eyes was bruised and half-closed and her hearing was temporarily impaired from a heavy blow."

"This is monstrous!" I interjected. "If this is true, the man should be dragged into court."

Holmes gave me a disapproving glance, but I chose not to see it.

"Has she not consulted the official force about these assaults," he asked after a moment, "with a view to getting her husband cautioned, or even leading to the end of the marriage?"

Our visitor shook his head. "When I asked her that question she replied, as you did Mr Holmes, that they would not interfere with goings-on in the marital home. Also, her husband has friends among the higher ranks of the police who would inform him of her complaint, leading to further punishment."

"You have presented me with something of a dilemma," Holmes took a cigar from the coal scuttle, then apparently changed his mind and set it down on a side-table. "I cannot approve of the friendship you describe with a married lady, for it can lead only to trouble and heartbreak. On the other hand, it would lie heavily on my conscience if this lady were to suffer further punishment after you have brought the situation to my notice." He regarded our client with a cool stare. "What then, would you have me do?"

Mr Barlow shifted uncomfortably in his chair, seemingly racked by an agony of indecision.

"Truly, I do not know what I was thinking of, by relating this to you. I must apologise again for occupying your time with such matters. What could I have expected? I really cannot conceive of any other way to assist Mrs Roper, yet to think of her subjected so is unbearable to me."

For a few moments there was silence, except for faintly heard shouting in Baker Street, as someone impatiently attempted to procure a hansom.

"We understand and appreciate your feelings," I said to our visitor, "but to intervene here would be to…."

"Perhaps," Holmes interrupted, "Watson and myself could call at the Mayfair house a little later. I can promise nothing, you understand, but I will attempt to convey to the husband that his actions are known and make him aware of the possible consequences."

For the first time, a strained smile spread across Mr Barlow's face. His relief was evident.

"I cannot thank you enough. To know that I have at least caused something to be done in her defence is of immense comfort to me."

"In return," Holmes continued a little sternly, "I must ask for your word that you will make no attempt to see this lady until after I have spoken to both her and her husband."

"You have it! My word on it!"

My friend nodded. "Thank you, Mr Barlow. If you will allow Doctor Watson to make a note of the lady's address and your own, and any other details that you may think relevant, I think we need not detain you beyond that."

We rose all three together, and I took up my notepad and pencil as Holmes crossed the room to stare from the window. I did not hear him answer our client's farewell, and the front door had closed before he spoke.

"I do not expect this to be the most interesting of cases, Watson. On reflection I would say that it is much nearer to your department than mine." He sighed heavily. "But, I have undertaken to look into this, and so I must. Be so kind as to hand me my hat and coat and accompany me, if you have nothing better to do."

A surprise awaited us as the hansom delivered us to a quiet side-street in Mayfair. A police coach waited near the gate at the end of the long garden, while the driver conversed with a burly constable. Holmes introduced himself and the constable saluted uncertainly while the driver, no doubt in disapproval of unofficial agents, stared into the distance.

"What is happening here, officer?" My friend enquired.

"I don't know if I should discuss police business, sir. Inspector Lestrade doesn't like too much to be known too quickly."

"Inspector Lestrade? He and I are acquainted. I have been of some small assistance to him from time to time."

The constable was suddenly more forthcoming. "Oh, in that case, sir, I can tell you. It's murder, for sure. There's blood all over the place. You'll find the inspector in the dining-room, straight through the garden."

Holmes thanked the man and we took the path, edged by roses and clusters of dahlias, to the front door. The constable on duty there asked us our business, but Inspector Lestrade appeared in the doorway before any reply could be made.

"Mr Sherlock Holmes, is it? He enquired unnecessarily. "I don't think we need your skills here, sir. It's all straight forward enough as I see it. Someone was burgling the house when Mr Roper disturbed them during the night. He's wearing his night-clothes you see, so I saw that immediately. Anyway, the burglar stuck a knife in the poor man's heart and made off with a few things. I've got men all over the district, looking out already, since there's been a number of robberies in the area, lately."

"Very efficient and commendable, Inspector. Would you object to my examining the scene? If you have finished, of course."

Lestrade considered briefly. "I don't see that it would do any harm, Mr Holmes. Mind you, I don't think you'll find anything, either. You've been a bit of help to Scotland Yard before now, so I suppose that's all right. I'll tell you what - I'll come with you."

Only I saw Holmes' irritated expression at this last remark, as we entered the house. Lestrade led us down a short passage hung with portraits to a large airy room containing a sideboard and a long table and chairs. Near its centre lay a grey-haired man of average height in a nightshirt, with a kitchen knife protruding from his chest. Blood had spread down almost to his waist, indicating to me that death was not instantaneous.

Holmes immediately whipped out his lens to examine the body and the surrounding area. He then extended his search to the perimeter of the room. Many of the panes of the full-length window at the far end of the room had been broken, probably by the bronze statuette lying on the carpet nearby, to the extent that a man could have passed through. Two of the sideboard drawers were half-open, and their contents disturbed.

Holmes ceased his inspection suddenly, replacing his lens in his pocket and standing in a pose of contemplation. No more than a few moments passed, before he turned to the inspector.

"Call off your men, Lestrade. The murderer of Mr Roper has not left this house."

"Did I miss something, Mr Holmes?" The official detective was aghast. "Surely, the entrance and exit of the intruder is obvious."

Holmes declined to comment on the question, but explained his findings. "The hole in the window is certainly of a width to admit a man, but the glass fragments lie on the loose soil *outside*. This indicates, as does the fact that there are no footprints out there, embedding shards of glass in the earth or otherwise, that the window was smashed from within. Also," he wore a condescending smile for an instant, "it has surely occurred to you that the noise resulting from this would have woken the household well before entry could be gained."

Lestrade looked over his shoulder, I thought to ensure that no one else, particularly a constable, was in earshot. "Quite right, Mr Holmes, I had of course taken that into consideration. In fact, I was about to confer with you about it. Would it be right then, do you think, to say that Mr Roper was killed as a result of a burst of anger, or something like that?"

"Undoubtedly, for if it had been planned in advance the scene would likely have been better prepared. There is no question in my mind that the decision to kill was taken on the spur of the moment."

"That was my conclusion, exactly."

"The household then, comprises of how many?" Holmes asked with a straight face.

"Three," said the little detective. "Apart from the murdered man, that is. Mrs Roper of course, then there is the butler, Danvers, and the maid, Carlotta. As you'd expect with a name like that she's Spanish, and speaks no more than a few words of English. I'm told she understands it, though."

"Naturally, you will want to interview these immediately, Inspector. Perhaps you would allow Doctor Watson and myself to be present, in order to learn from your expertise and possibly to add a different point of view. In addition, Watson may be able to assist if Mrs Roper or the maid are excessively distraught."

This time, Lestrade needed little time to consider. "Very well, gentlemen. I have asked them to remain in the parlour together for the time being, under the watchful eye of one of my constables." He covered the body with a sheet that someone, presumably a constable, had obtained and left for the purpose, and strode over to the door to call out. "Newton, ask Mrs Roper to step in here, if you please."

We heard a distant door open and close, before she entered. I had once been enthralled by her in a performance at the Theatre Royal in Drury Lane, and the magnetism she had exuded then had not diminished. Even in these sad circumstances, and in distress, her personality seemed projected before she had uttered a word. She appeared more mature, it is true, but her hair had retained its gloss and her face much of its beauty. She was dressed in a simple dark-coloured frock, and her features were swollen by the tears of her grief.

"Please be seated, Mrs Roper," Lestrade said in a kindly voice, which was unusual for him. "Let me first express our condolences at your loss. You will appreciate, I'm sure, that these gentlemen and I will need to ask you certain questions, in order to discover who has done this terrible thing."

As she sat tears welled up in her eyes, but she spoke bravely. "Do not spare my feelings, Inspector. This man must pay for his crime. Ask me whatever you wish."

"When did you first become aware that someone had entered your house?" Lestrade enquired after allowing a short while for her to compose herself.

"I awoke early, and realised at once that my husband had gone downstairs. I heard movement, which I thought must be him since it was too early for the butler or maid to have risen. After a while, as he had not returned, I went to look for him. I found him as you see him now."

"You saw no one fleeing from the house, or attempting to hide within?"

Her expression was one of extreme melancholy, as she shook her head. "There was only my poor dead husband. I cried out to raise the alarm, and Danvers came out of his room half-dressed. When he saw what had happened, he went to the local police station."

"Who promptly called us." Lestrade's bulldog-like face wore an expression that appeared as confused as ever.

"If I may ask," Holmes looked at Mrs Roper, and spoke in his most soothing voice, "about something that puzzles me. We have seen how the murderer apparently entered your premises, searched through your sideboard drawers and disturbed your husband. This must have entailed considerable noise, which doubtlessly woke him. Did you, yourself, hear nothing, or either of your staff?"

She looked at him silently, for what seemed to me a long time. Lestrade had made no introductions, so she probably assumed that we were his colleagues from Scotland Yard.

"As I indicated, I heard nothing," she said at length. "As for the butler and the maid, they will answer for themselves."

"Indeed they will," confirmed Lestrade. "I think that we have troubled you quite enough, Mrs Roper. I will see the butler now."

She rose and left slowly, still visibly distraught. Some minutes passed, during which Holmes remained impassive while Lestrade became increasingly impatient. I believe that he was about to utter some remark about having to wait while a servant condescended to join us when the door, which had been left ajar, opened fully. The man who entered, wearing butler's attire, was more elderly than I had imagined, tall but bent and darkly saturnine. His harsh demeanour was belied by his calm and gentle voice.

"Gentlemen, I cannot apologise enough. Earlier, I was sharpening the cutlery and, unfortunately, I was careless. I was obliged to bandage my hand," he indicated a dressing stained with a spreading spot of blood, "before I could present myself."

"If you wish," I said at once, "I could assist if the bleeding is profuse. I am a doctor."

"My thanks to you, sir, but it is nothing. It will heal in a day or two."

"Listen, my man," Lestrade interrupted then, "Danvers, is it?"

"It is, sir."

"Very well. I want you to tell me all that you know about this business. Don't try to lie or mislead me – we take a very dim view of that kind of thing, at Scotland Yard."

"Yes, sir. I was alerted by Mrs Roper's screams, and got to her as soon as I could. She was very upset of course, and instructed me to go to the local police station to report her husband's death."

"How did you get there, so quickly? We were called in soon after."

"I have a bicycle, sir."

"I see. What happened then?"

"Sergeant Hollis came out here in a borrowed cart, but he didn't stay for long. He looked at Mr Roper, said that this was a matter for his superiors to deal with and left."

Lestrade scratched his head. "Did you return on your bicycle?"

"I did, sir."

"Then how did you occupy yourself from the time you got back to the house, until my constable ordered you to remain in a room with the maid and under guard."

"I spent most of the time doing what I could for Mrs Roper, which was very little I'm afraid. I found a clean sheet which I gave to your man, since I knew it would be needed. I also acquainted the maid with the situation as best I could, which was difficult because the girl is foreign. I think she knows now, though."

"All right," Lestrade viewed the man suspiciously. "You can go, but I'll want to talk to you again, I don't doubt." He looked at my friend. "Do you have any questions for this man, Mr Holmes?"

"Only two." He looked directly at Danvers. "Did you, at any time, approach the body?"

"No, sir."

"And how long have you been in Mr Roper's employ?"

"Fifteen years, sir. I served with Mrs Roper's family for many years previously, since she was no more than a child."

"You came with her, as it were, when she married?"

"That is correct, sir."

"Thank you, Danvers, that is all I need to ask."

"Be good enough to send in the maid," Lestrade said to the butler's retreating back.

Shortly after, the maid entered. She was far from the exotic beauty I had imagined, being short and rather narrow-faced. I saw at once that her most noticeable features were her shining black hair which she had tied with a ribbon, and her dark eyes which seemed to hold a resentful glitter.

Lestrade did not invite her to sit, but launched immediately into his questioning.

"What can you tell us about this dreadful business, girl?"

It took her a moment to answer, perhaps to understand the question in a tongue that was not her own.

"I know nothing of killing, sir."

Now it was the inspector's turn for slowness, the girl's English was so heavily-accented.

"Oh, yes. Have you seen your master quarrel with anyone, or did you happen to see whoever broke in here?"

She shook her head vigorously. "I see nothing."

"You heard no raised voices, or noise of someone smashing their way through that window back there?"

"Nothing," she repeated. "Mr Roper was a good man."

Lestrade was finding communication difficult and he fell silent, I thought while he decided whether to continue.

"Senorita Carlotta, did you see anyone watching the house, beforehand." Holmes asked suddenly.

Again, the girl took some little time to reply. "I saw the man who is my mistress' friend."

"Yesterday?"

She shook her head again. "It was days ago. I saw no one after."

"Did this man enter the house?"

"No. I saw him walking past, two or three times. He was always looking at the windows." She hesitated, as if uncertain whether to elaborate. "I saw mistress wave to him once, when my master was not there."

"Thank you," Holmes said.

"You can return to your duties, for now," Lestrade told her, evidently with some relief at not having to struggle to understand her further.

"Well, I don't know, Mr Holmes," he confessed when the door had closed behind her. "It seems as if we have someone else to consider here. I shall have to speak again to Mrs Roper of course, but the lady is too distressed at the moment. I will return to Scotland Yard, where I will consider your observations also."

Holmes nodded. "Quite so, Inspector. It is always best, I find, to think at some length about the facts and their implications before reaching any conclusions. Doubtlessly our paths will cross again before long, but for now we will bid you good-day."

"Well, Watson, what do you make of this?" Our hansom was on its way back to Baker Street, and my friend had spent some time in contemplation.

"I have solved it," I answered triumphantly.

"Indeed?" His suppressed smile did not deter me, for I knew that my theory was sound. "Pray explain."

"The butler, Danvers, explained his injured hand as the result of his carelessness while sharpening knives. I am inclined to think that the damage was incurred by broken glass as he smashed the window to create the apparent means of escape."

Holmes raised his eyebrows. "Excellent. Watson, you go from strength to strength. All that you have said is correct, but I do not think that the butler is responsible for Mr Roper's death. I watched his response to Lestrade's questions carefully, and they convinced me that there is no malice in the man, and certainly no reason for him to take the life of his master."

"Then I confess to being in the dark as to who actually killed Mr Roper. The maid seems an unlikely prospect."

"Perhaps, but do remember that we know little about her. However, it has crossed my mind that our client may be more deeply connected to this affair than he would have us believe, whether or not he is aware of it."

"What then, is your intention now?"

Holmes adopted a thoughtful look and, as our cab turned into Baker Street, he replied briefly: "I suppose I shall have to keep an eye on Mr Barlow for a day or two. However, that is for later. First, we will partake of the fresh salmon which I know that Mrs Hudson has procured for our luncheon."

We did indeed enjoy an excellent lunch. As soon as it was over, Holmes vanished into his room, to emerge a short while later in the guise of a rather well-dressed man-about-town.

"I think this will suffice," he remarked as he studied himself in the full-length mirror. "Kindly inform Mrs Hudson that I am likely to be a little late for dinner."

There my friend was mistaken, for he reappeared at the moment our landlady served my chicken pie. He quickly shed his disguise and in moments we were eating a steaming meal together.

"Were you successful in finding Mr Barlow?" I enquired when the coffee pot was empty.

"There was no difficulty there. I simply waited near Berryman's until he left, and then followed him to his home in Highgate. It appears that he has kept his word to us in not attempting to approach Mrs Roper, at least since this morning. He sent no telegram on his way home, and posted no letter although, as this evening's newspapers are full of the incident, he must know of Mr Roper's murder by now. I must return to Highgate this evening, tomorrow and possibly the next day for, if our client is involved he will certainly wish to ensure that everything in Mayfair has turned out as he intended. I do not think he will visit her otherwise, despite her apparent need for comfort, because this will not only bring their friendship into the open and cause a scandal for them both but will, in the eyes of some, implicate him in the crime. Now, a change of appearance again I think, and I must spend the next few hours in a rather uninteresting fashion."

I saw little of him during the following day or two, except for some meals and his brief appearances in a variety of different guises. A plumber, a window-cleaner, a tramp and a tinker all came and went until finally, once more at breakfast, he sat at the table restored to himself.

"Have you been successful in discovering our client's connection to Mr Roper's death?" I asked when our meal was over.

"I have been successful in establishing that he had nothing to do with it. He has made no attempt to see Mrs Roper, or to be anywhere near Mayfair, as far as I can tell. It was a false trail, Watson, but I am glad to discount it from our list of possibilities."

I nodded. "How then, will you proceed?"

We heard the door-bell ring, and were immediately still to listen. The caller spoke briefly to Mrs Hudson, before we heard the door close and she returned to the kitchen. For once, this did not concern us.

"I have an appointment," Holmes continued, "with Mr Artemis Blunt. From him I am expecting to learn the reason behind this crime and possibly how to obtain a confession."

"But who is this Mr Blunt, and who are you expecting to confess?"

"He is Mr Roper's solicitor, who controls the estate. As for the murderer, I must confess that I was in no doubt from the beginning. The difficulty was in obtaining some sort of proof that would convince Lestrade, before his blundering obscured or ignored every indication."

"Who, then, is responsible?"

He consulted his pocket-watch. "You will find out very shortly, old fellow. For now I must depart to avoid keeping Mr Blunt waiting. I will however, leave you with one thought: what evidence did you see of our client's claim that Mr Roper was a violent man?"

With that he was gone, and from the window I saw him board a passing cab. After a while I settled myself at the table to perform the long overdue task of bringing some of my medical notes up to date. Less than an hour had passed, when the door-bell rang once more.

I strained my ears to listen, as I had seen Holmes do in order to prepare himself for a visitor, and heard a woman speak briefly to our landlady. The door closed and I heard footsteps on the stairs before Mrs Hudson knocked and entered our sitting-room.

"Doctor Watson," she began, "A lady downstairs is here to see Mr Holmes. I have explained that he is out, but she insists on leaving a message. Will you see her?"

I put aside my pen. "Of course. Please show her in."

A moment later the lady entered. She was dressed completely in black, her bonnet and veil hiding much of her features, and she said at once that her message was brief. I introduced myself and offered her a chair.

"No, thank you, sir. I have little time. As you see, I am here to attend a funeral. I must return to Norwich on the afternoon train."

"Very well. What is it that you would like me to tell Mr Holmes?"

"Simply this. I am Miss Jane Roper. My brother, Mr Andrew Roper, was a good man. Whatever you are told to the contrary, I beg you to disbelieve. Please do not proceed with your investigation deceived by anyone who would tell you otherwise. That is all I have to say, sir."

"Yes, but...." I said no more, for I was speaking to an empty room. She had fled abruptly, and I heard her descend the stairs and close the door.

For some time after I wondered how that distressed and tearful lady could know that Holmes was concerned with the affair of her brother's death, and concluded that she had probably visited Scotland Yard and learned it from Lestrade. I wondered also whether she was acquainted with Mr Ebenezer Barlow, our client, or if Mrs Roper had remarked about her late husband's ill-treatment.

It was almost time for luncheon when Holmes reappeared, and he listened intently as I described Miss Roper's visit.

"You may take the lady at her word, Watson," he said as I concluded my account. "As I suspected, and Mr Blunt confirmed, Mr Roper was not known to be violent."

"Then what of our client's fears?"

"Unfounded, all of them. I hope to demonstrate this, later."

"The visit to Mr Blunt was satisfactory, then?"

"Very." He hung up his coat and we repaired to our armchairs to await Mrs Hudson. "He confirmed much that I had surmised. Mr Barlow will be distressed to learn that Mrs Roper has no affection for him nor any use, save to rid her of her husband."

"Our client is the killer, after all?"

Holmes shook his head, smiling at my lack of comprehension. "Not so, old fellow, but that was Mrs Roper's reason for allowing a friendship between them to develop. I believe that she was making him progressively anxious for her by means of her accounts of ill-treatment, intending to do so until he felt bound to act in her defence. His feelings for her would have dulled the enormity of taking her husband's life, had it come to that."

"Did he refuse then, necessitating her use of another?"

"There was no need. According to Mr Blunt, the marriage of Mr and Mrs Roper had been faltering for some time, despite the image they projected in public. Mrs Roper made several attempts to induce her husband to sign a large part of his fortune over to her, but to no avail. When she met Mr Barlow she saw her opportunity to take it all, since it would revert to her on her husband's death, but she needed time to convince our client gradually. Then an event occurred which compelled her to act immediately. You see, Watson, Mr Roper had a previous marriage, he was in fact a widower when he met his current wife. From that first marriage came a son, Anthony, from whom his father has been estranged for years until a chance meeting in a London club saw them restored to an amicable state."

The situation was now clear to me. "Whereupon Mr Roper intended to change his will in favour of the son, leaving his present wife with much less?"

"Precisely. He had intended to do this the day after Mrs Roper put a knife in his heart, which is why she acted so quickly. He made a fatal error by informing her. She would still, on his natural death, have inherited a substantial sum but, as in many situations that I have encountered, that was not enough – she wanted it all. The timing of the murder made Mr Blunt suspicious, and so it was easy to persuade him to assist in obtaining a confession, which he and I will do this afternoon. As I have indicated, it was obvious from the first: you will recall our client's description of Mrs Roper's facial injuries, of which there was no sign when we met her."

"Her skill with theatrical face-paint, from her previous profession."

"Exactly."

"But Danvers, the butler, was he a party to this?"

"Yes, but I doubt if he will suffer for it. The man has loved her since her childhood – you will recall that I questioned him about the length of his association with the family – and it may well be that she somehow presented him with another explanation of what had occurred."

"But for such a great actress, admired by many, to have done such a thing. I would never have believed it."

"That, if I may say so, has also been obvious to me from the outset. As I have stated before now, there is no place for sentiment or preconceived impressions in the methods of the ideal reasoner. Now, the only missing piece for the case to be complete is the lady's confession." He inclined his head, listening. "Ah! But I believe our luncheon is on its way. Let us take our seats and see what our good landlady has prepared for us."

He could hardly contain his impatience to begin upon his plans for the afternoon, although it was with some surprise that I watched him consume his meal since I had become used to him eating only a small amount or leaving his food entirely untouched.

No sooner had he replaced his teacup in its saucer than he sprang to his feet.

"I regret, Watson, that I cannot ask you to accompany me on this occasion. However, you have my solemn word that I will relate the occurrences of this afternoon in their entirety to you, upon my return."

With that he withdrew to his room, emerging in a remarkably short time as a rather prim young man in the subdued dress of the legal profession.

"Mr Blunt requires a clerk to be present to witness his dealings with Mrs Roper," he explained. "He and I have come to an agreement as to what she should be told."

With that, he picked up a battered briefcase and left without another word. I confess to feeling disconcerted at my exclusion, but I could not see how I could have been of service in Holmes' plan. I resumed my study of my medical notes but found concentration difficult, so that I took up my book after a while to lose myself in the exploits of the great explorers in the days of sail. After a chapter or two I became drowsy but shook myself awake, as I had heard the door close loudly before quick footsteps sounded upon the stairs.

"Ah, there you are, Watson!" Holmes said as he entered. "Did I not say that I would be away for no more than a short time?"

"It all went well, then?"

"Exactly as I anticipated. Pray contain your impatience until I have resumed my normal appearance, and I will tell you all."

He vanished into his room abruptly, and I heard water splashing as I retrieved my notebook. Shortly after he reappeared, having shed his disguise, and I poured us each a glass of brandy as we seated ourselves.

Holmes consulted his pocket-watch. "I see that there remains almost an hour before dinner. Ample time, I should think, for me to acquaint you with all that has transpired." He took a sip from his glass, before replacing it on a side-table.

"Mr Blunt and I discussed our intentions further during our journey to Mayfair," he began. "By the time we arrived he was quite clear as to the part he should play, and I must say that he did so faultlessly. We were admitted by the Spanish maid, Carlotta, and shown into the room where Mr Roper died. I observed that the window had been repaired. Mrs Roper appeared in high spirits, apparently having convinced herself that her role as a grieving widow could be dispensed with, now that the funeral is over. I believe that she had also deluded herself that her crime was undiscovered, possibly encouraged by Lestrade's erroneous conclusions."

"The Inspector has made further investigations, then?"

"Apparently he could make nothing of my recommendation that he search for the intruder within the house, and decided to concentrate his efforts externally. At Mr Blunt's suggestion, and after he had introduced me as his clerk, we sat around the table and he produced documents relevant to the estate. I watched as the expression of expectation grew on Mrs Roper's face. Seldom have I seen more pitiless greed than that which filled her eyes. When the solicitor reached the clause that I had convinced him to insert, stating that her husband had already altered the beneficiary of his entire wealth, her face froze as if encased in ice. All animation drained from it and she exhibited symptoms of profound shock. 'Anthony,' she whispered. 'No, not him. Why did I not act sooner.' She jumped to her feet and hammered on the table with her fists, terrifying Mr Blunt and making it apparent that she had lost all reason. Eventually she became calmer, and I asked her when she had decided to kill her husband and she replied that it had not been her original intention. She had, as I suspected, begun to prepare Mr Barlow for that role. 'What would I want with a penniless clerk, otherwise?' she enquired of herself. I saw then that she was probably unaware that she was confessing, but she surprised me by fixing me with a hateful stare and saying that she knew that she had met me before."

"She must be a most perceptive woman. I would not have recognised you."

"I can only suppose that it was a similarity in the voice I had adopted. Playing so many parts on the stage, she would be sensitive to such things."

I nodded. "Doubtlessly. Did you then send Danvers to the local police station?"

"It was unnecessary. I had telegraphed Lestrade earlier, and he arrived at precisely the right time accompanied by two constables. Mrs Roper, I fear, will spend some time in the cells at Scotland Yard before the trial. I have no doubts that her performance then will equal any of those enacted upon the stage, but let us hope that the jury is composed of level-headed men." He sat back in his chair and inhaled deeply. "But Watson, today is one of those rare times when my appetite has become considerable. Let us finish our brandy, before doing justice to the fried chicken that I smell as the aroma increases with Mrs Hudson's approach."

The Adventure of the Incessant Workers

During my long association with my friend Mr Sherlock Holmes I was privileged to witness his dealings with clients of all classes and from many walks of life. Not all visitors to our lodgings in Baker Street sought his attentions, however. I recall a stormy May morning when our landlady, Mrs Hudson, ushered a windswept lady with quite a different purpose into our sitting room.

"Mrs Clementine Durrell, to see Doctor Watson," she announced. "Shall I bring tea, gentlemen?"

Holmes assented, with a faint air of disappointment. "You seem to be more in demand than I today, Watson," he said. "If you and your patient have no objection, I will remove myself to the far side of the room to continue my reading while I drink my tea."

"Please do not inconvenience yourself on my account," the lady said at once. "There is nothing of a personal nature to be discussed. I merely seek a second opinion about something which my own doctor is unable to clarify."

"Very well." I gestured to her to take one of the armchairs. As we seated ourselves Mrs Hudson brought in the tea-tray, and I waited until she withdrew before pouring for the three of us. Holmes took his cup and resumed his perusal of *The Standard.*

"How is it, Mrs Durrell, that you have come here to consult me, rather than at my practice?" I asked her then.

She replaced her cup in its saucer, which she stood carefully on the tray. I noticed that her hand shook. "I should explain that my usual physician is Doctor Selby, who I have consulted several times about my ailment. He is an elderly man, due to retire soon I think, and appears perplexed as to my condition. He suggested that I seek a second opinion but was not specific and, knowing of no other medical men or anyone who could make a recommendation, I was at a loss to know where to turn. Then I read a newspaper article about one of Mr Holmes' cases and you were mentioned. I resolved then to visit you here as I had no other address, in the hope of receiving the benefit of your advice."

While she had been speaking I noticed Holmes look up briefly at the mention of his name. I had no doubt that he had heard every word, and made his usual observations about my patient.

As for my own observations, I would have placed Mrs Durrell at about thirty years of age. There was a delicate air about her, and indeed that describes her looks also. A tall woman, her dark hair was unfashionably long, surrounding her elfin features and lying easily on the shoulders of her green costume. Her eyes appeared slightly sunken, her expression drawn, and her every movement betrayed a heavy weariness.

I put down my own cup. "I understand. Pray tell me than, what it is that troubles you."

"It seems so absurd, when put into words," she said after an embarrassed hesitation, "but it is simply that I awake every morning in a state of exhaustion. I am more weary then than on retiring the previous night. Doctor Selby prescribed a tonic at first, but it had no effect."

I nodded. My first thought was that this lady had fallen prey to somnambulism. Previously, over the years, I had been consulted by several sufferers, usually former military men haunted by memories of violent action.

"Has your husband been disturbed by your movements during the early hours, perhaps by you walking around the room?"

"I am a widow sir," she said sadly. "My Richard was taken by consumption, three years ago. Nevertheless, I am able to tell you that I have considered this and found nothing to suggest it. Nothing was out of place throughout the house, and the front door was locked as I had left it."

"I am sorry to hear about your husband," I said with feeling. "For how long has this tiredness persisted?"

"Almost four weeks, and I am aware that my appearance has begun to show it. I suspect that it could have been longer, and that I may not have been aware of it at first."

There was a long moment of silence as I considered Mrs Durrell's account. Clearly, the tonic prescribed by Doctor Selby had not helped, nor could I see that a stronger preparation was the answer. Laudanum perhaps? No, for that would simply be a temporary solution that would not attack the source of her complaint.

Suddenly, Holmes put down his newspaper and strode across the room.

"Pray excuse my interruption," he began, his eyes moving from my patient to myself, "but I feel that I may have something to contribute, here."

I glanced at Mrs Durrell, who nodded her acceptance of my friend's inclusion in our conversation. "Do join us, Holmes, please."

When he has settled himself in the basket chair, we looked at him expectantly.

"I believe that this may be in my province as well as yours after all, Watson. During the past two weeks I have been consulted twice by prospective clients with exactly the same symptoms, if I may put it like that. Mrs Durrell, if you could tell us what you are able to recall of your dreams throughout the nights before awakening in a state of exhaustion, it would be most helpful."

The lady appeared somewhat surprised by this request, and looked to me for confirmation that she should take this seriously.

Then a new expression crossed her features. "It has just now occurred to me as strange, that my dreams have not varied at all. I dream of the same event each night."

"And what event is that, pray?"

She shook her head, wearily. "My only impression is of sitting at a desk or table, surrounded by banknotes of a high value. I am sorting the money into piles of equal number and someone is watching constantly. The only sounds that I recall are of being urged to work faster, ever faster."

"Precisely the descriptions of the two men who asked my advice previously," Holmes cried triumphantly. "You mark my words, Watson, there is something strange afoot here."

"What advice did you give to these men?" I enquired.

"My first inclination was to recommend that they seek out a priest, for I have had many similar situations put to me to which that was the solution. When the second man approached me however, I realised at once that more was involved because his account was identical to the first. I then resolved to treat both as unsolved cases, which would bear investigation when additional evidence came to light. Mrs Durrell has now supplied such evidence."

71

"Then I am not going mad," she said in a voice heavy with relief. "I considered that as a possible explanation, for these experiences are distressing and I have not known their like before."

"That is certainly not the case," I reassured her. "But Mr Holmes and myself will spare no effort until the true cause is found."

"That there is some human agency behind this I have no doubt," Holmes added. "I have no inclination as to how this can be as yet, but you may be sure that no stone will be left unturned until all is revealed."

The lady got to her feet. "I am so grateful to you both for setting my mind at rest. Is there anything more that I can tell you?"

Holmes looked thoughtful for a moment. "You are a widow, are you not"?

"I have said as much, sir."

"Then tell me, pray, has the loss of your husband compelled you to earn your own living?"

"It has."

"What then, is your present occupation?"

"I work in a laundry."

"That was one of the possibilities that presented themselves to me after examining your hands while we spoke. Thank you, Mrs Durrell, you will hear from us presently."

It was left to me then to show our client out. On the stairs she gave me a glance that told me she had not understood the relevance of Holmes' observation, and that she found him to be curious among men. I was glad to see that the storm had subsided somewhat as I secured a passing hansom for her.

I re-entered our sitting room to see Holmes watching from the window as the hansom departed.

"It seems we are on the same track, Holmes."

"It never ceases to surprise me how the situations that confront us can alter in an instant, after facts are brought to light during discussion." He lowered his head, still peering through the window. "But I see that the dark clouds are passing and the wind has definitely dropped. I think, Watson, that with your permission our enquiries can begin immediately."

Within the hour we found ourselves in the waiting room of Doctor Selby's surgery. The three patients ahead of us had been dealt with quickly, emerging from the doctor's presence after far less time than I would have allowed. I recalled that he was elderly and on the brink of retirement.

The last of them, a one-legged man with a crude crutch fashioned from a tree branch, re-entered the waiting room and sullenly limped out into the street. The doctor called for us to join him.

Doctor Selby was indeed elderly. A grey and bleary-eyed man, he sat half bent over his desk. At our approach, he looked up sharply.

"I had not expected two patients at the same time. Which of you gentlemen requires my attention, or is it both?"

We removed our hats.

"That is not the cause of our visit, sir," said my friend. "My name is Sherlock Holmes, and this is my friend and associate, Doctor John Watson."

"A medical man also. If there is no ailment, what can have brought you to me?"

At Doctor Selby's invitation we settled ourselves in the two worn chairs before us.

"We are making enquiries about one of your patients," Holmes began. "Mrs Durrell, I understand, consulted you recently regarding her exhaustive state."

The elderly physician nodded. "Ah, I recall the lady. She did indeed appear exhausted. My examination revealed nothing to be physically amiss, so I prescribed a tonic of herbs with a recommendation that she should drink plenty of strong coffee. She returned not long after, but I felt there was little else I could do for her apart from adding a sleeping draught to be taken on retiring to increase the depth of her slumber. She declined this, and I have not seen her since."

"Did she mention the repetitive dream that haunts her?" I enquired.

He looked thoughtful briefly, before the recollection came to him. "She did speak of something of the sort, but I attached no significance to it. I am not a doctor of the mind, but it seems obvious that an unhealthy obsession with money is involved, having no connection with Mrs Durrell's excessive tiredness."

"Did she disclose anything more, about her dream or general condition?" Holmes asked.

"I can recall little else of what transpired during our interview." Doctor Selby shook his head slowly. "Her ailment is most peculiar, though. I have not come across the like of it, in all my years in the medical profession."

Holmes and I rose together.

"Strange indeed. Our thanks to you, Doctor, for a most informative conversation," my friend said. "We will now take our leave of you and wish you a very good morning."

Holmes' remark about the time of day was only just correct, for it was almost mid-day. We returned to Baker Street to consume our luncheon, which was for me a good helping of Mrs Hudson's curried chicken. Holmes, as was usual when he was in the midst of an enquiry, dealt with his food less enthusiastically.

"We seem to have learned little from Doctor Selby." I observed as I pushed away my empty plate.

"Much to the contrary, Watson," Holmes replied thoughtfully. "We have had confirmation of much that Mrs Durrell told us."

"That would seem to be so, but I cannot see how we can proceed."

"A visit to Mr Michael Brewer would doubtlessly help to set us on the right path."

After a moment of recollection, I shook my head. "I have not heard that name before."

"That is because I have not mentioned it. He is one of the two previous clients whose account was the same as that of Mrs Durrell."

At my friend's direction, the driver brought the hansom to a halt near the entrance to a decrepit alley somewhere in Whitechapel. The decaying buildings on either side were tall enough to prevent much of the newly-appeared early afternoon sun from lighting our path, and the smell from the occasional piles of rubbish caused us to take only shallow breaths.

Holmes' knowledge of London has always been a source of amazement to me, and now he led us through what became a maze of narrow backstreets as if they were thoroughly familiar to him. Presently we emerged into a tiny square courtyard. It was a dismal place, containing six houses in poor repair with tiny barren gardens before them. My friend peered at the faded numbers briefly, then opened the low and rickety gate and approached the front entrance. He rapped upon the door with his stick, receiving no response at first. I was about to suggest that he repeat the summons when it swung open, its hinges squealing in protest.

"What do you want?" Asked the dowdy and solemn woman after a moment of staring at us suspiciously.

"Mrs Brewer?" Enquired my friend.

"What if I am?"

Holmes put on his most charming smile. "My name is Sherlock Holmes. Your husband may have mentioned to you that he consulted me on an unusual matter concerning his health."

I noted that he made no reference to his true profession, doubtlessly because any connection to the law would automatically be met with resistance here.

"He said something," she replied unsmilingly, "but it seems you did him no good. He acts as if he's worn out all the time, and I can't get him out of his chair. We'll have no food soon, if he doesn't change his ways."

"Does he, by any chance, leave the house during the night?"

"I don't know how you found that out, unless he told you. It's true, how he can do it when he says he hasn't the strength to stand up during the day I don't understand."

"It may be that I will soon be able to throw some light upon this curious condition," Holmes told her. "Can we now come in and speak to him?"

"If he's awake, you can." She stood aside and we entered the dwelling. Halfway along a dusty corridor she pointed to a door ahead and said "There," before disappearing into a nearer, shadowy chamber.

We approached the room she had indicated and Holmes knocked on the ill-fitting woodwork, announcing us. The reply that came from within was more a kind of weary growl than a bid to enter, but we took it to mean the same. The room held little that was unexpected, tattered curtains hung around smeared windows and the single armchair contained a sprawled figure.

"Mr Brewer," Holmes began, after introducing me. "I am sorry to see that your situation has not improved. We are here because we have learned something more, and are getting closer to a solution."

Mr Brewer made a gesture which Holmes interpreted as permission to sit, and we settled ourselves in the two straight-backed chairs near the worn table. This man did indeed look tired to the point of being ill. He was in a worse state, I thought, than I had observed Mrs Durrell to be. His unshaven face and disarranged hair contributed to his appearance of absolute hopelessness, and I would have wagered that his shapeless trousers and collarless shirt had adorned his body for many days.

"Have you yet discovered the cause of this?" His voice was barely a whisper, like someone who is barely conscious.

"We have made some way forward," Holmes answered. "You may be assured that what ails you is not natural, but is caused by the actions of another."

In the gloom I saw Mr Brewer's eyes widen. "But how is that possible, and why? To my knowledge, I have no enemies."

"Those are among the questions we seek to answer. Pray tell us, are the dreams you spoke of before continuing?"

"They are, and worse than before. In the midst of a restless sleep I am surrounded by more money than I have ever known, and on awakening my strength, my will to live, grows less every day."

Holmes nodded. "Your wife had said that you leave the house every night, and you refuse to explain how this is possible. What have you to say to that?"

"I cannot explain it. Neither can I remember doing this. As I told you before, Mr Holmes, I go to my bed exhausted and awake the next morning feeling ten times as weary. I know nothing more."

"When you consulted me in Baker Street, you did not mention the recommendation of your Doctor. What was his advice?"

"Doctor Queller insisted that these effects are part of the normal process of ageing, for some men. He assured me that they would pass, after some little time."

"Then he must have rare knowledge indeed," I said. "Never in all my years in medicine have I come across such nonsense. Has he perhaps travelled in the East, and adopted some of their attitudes towards healing?"

"That I do not know, Doctor. I am mostly unfamiliar with the man. He has recently taken over the practice of Doctor Barker, who is now deceased."

"Be so good as to describe him for us," Holmes requested.

Mr Brewer hesitated, as if the effort of recalling Doctor Queller's appearance was immense, as it probably was to his sluggish senses. "He is tall, and very thin. His nose is sharp and pointed and his hair longer than is usual, and grey. His manner is what you would call aloof."

I saw a glimmer of excitement in my friend's eyes. "Did he, by any chance, have a missing left forefinger?"

"I am sorry, Mr Holmes," Mr Brewer shook his head slowly. "I was in no condition to notice, at the consultation."

"No matter," Holmes hid his impatience well, I thought. "you have given us a new line of enquiry, for which I thank you. I have every expectation that matters will be put aright soon, and you have my word that I will not rest until then. May your recovery be swift. Good afternoon to you, Mr Brewer."

Holmes took us back through the labyrinth of alleyways, and as we regained the streets of Whitechapel I saw that the look of triumph that I had come to know well had entered his expression.

"Have you found the solution to this curious business, Holmes?" I asked him as he raised his stick to attract the attention of the driver of a passing four-wheeler.

He made no answer, but I saw a secretive smile steal across his face as we took our seats. He shouted the address of our lodgings and the carriage moved off at once.

"Yes, Watson, I believe I have it now," he said as we passed a group of urchins who were begging from passers-by. "I will however require confirmation, but that should be settled by means of a couple of telegrams." He then instructed our driver to stop at the nearest Post Office.

#

That evening we ate an excellent dinner, and I was pleased to see that the solving of this affair had improved my friend's appetite. About two hours must have passed, and we sat in our usual armchairs reading, he the latest *London Evening News,* and I a medical journal, when the answers to his telegrams arrived.

"Capital!" he exclaimed as he tore open the envelopes. There was a moment of silence between us when the only sounds were of a passing carriage beneath our window and Mrs Hudson's retreating footsteps on the stairs. "Mr Stephen Lang confirms that he also consulted Doctor Queller, and that he noticed his missing finger."

"I take it that Mr Lang is the other client who previously consulted you on this matter?"

"You take it correctly, Watson. The other message is from our current client, Mrs Clementine Durrell, who informs us that a man of similar description to Doctor Queller was present as an unidentified observer, during one of her visits to Doctor Selby. This is all taking shape rather well, I think."

"Who is this Doctor Queller, Holmes? That you have had previous dealings with him is obvious, since you knew of his missing finger. I cannot recollect you mentioning him before now."

My friend reached for the Persian slipper on the mantle-shelf and filled his clay pipe. "You will recall Barker, the private enquiry agent with whom I have had some dealings?"

"Of course."

"It was he, not I, who encountered the so-called Doctor Queller in the course of a case of extortion. I understand that Queller narrowly escaped a prison sentence, due to the disappearance of a witness who was never traced."

"It sounds as if he could have been done away with."

"Most probably, but it was not proven." Holmes blew out a cloud of smoke and leaned back in his chair. "However, if Queller was innocent of that, I'll wager that he had it done. He is no more a doctor than I am, in fact he was dismissed from the Royal College of Physicians while still in the early stages of training. His real name is Elisha Cobb, but he has not been known as that for years. During the case involving Barker, I added much that the dailies reported to my index."

"Should we not inform Inspector Lestrade of this man's activities?"

Holmes shook his head slowly. "As yet, we have little to charge him with. However, if you would care to continue reading for a while, I believe I have the means to set things in motion."

I took up my medical journal again, as I was bidden. Holmes sat in silence until he finished smoking, then returned his pipe to the rack before crossing the room to stare out of the window. After a short while he suddenly exclaimed "Aha!" and dashed out into the street. I rose and looked down at the passing hansoms and people out for an evening walk, to see my friend in conversation with a ragged urchin who saluted smartly and ran off. Seconds later I heard Holmes on the stairs, and he quickly resumed his seat.

"I was fortunate enough to see one of the Irregulars out there. They have been instructed to watch Doctor Queller's house from now until the early hours. That should be sufficient time, I think, for him to take the action that he must if my presumptions are correct. As for us, my dear fellow, we have work to do this evening."

"What have you in mind?"

A quick smile. "A little matter of burglary."

"My dear Holmes!" I exclaimed, surprised.

"You really shouldn't be so shocked, Watson. We have, in the course of some enquiry or other, undertaken such a course before, have we not?"

"Yes, but…."

"But are you with me now, as you were then?"

I allowed myself to smile, at the memory. "As ever."

"I thought I knew my Watson."

#

A distant church clock chimed eleven as we took up our position beneath a sprawling beech in a well-to-do side road off Hammersmith High Street.

"We are in deep shadow here, Watson. Even from a few yards away, we are invisible."

"That is reassuring but the street is deserted, fortunately."

"Yet the Irregulars are here somewhere. I gave Winters, the boy you saw me with, most specific directions. Apparently, my training was not wasted on them."

From then we stood in silence. An occasional fellow, dressed for an evening out, walked or staggered along the street, and once a cat ran madly across, but at no time was our presence detected.

Presently, the clock chimed again. It was now midnight and no more than a few minutes later the front door of the house we watched opened to reveal a man in a tall top hat who struck off smartly along the street in the other direction.

"That was Queller," Holmes whispered when the man was almost out of sight. We saw a shadow detach itself from a nearby wall, and move quietly in pursuit.

"Your unofficial detective force have not failed you," I said quietly.

"We will enter by the front door, I think, since the street remains deserted."

"Holmes, what if the man has a wife, or there are servants within?"

I sensed his eyes upon me, in the darkness.

"You surely do not imagine that I would have brought us here with such intentions, had I not first ascertained that Queller lives alone. An elderly couple attend from morning to late afternoon, to care for his needs and the simple maintenance of the house, but that is all."

We spoke no more until my friend had produced and made use of his pick-lock, while I kept watch in both directions. We entered slowly and without a sound. The house was quiet except for the loud ticking of a tall casement clock standing in the hall. Holmes ignored all four of the doors facing us and noiselessly climbed the stairs two at a time. Three more doors on the landing were opened and quickly closed again, until he entered the fourth room and beckoned me to follow.

"The study," he whispered. "That is where it will be."

"What are we looking for, Holmes?"

"Proof of my theory. Proof that Queller is responsible for the exhausted condition of Mrs Durrell, and the others."

He produced a dark lantern, and by its light examined the contents of the bookcase and those of a locked desk drawer, which again required the use of his pick- lock. After a surprisingly short time, but to my relief, he announced that we were leaving.

"Already? Have you found what you were searching for?"

"Everything."

"Is it as you supposed?"

"Exactly as I supposed."

"Then we can return to Baker Street?"

"By the first carriage that presents itself."

We took our leave of the place, ensuring that everything was as it had been before.

#

Holmes seemed in an extraordinarily cheerful mood the following morning. I attributed this to the obvious satisfaction he derived from bringing some understanding to this strange affair, and on my mentioning this, he immediately concurred.

"It is always gratifying to be proven correct in one's suppositions, Watson," he answered. "The final piece of the puzzle will be within our grasp when my unofficial force bring me the results of their activities."

"What is it that you expect them to have discovered?"

"The location of the factory."

I looked up from the morning edition of *The Standard* at this unexpected prospective development. "The factory? How does such a place concern our investigation, Holmes?"

"It is where Queller was bound for, when we saw him leave his house last night. If not that, it has to be a fairly large room to contain all his victims. You can be sure that the three we are aware of do not represent the extent of his villainy."

The steely look in my friend's eyes told me that it would have been unwise for me to enquire of him further for, as was usual for him, he would enjoy revealing all at the time he considered appropriate. Showing a little impatience, he wandered across to the window before resuming his seat.

I was about to ask when he expected to hear from the Irregulars, when the door-bell rang, answering my question before I posed it. I heard Mrs Hudson answer the summons and her voice rose critically, before quick footfalls echoed on the stairs and a hurried knock sounded upon our door.

"Come in, Wiggins!" Holmes cried, and I knew he had seen our visitor approach from the window.

The leader of the Irregulars entered, looking slightly taller and older than when I had last seen him. He snatched his cap from his head and stood stiffly at attention, before us.

"Did you succeed?" Holmes asked him at once.

"We did sir. It was just as you said."

"And where was the place?"

Wiggins produced a crumpled paper from his pocket and handed it to Holmes. "There is the address, Mr Holmes. It is some distance away, in Hammersmith. The gentleman arrived not long after half past midnight as far as we could judge and spent about twenty minutes inside the building, which was a place that used to make bicycle clips. When he came out, it was with a big man, a really nasty-looking cove, I can tell you, and together they sent twenty two people, both men and women, in different directions. Did we do well, sir?"

"You conducted yourselves without fault or error," Holmes assured him. "Here is twice our agreed rate, together with enough money to cover the additional inconvenience of travelling further afield. Kindly express my appreciation to your companions."

Wiggins gave a slight bow as he accepted he coins, before mumbling his thanks. A moment later we heard the front door close as he departed.

"I presume he spoke of the factory that you mentioned earlier," I enquired, as Holmes glanced at the paper.

He nodded. "I think we can safely spend today reading, or perhaps partaking of some exercise. I may take it upon myself to conclude the series of chemical experiments that I have been conducting of late, for we can do nothing more until tonight. Then, I have great hopes that we can bring this affair to its conclusion."

And so it came to be. As it was a fine day we passed the morning in a pleasant stroll in Hyde Park, and the afternoon as Holmes had suggested. Our mealtimes came and went, slowly for me as I found myself eager to discover the true nature of this adventure. I would certainly add it to the chronicles intended for my publisher, but whether Holmes would allow this was, as usual, quite another matter.

After dinner, we had begun a long discussion concerning the current political situation, particularly the rising influence of Imperial Germany, when Holmes paused abruptly and took out his pocket-watch.

"It is time, Watson. If we leave now, we will be in Hammersmith just after midnight."

So involved had I been in our discussion that the lateness of the hour had quite escaped me. We rose and retrieved our hats and coats, before leaving quietly so as not to disturb Mrs Hudson.

Because of the lateness of the hour hansoms were not so much in evidence, and we had walked almost to the end of Baker Street before one drew up beside us in answer to Holmes' call. I formed the opinion that the cabby was anxious to get to his bed, so rapidly were we conveyed to Hammersmith.

Before long we stood at the end of a long street, poorly lit by the glow from regularly-spaced lamp-posts. The departing hansom left in the direction of the High Street, and we exchanged no word until the sound of the horse's hooves on the cobbles had ceased.

"There appear to be no houses here, Holmes," I observed with difficulty. "These buildings are factories and business premises, some of them disused I would think."

In the poor light, I saw him nod. "And there is but one showing any sign of habitation. I can just make out a lighted window above those rather decrepit gates. Come, I see a deep doorway a little way further on. From the opposite side of the street we should have a clear view."

"But what are we looking for?"

"We are watching for the workers to leave, of course."

"I was under the impression that we were waiting for Doctor Queller."

"And so we are. Have patience, Watson, and all will be revealed soon."

We stood still and in silence in the doorway of the old building. The only sound, apart from an occasional bird-cry, was the faint throbbing of machinery from the lighted factory before us. It seemed hours, but in reality was probably less than an hour, that we waited. I felt cramp in my shoulder, a legacy of the Jezail bullet from my service days, and shifted my position to ease it as Holmes spoke:

"Any moment now, Watson. Try to limit your movements, if you can."

Before I could reply the doors opposite were flung open. A burly roughneck who was probably the man described by Wiggins stepped out into the street and looked cautiously in both directions. Seeing that he was apparently unobserved he made impatient gestures accompanied by a series of oaths, shouting back into the building.

For a few moments nothing happened, then a procession of about twenty people filed out. I recognised at once our client, Mrs Clementine Durrell, and Holmes murmured the names of his two recent clients also. The little group arranged themselves along the pavement with no word having been spoken, and I became aware of the unnatural posture of them all.

"Holmes," I whispered. "They are sleepwalking."

"As I suspected. Ah, here is Queller."

The man who Holmes and I had briefly seen near his house strode out and ordered the group to be ready to leave. About five minutes elapsed before a cart drawn by two black horses appeared at the end of the road and approached. The instant it came to a halt Queller, the other man and the driver pushed and prodded the group until everyone was aboard. I noted that they were about to embark on an uncomfortable journey, for there was little room for half their number. But not a sound, not a cry of complaint, came from their lips, as the cart took them slowly out of our sight.

Queller and the other man, who I presumed to be some sort of factory foreman, exchanged a few words before going their separate ways, each in search of a cab. Only when the street was empty did we emerge from our concealment.

"Holmes, those people looked more dead than alive. What does it all mean?"

He smiled grimly. "First let us see if we are to be fortunate enough to find a hansom at such a late hour, for the second time tonight. A brandy, I think, would be in order on our return to Baker Street."

I knew that to press him for an explanation would be pointless, for it had long been his custom to decline to disclose his theories and deductions until his own chosen moment. Hammersmith High Street was devoid of traffic and we were about to resign ourselves to a long walk with the prospect of finding a cab on the way, when the doors of a tavern burst open and a thick-set and obviously drunk customer was forcibly ejected onto the pavement. We watched as he staggered to his feet and shook his fist at his assailant, then made his way to an open cart nearby. The tethered horse scraped the road impatiently with well-shod hooves, and his master murmured words of affection into the animal's ear and took up the reins.

"Come on, Watson." Holmes strode across to the other side of the street, and I followed closely. In minutes he had come to an agreement with the man and we were on our way back to our lodgings. My friend constantly issued instructions, and despite the inebriated state of our driver we arrived without incident. We thanked him and my friend rewarded him handsomely, and then we were climbing the stairs to our sitting room.

"Holmes, will you now explain to me what this man Queller has done to those people?" I asked when we were settled in our armchairs with glasses of a fine cognac.

He took a sip before placing his glass on a side-table and leaning back in his chair. "Ask first the purpose of our visit to his house last night, and I will reply with one word which will reveal much to you."

"Very well. What is the word?"

"Mesmerism."

"That is how Queller controls them?"

He nodded. "I suspected it almost from the first, and on examining his notes and books on the subject in his study last night, it became a certainty. By means of that practice he is able to cause these individuals to rise from their beds and work for him in that place we watched tonight. I suspect that the work involves the processing and packing of large amounts of counterfeit notes, but that is something for Inspector Lestrade to confirm when I lay the full facts before him."

"This certainly explains the weariness of Mrs Durrell and the others."

"That was to be expected, when they were allowed so little rest. The dreams of course, were the fragments of memories of their unpleasant experiences. They were returned to their homes where, after a few hours, they would awaken exhausted with no recollection of having left."

"And the labours of the day to contend with," I finished. "Little is known of mesmerism as yet, but I would not have thought it possible to manipulate others to this degree."

"It seems it is, old fellow. You cannot have forgotten that scoundrel Marcus Davery, who employed a similar technique."

"No, indeed," We sat drinking in silence for a while, Holmes' mind elsewhere and mine on the incredibility of this affair.

Presently he drained his glass and rose, and I did likewise.

"I do believe we will visit Lestrade at Scotland Yard tomorrow, Watson, after we confront Doctor Queller. But for now, I wish you a very good night and a peaceful sleep during the remaining hours."

He turned and disappeared into his room before I could reply. I realised then that fatigue had claimed me, and followed his example.

#

We set out for Queller's house immediately after breakfast next morning. Holmes had hardly rapped upon the door with his stick when it was opened by Queller himself, his top hat in his hand.

"Ah, I see that you were about to go out, Doctor Queller," said Holmes. "Pray spare us a few moments of your time, beforehand."

Queller stared at us, surprised. "I do not see patients, in my home."

"But we are not patients. My name is Sherlock Holmes, and this is my friend and colleague, Doctor John Watson."

"The consulting detective," his eyes narrowed with suspicion. "I cannot see that you could have dealings with me."

"Perhaps things would become clearer if I mentioned mesmerism, counterfeit bills and the exhausted state of twenty people or more."

"You can prove nothing." He adopted a sly expression. "If it were true, what crime can you accuse me of? I know nothing of mesmerism, nor of the production of false money."

"We have a client who will be an excellent witness," said I.

"I doubt that. He or she will remember nothing."

"And how, knowing nothing of mesmerism, would you have ascertained that?" Holmes enquired. "Also, nothing was mentioned of the *production* of counterfeit, nor of your band of victims comprising of both men and women."

"Any fool would have assumed those things, from what you have mentioned."

"True," my friend agreed. "But what of murder?

Queller's eyes were now full of alarm. "What are you referring to?"

"I am simply stating that we intend to pursue the disappearance of a witness in a case that would certainly have resulted in your conviction, Mr Elisha Cobb."

Queller's thin face was contorted with shock. Doubtlessly he had thought the case investigated by Barker was behind him and no longer a threat. He saw his past catching up with him and shook his grey head as if to dispel the possibility like a cloud of smoke. He made as if to reply and raised his top hat, and for a moment I thought he was about to accompany us, but then he retreated into the house in a rush before slamming the door.

"Quickly, Watson," Holmes cried. "He knows he is finished. That gate at the side of the house will lead to the garden. Doubtlessly that is his escape route. Hurry and intercept him, while I wait here in case he attempts to double back."

I was prepared to use my service revolver on the lock, but it proved unnecessary. I flung the gate wide and rushed through, to find Queller in the act of leaving by the rear entrance. He spat out a foul oath and turned back, once more slamming the door with a mighty crash. I drew my weapon again after failing to gain entry, and blew the lock out. I was about to enter cautiously when sounds from above reached me. I retraced my steps and stepped back outside. Queller stood above me, framed in the full-length window. I imagined his intention to have been to leap to the ground while I searched for him within. He was balanced precariously, his expression fearful and uncertain.

"Queller!" I cried. "Stop! You will not survive."

I was about to call my friend, but Holmes appeared by my side in an instant. Before we could do anything more, Queller had retreated and was gone.

"Back to the front of the house."

I followed at a run, as Holmes set off at full-pelt. Here there were no large windows to accommodate Queller, and he had already used a chair to smash his way through before we arrived. This time we had no opportunity to make an attempt to reason with him, for he had launched himself into the air with his arms outstretched. Holmes and I watched in horror as we realised that he would never reach the ground. He screamed once as he became impaled upon the iron railings that ran along the front of the building, then his body writhed briefly and was still.

His blood pooled around him as we approached.

"An awful way to die," I commented after the briefest of examinations.

"Indeed." Holmes turned away and we left. The white-faced driver of our waiting hansom said nothing as we entered but took up the reins at once.

"However," my friend continued, "I would not waste too much sympathy here, Watson. The way my accusation was received suggests that he was guilty of murder, and his use of others reveals a cruel and insensitive nature."

I nodded, as the driver urged the horse onward. "I suppose, Holmes, that justice is not always decided by the courts."

"Sometimes, I am sure, fate takes a hand in our affairs, although I shall not include such an opinion in my report to Lestrade, when we reach Scotland Yard. After that, I think, a hot meal in a newly-opened restaurant that I have noticed, should act as a restorative."

The Adventure of the Injured Man

The past few days had been, as I recall, a Christmas that was quiet and without incident. My friend Mr Sherlock Holmes and I had done nothing but converse, smoke and read, with no disturbance or distraction other than our good landlady producing her excellent fare at mealtimes. Holmes refuted my suggestion that we should leave our lodgings for a walk through the nearby streets of the capital, reminding me that he deplored exercise for its own sake and drawing my attention to the dark clouds that had hung over London for many days past.

"You expect that we will have snow then, Holmes?"

He blew out a final smoke ring and knocked out his old briar. "I am certain of it, and before long. This persistent bitter cold can mean nothing else."

"I have probably presumed unjustly," I confessed, "since I had imagined that you wished to remain here for no other reason than to receive an unexpected client. Your growing restlessness since your success in the Justice Master affair has not escaped me."

"You know me too well, Watson." He replaced his pipe in its rack. "But my ordeal, I think, is over. My client of this morning is not unexpected, but the appointment was arranged in response to his letter of Christmas Eve." He took out his pocket-watch but the door-bell rang before he could open it. "Mr Fitter is prompt," he said with approval.

Our landlady showed in a tall young man with a sallow face and thin moustache. "Mr Linus Fitter to see Mr Holmes."

"Thank you, Mrs Hudson. Kindly bring a fresh pot of tea and an extra cup."

Our visitor held up a hand. "Not for me thank you, sir. My work will have accumulated significantly during the holiday, and I must return to it at the earliest possible moment."

"Very well then," said my friend as our landlady withdrew. "Pray be seated. I think you will find the basket chair comfortable as you explain your difficulty. This," he gestured in my direction as I rose in acknowledgement, "is my friend and colleague, Doctor John Watson. Be assured that you can speak as freely before him as you would to me. He has been instrumental to the success of many of my past cases."

I felt slightly embarrassed at this exaggerated praise as I shook hands with Mr Fitter, a very brief experience as he withdrew his hand rather hurriedly. When we were settled I saw that Holmes was drawing his conclusions from our client's appearance, though he revealed but one.

"You may, if you wish, partake of your usual snuff, Mr Fitter, provided that you do not object to the aroma of strong tobacco."

"Not at all, Mr Holmes, for I am accustomed to it from my business partners." His expression changed to one of curiosity. "How, may I ask, did you know that I am in the habit of taking snuff?"

"The tiny amount remaining upon your moustache led to that unmistakable conclusion."

"Of course. Quite an obvious observation, really."

Holmes shrugged. "In my profession, it is as natural as breathing."

"As I would expect," Mr Fitter replied in a slightly arrogant tone. "The matter which brings me here, is one that you have doubtless met before. It is a case of blackmail."

"And what crime or indiscretion have you committed, that could allow such a situation?" Seeing our client's hesitation, my friend prompted: "I must know this, sir. If you have been subjected to blackmail, I must be aware of the reason. I cannot begin an investigation blindfolded."

The reply came reluctantly. "A week ago I rode my mare in Hyde Park. Somehow I struck a man in passing, although I recall no sense of the impact. He lay upon the ground, dead I thought, and I looked around me and saw no other soul. My horse appeared not to have suffered any harm, or even to have become alarmed, so I urged her into a fast trot and left the place quickly."

"You did not attend to the fellow?" I said, my tone a mixture of disgust and dismay. "I am shocked at such deplorable conduct, sir."

"I am not proud of my actions, but at the time I felt they were appropriate. You see, gentlemen, by profession I am a lawyer, a junior partner at the firm of Lenstrom, Fitter & Parker, and any legal repercussions from the incident would not sit well with our reputation."

I started to further express my strong disapproval, but was silenced by a gesture from Holmes.

"But you have stated that the unfortunate man was dead, and that no one witnessed the incident."

"That is how I perceived the situation, and I endeavoured to put it out of my mind. However, I was at home in Hampstead Heath, no more than two days afterwards, when a surly ruffian called upon me and demanded money in exchange for his silence regarding the affair."

"Did he offer any proof of what he knew?" Holmes enquired.

"He related the incident as if it had taken place before his eyes."

"How much did he demand?"

"Five hundred Pounds."

"No doubt he claimed that you would hear no more of it, after the payment of such a large sum. In fact, it would have been the first of many demands. I take it that you refused?"

Mr Fitter produced a shiny new snuff-box, breathed in some of its contents and blew his nose loudly into a handkerchief.

A few moments passed while he resumed a respectable posture, in silence except for the faint sounds of passing vehicles along the street and the occasional sigh of the wind.

"Excuse me, gentlemen. This is something of a habit, which I have entertained for years." He returned the snuff-box to his pocket. "I told the blackguard that I would require some little time to withdraw the money, and that he should call again this very evening, but he was too astute. He said that I should acquire the amount, but he would choose his time for another visit."

"You intended that he should call again, but after you had consulted me?"

"Exactly that. I thought that we could lie in wait."

Holmes leaned back in his chair. "That would not be practical now, since the date of his intended return is unknown to us, and he may be keeping your house under observation. Did he give you any indication as to how he traced you to your address?"

"None. I have wondered about that, since."

"Can you describe him?"

Our client pondered for a moment. "Short, unshaven and not too clean, as you would expect from those of his class. His hat was pulled down almost over his eyes and a thick muffler obscured much of his lower face. I could make little of his looks."

"The man you injured," Holmes said after a short silence. "What of his appearance?"

"That is much easier. He was short and muscular. His head was completely bald and tattooed with the figure of a bird."

At this, I saw Holmes' expression change.

"I think that is all I need to ask, for now." he said in conclusion. "Mr Fitter, kindly give Doctor Watson your address. If you hear any more from this blackmailer, or anything else of this incident, you must not fail to inform me at once. You will hear from me, I think, in the very near future. Good-day to you, sir."

Holmes turned abruptly and strode over to the window. He looked down on Baker Street as our client produced an engraved card before leaving.

When we were alone again, I remarked to my friend:

"Objectionable fellow, don't you think, Holmes? I did not like the arrogance of him, nor could I approve of any man who would abandon someone to whom he had caused injury."

"My dear Watson," he shook his head and smiled. "How many clients would I never have had, if I dismissed them because of their peculiarities or because of some annoying trait? I have mentioned before now that I regard each as a unit, a conduit to the little puzzles that illuminate my life, and nothing more."

"When Mr Fitter described the injured man, I saw recognition in your face."

"Yes, indeed. Unless I am much mistaken the victim, if I may call him that, is one Milos Narvik, a Hungarian émigré who has retired from circus life and makes his living in ways as yet unknown to me. He is often seen in various districts of the capital."

"For no longer, if Mr Fitter's account is accurate."

He nodded. "Our client's caller who proposed blackmail was undoubtedly Silas Norris, a common figure in the London underworld and a known associate of Narvik."

"So," I said lightly, "the case is all but solved."

"Perhaps, but I think a little excursion to Lambeth, where Narvik most often plied his trade, might settle some doubts that I have developed. Mrs Hudson will serve luncheon within the hour, after which we can set off."

I spent the next hour or so perusing an issue of *The Lancet* but curiosity as to Holmes' intentions dominated my thoughts, so that much of what I read was lost to my memory. Luncheon was over quickly and my friend jumped to his feet and handed me my hat and coat the instant that I drained my coffee cup. We stood under persisting dark clouds in Baker Street, our faces reddened by the keen wind, until a hansom appeared and the driver responded to my signal. He nodded silently in acknowledgement to Holmes' direction, and the horse took off at a fast trot.

We had passed through Charing Cross when, having failed to understand his reasoning, I enquired as to our purpose.

"There is something which disturbs me about Mr Fitter's accident, Watson. It could be the instinct I have which often warns me when I am not hearing truth, or perhaps that he mentioned no visible injury, such as a spreading pool of blood, to Narvik after he collided with the horse. If it is nothing, then we have had a pleasant journey after our recent confinement to our rooms, and no harm can come from it."

Nothing more passed between us until the hansom left us in Lambeth High Street. We were surrounded by folk going about their daily business, but Holmes strode through the crowd with clear purpose.

"Where are we bound for?" I asked him.

"If we visit some of the local haunts of Narvik. We may encounter someone who has seen him recently."

We turned a corner, and I chanced to look back. "Holmes, surely that is the man whom Mr Fitter described?"

As we watched, a fellow conforming exactly to our client's description sauntered along the pavement studying the passing conveyances carefully, as if expecting a particular carriage. A landau approached at speed, and at that precise moment he stepped into its path. The impact flung him down, and the coach came to a halt at once. A crowd gathered quickly, and the landau's occupant and the coachman stood near with faces full of concern.

Holmes stood silent and very still, peering at the spectacle before us. Then a slow smile crept across his features and he gave way to a fit of mirth.

A few faces among the crowd glanced at him in annoyance and disapproval, and I found myself totally astonished.

"Holmes! There is no humour in this. I must go and do what I can for that poor fellow. He evidently survived his encounter with Mr Fitter, but I doubt he has done so now."

I would have rushed to push my way through the crowd, had not my friend grasped my arm while struggling to contain his laughter.

"Oh, that was superb! He timed it beautifully! I do not wonder that our client was deceived, but I see it all now. Do not trouble yourself, Watson, for he has no need of you."

I stared at him in disbelief. "Do you mean because you believe he is beyond help?"

"No, old fellow, that is not it at all. Come, let us find a hansom and return to Baker Street. Trust my judgement, I beg you, and I will explain the situation."

We were more than halfway back to our lodgings, in the company of a cabby who sang to himself or to his horse constantly, before Holmes had collected himself sufficiently to satisfy my intense curiosity.

"I would be grateful if you would elaborate on that disgraceful exhibition that I have just witnessed, and your reason for preventing me from doing my sworn duty and attending to that stricken man," I said when I was certain that he had calmed himself.

"Watson, let me tell you at once that I am innocent of that charge, for the reason that there was nothing for you to do."

I shook my head in perplexity. "Holmes, what can you mean? I saw the man who you have called Narvik lying there, probably severely injured."

"Lying there, yes, but no more injured than you and I are at this moment."

"But….. I confess to being completely bewildered."

"That is because you have likely never seen that trick before now. It was an acrobatic somersault, a backflip I believe is the correct term, executed at the precise instant necessary to produce the effect of being struck by the horse. You will recall that Mr Fitter stated that he felt nothing when his mare struck Narvik. That was because Narvik was not struck."

"Then this, and the incident of Mr Fitter, was all a trick?"

"Indeed it was, and an ideal opportunity for extortion, in one way or another. Heaven alone knows what Narvik intended to hold over his victim just now. Doubtlessly he studied and selected his prey carefully, always choosing men whose reputation was precious to them. Why, I even glimpsed Silas Norris, Narvik's accomplice, among the crowd. There can be little doubt that Narvik performs this feat regularly, perhaps even daily in various places."

I sighed, both at my own lack of observation and my failure to trust Holmes' judgement when he had responded so.

"Then we can tell our client that he has nothing to concern himself with, after all. Should we not inform the official force of this?"

He nodded. "It would be as well to send a telegram to Lestrade a little later, so that he can put an end to Narvik's tricks. I doubt if Mr Fitter will care to be a witness in court, though."

This proved to be unnecessary. We returned to Baker Street to find the good inspector awaiting us in our sitting room, Mrs Hudson having had standing instructions to admit him in our absence.

"Good afternoon, gentlemen." He greeted us, beaming as we entered. "I do hope you have no objection to my calling on you unannounced."

Holmes gave him a wry smile. "None at all, Lestrade, after all you have visited us many times before without warning. However, you do not usually make a point of mentioning it. Would you care for tea, or a cigar perhaps?"

"Thank you no. I am here only to convey my appreciation. Immediately afterwards I will be on my way to Edmonton in a police coach which will shortly present itself. A local burglar has at last been apprehended."

We settled ourselves around a blazing fire.

"I am exceedingly glad to learn of that," my friend said, "but what, pray, are you here to thank us for?"

"For your assistance in the Justice Master case, of course. It is true that I would have had the fellow behind bars quickly enough had he not met with the end that he did, but you were a great help during the investigation and The Yard is grateful."

"Thank you, Inspector," Holmes replied with a straight face. "It is good to know that my enquiries sometimes produce useful results."

"Indeed they do, sir. Incidentally, just as I was leaving my office I chanced to meet Bowman, one of our more observant constables. He told me that he saw you in Lambeth earlier, as he was on his way back to The Yard. There's nothing in this that I should know about, I suppose?"

Holmes nodded. "I was, in fact, about to send you a message. Milos Narvik, who you are aware of, seems to have adopted a new trade. I know of two instances when he has feigned injury after falsely appearing to be the victim of an accident. He then arranges to blackmail the unfortunate who believes himself responsible."

For the second time that day I found myself astonished, for Lestrade's response was as unforeseen as Holmes' had been earlier.

He looked at my friend with an incredulous expression, which after a moment became a superior smile.

"I am afraid, Mr Holmes, that this time your conclusions are way off the mark. What you suggest is quite impossible. Whoever is responsible for these crimes, it cannot be Milos Narvik."

Holmes raised an eyebrow. "You seem very certain of that, Lestrade."

"Oh, but I am, sir. You see, the body of Milos Narvik was discovered yesterday morning, beneath a pile of rotten vegetables in an alley near Waterloo Bridge. He had, by my estimation, been dead for a few days. Someone put a knife in him, it seems."

"How very curious. I would like to visit the scene of his unfortunate demise."

"The body has been removed to the mortuary, naturally."

"As I would expect. But I would like to examine *the place* where he died."

Lestrade adopted an incredulous look, but conceded. "Very well, but my men have already been there and found nothing."

"Nevertheless."

The inspector produced his notebook and riffled through the pages. "It was the north end of Needler's Alley, near a house with a broken-down garden fence."

"Thank you, Lestrade. I do believe that your coach has arrived near our front door. I wish you well with your enquiries in Edmonton."

Having declared that the lack of light at this late hour would hinder his investigation, Holmes postponed our visit until the following morning. Dinner, our evening and breakfast were spent with him in a largely morose frame of mind, doubtlessly brought about by this unexpected turn of events.

We left our lodgings early, and I was glad to see the sun emerge at intervals from the heavy clouds as we neared Waterloo Bridge. The hansom having left us, we found ourselves confronted by a street of dilapidated terraced houses, and he amazed me once again by striding to the entrance to Needler's Alley without hesitation.

At the entrance we hesitated, for the smell of rotting vegetables lay thick in the air.

"Hold a handkerchief to your mouth if you must, Watson. Ah, we are fortunate. It is unnecessary to venture very far into this odious place for there, if I am not mistaken, is the damaged fence that Lestrade described."

I did as he suggested, although he seemed unaffected. As I watched, my friend peered along the walls of both sides of the alley before pacing further in and returning several times. He scrutinized some muddy imprints, before making a hopeless gesture.

"If only Lestrade and his men had refrained from dancing all over this patch of ground, what might we have learned from it."

I was about to reply with some conciliatory remark, when he knelt suddenly to retrieve a small object from a stagnant pool near the fence. The ray of wintry sunlight that had weakly penetrated this dismal corridor shone briefly upon it, before Holmes dropped it into his pocket without comment.

I sensed that this was not the time to ask questions of him, but I imagined his find to be a ring or brooch, although the part that such baubles could play in our enquiry I could not imagine.

After a further few paces, during which he several times poked at little piles of rubbish with his stick, he shrugged and turned away abruptly.

"I can see nothing more of interest here. Let us hope that it will not be too difficult to procure a hansom."

Holmes proved to be more cheerful during luncheon, from which I gathered that he had learned something of significance from our excursion of the morning. I had hardly finished my blackberry and apple pie, and noted with surprise that he had consumed all of his, when he left the table hurriedly with the air of having come to a decision.

"Perhaps you would care to accompany me again, Watson, to Fulham this time. There is someone who I wish to see who may be able to throw some light on this matter."

I rose and put on my greatcoat. "I wonder whether Lestrade will discover the identity of Narvik's killer."

"If he does not, then I must remember to point him in the right direction when we see him next."

"You know this, now?"

He smiled grimly. "I do. It was elementary. I am more interested, however, in ascertaining how Narvik performed the feat we saw yesterday, while apparently lying in the mortuary. There can be only one solution of course, but I must have other aspects of my theory confirmed before I share it with the good inspector. We are about to visit a man who I believe can assist us."

We had almost arrived in Fulham when our conveyance was delayed by an overturned cart. Two young men were frantically attempting to retrieve vegetables that had been scattered across our path from burst sacks, while a third calmed a frightened horse.

I was about to use this opportunity to ask Holmes about our destination when he looked at me thoughtfully, as if he had defined my intention.

"Mr Piotr Kavanski is a retired circus ringmaster, Watson," he began. "I wonder that it did not occur to me before, that he might be useful in our enquiries. After all, who else would know more of those skilled in acrobatics than someone such as he? Ah, but I see that the way has now been cleared, and we can proceed."

We alighted in a side-street before a red-brick house that was almost completely covered in ivy. I paid off the hansom while Holmes rapped upon the door with his stick, and received a response as I approached. An elderly man, slightly stooped, stood before us. He regarded us with a blank expression, fingering his untrimmed moustache before recognition dawned and his face lit up with a broad smile.

"Why, it is Mr Holmes!" he exclaimed in a voice tinged with an accent that was unfamiliar to me. "I had not thought to see you again, but I am exceedingly glad to renew our acquaintance. Come in, please, with your friend."

We removed our hats and entered, to be led into a room with walls that were decorated with posters depicting circus performances in half the countries of Europe, from bygone years. Two large and overfull bookcases stood near a low table and several armchairs.

"Be seated gentlemen, please," invited our host, settling himself opposite us. He offered glasses of a clear spirit, but both Holmes and I refused. His pleasure at my friend's visit was obvious.

"After so many years, I am glad to see that you are still in good health," Holmes said after he had introduced me.

Mr Kavanski brushed a lock of grey hair back from his brow. "I am most fortunate. I suffer from occasional indigestion, but that is all. It is good to be retired when you have some years left to you, although I miss the circus still. Pavelli the tightrope walker and Valentini the juggler, and a few others come to see me when the company is in this country, and it is enough. I spend my time reading and among my many memories."

"There speaks a man who is content." I remarked.

"Indeed I am, and that is no small thing as the end of one's life grows nearer. How long is it, Mr Holmes, since you helped me? Were it not for you, that scoundrel Morgandahl might still be continuing with his sabotage. More of my people would have been killed, and I could easily have been ruined!"

Not having heard of this before now I turned to my friend questioningly, but received no response.

"It was a simple matter," he assured our host. "Concluded long ago."

"There can be no connection surely, to your visit today?"

"None. We are here because we need information regarding a performer who may have appeared in the circus during your travels, or you may know of him from others. He features in an affair which I am currently investigating."

Mr Kavanski leaned forward in his chair, his eyes bright. "Of course I will help, if I can. Who is this man?"

"We know him as Milos Narvik."

"Oh, yes. He is an acrobat who once worked for me for a time, and for many other circuses. I am not surprised that it is he that you seek, for he was always the sly one. I will tell you all that I know of him, but little of it is pleasant."

The time for dinner was fast approaching as we left Fulham. Holmes bade the cabby to wait at the first Post Office we passed, and was gone for a short while.

"Telegrams, I presume?" I ventured when he had resumed his seat and we were once more on our way to Baker Street.

"You presume correctly."

"To Lestrade?"

He nodded. "And to our client."

"Ah. You have told him that Narvik still lives?"

"I have invited both of them to visit us, this evening."

We regained our rooms in time for a warming glass of brandy before dinner. A bleak cold had settled upon the capital and, as Holmes had predicted, it seemed certain that we would see snow soon.

Holmes barely touched his rainbow trout, being unsettled and full of the enthusiasm that was typical of him as a case drew to its close, but I did justice to mine and to the dessert that followed.

He said little as we ate, but his eagerness was apparent. He left the table the moment our meal ended, and we seated ourselves around the fireplace as Mrs Hudson cleared away our plates.

"I am expecting Inspector Lestrade and two others, very soon," he informed her and rose impatiently to look out of the window. "In fact I see the good inspector passing beneath the lamp across the street."

"Very good, Mr Holmes. I will show him in."

She withdrew, carrying the laden tray, to reappear after a few minutes had passed looking bemused. Lestrade was announced, and he entered handcuffed to the acrobat who we had seen in Lambeth.

"Good evening, Lestrade," Holmes said as our landlady withdrew once more.

The little detective removed his hat. "Good evening, gentlemen. As you can see, Mr Holmes, I have acceded to your request to arrest Narvik. We have him for blackmail, and Silas

Norris will shortly be joining him in the cells, but you hinted that there is more to this."

"Indeed there is, and if you will be so good as to conceal yourself behind that door to your left, I think I can promise that you will hear a confession to a more serious crime. You will leave us tonight with two prisoners, which is not a bad night's work I think you will agree."

"Yes, Mr Holmes, and thank you, but...."

"The door-bell has rung, and I hear Mrs Hudson rushing to answer it. Retreat if you please, inspector."

Appearing incredulous, Lestrade looked at his sullen prisoner. "If you know what's good for you, stay silent."

They disappeared into Holmes' bedroom, before footsteps sounded upon the stairs. Our door swung open.

"Mr Linus Fitter, to see Mr Holmes." Our landlady announced.

When all three of us were seated before a crackling fire, greetings having been exchanged, our client stared at Holmes expectantly.

"As you have summoned me here, I imagine that you have something to report."

"Indeed we have. There are several things, in fact, that must be brought to your attention. The first of these is the murderous attack that you made upon a man in Needler's Alley, the man you believed was blackmailing you."

The effect on our client was dramatic. His body went rigid in his chair, and all colour drained from his face. His mouth fell open, as he fought for breath.

"What.... What are you saying?" he spluttered. "Did I not consult you to put this matter straight?"

Holmes nodded. "You did, doubtlessly with the intention of concealing your actions, since it would be considered unlikely that a murderer would set in motion enquiries in pursuit of his own crime. Oh, do not bother to deny your guilt, Mr Fitter, your response to my accusation was sufficient to convince me, even had we not acquired further evidence."

"What evidence?" His voice was a croak, his face ashen.

Holmes took something from his pocket and set it down on the coffee-table. "Your snuff-box, I believe, found at the scene of the murder. I noticed that you were using a shiny new replacement during your original visit. If Scotland Yard were to examine the contents of the old one, would they not find them to be an identical mixture to that in the snuff-box you currently use?"

"There are hundreds of snuff-boxes, and many who use them, in London."

"Quite so, but there is more. I have determined that your snuff mixture is unusual, probably your own invention. Again, comparison with the box that I recovered should be revealing. And there is yet more evidence to come." Holmes gestured towards his bedroom door. "Watson, if you would be so good…"

I got to my feet, opened the door and stood aside to allow Lestrade and his prisoner to pass. Our client half-rose from his chair, then fell back into it as if he had swooned.

"This is impossible," he gasped, in a voice that was little more than a whisper.

"Not at all," my friend assured him. "This is Inspector Lestrade of Scotland Yard. The other is the man who attempted to blackmail you, Milos Narvik."

Narvik looked at his former victim, scowled and remained silent. Our client trembled visibly.

"No, you are not in the presence of a ghost," Holmes continued, "nor of a man who has returned from the dead. Earlier today, Watson and myself visited a man who has spent his life in the circus, his information regarding this man and his identical twin, Janos, was most illuminating."

"You seem to have murdered the wrong twin," Lestrade informed Mr Fitter.

"Precisely," Holmes confirmed. "They were born to a half-gypsy woman whose function within the circus was to ride an elephant, and a clown with an outrageous act that appealed to the lower classes. From the first, not even their parents could tell the twins apart, until their rather insensitive mother had a blue swallow tattooed upon the head of Milos, and a red one upon that of Janos."

We all turned to look at Milos Narvik's bald head, to confirm that the bird was blue.

"As well as their appearance they also shared the unfortunate peculiarity of never growing any cranial hair. After leaving circus life behind, the brothers settled in Lambeth. They lived apart and pursued their different illegal professions independently. Janos became a professional card cheat, it is true, and Milos derived his income from his acrobatic skill followed by blackmail such as you have experienced."

Our client sat slumped in his chair, his hands covering his face. "No, no, no!" he wailed.

"I am aware," said Holmes after a moment, "that your irresponsible actions in the past have several times brought the legal practice in which you are a partner near to disrepute. This additional incident, had you been genuinely at fault, could scarcely have avoided a scandal for them. That you became suspicious about the 'death' of Narvik, possibly because of a slip of the tongue by Norris, and made use of agents known to you through your position to discover whether he still lived, I have no doubt. But they identified the wrong man."

Milos Narvik leaned towards Mr Fitter, so that Lestrade had to restrain him by means of the handcuffs.

He glared hatefully at our client. "So, now I know why I have not seen my brother recently. You better hope they hang you, Mister, because if they don't you'll be a lot sorrier. I have friends in prison who'll be glad to meet you, but if you ever get out I'll be waiting."

"That's enough out of you," said the inspector.

Holmes rose and went to open the window. "I see that you have brought others to assist you as I suggested, Lestrade. Capital!" Whereupon he called out before shutting out the cold blast.

Moments later heavy footfalls on the stairs preceded our door opening to admit two burly constables.

Lestrade took out a key and unlocked the handcuffs before handing his prisoner to the tallest of the officers. "Take him straight

to the Yard, Simmonds. I want him in the cells by the time I return."
To the other constable, after indicating Linus Fitter, he spoke also.
"This one, too. I presume that you have arranged for the police
coach to meet you here?"

"It has arrived, sir."

"Good. Get on with you, then."

Both officers saluted and, with their prisoners, were quickly
gone.

When the protests of the prisoners and the rattle of the
conveyance had faded from our hearing, Holmes addressed
Lestrade, whose expression was one of satisfaction.

"The arrest of those two should add, I think, to your already
formidable reputation, inspector."

"Again, I am in your debt, Mr Holmes."

"Not at all. You really must not feel obliged." My friend smiled
warmly. "You could, perhaps, consider our contribution as a sort of
belated Christmas present. But for the moment, I am sure that you
will not be averse to taking a glass of brandy, with Watson and
myself."

The Adventure of the Maligned Mineralogist

According to the records stored in my despatch box, Christmas was but a week away when my friend Mr Sherlock Holmes finally put an end to a persistent situation which, had it ever been made public, would have caused a scandal and considerable embarrassment to our Royal Family.

I was in a state of near-exhaustion, since the recent influenza epidemic had produced many more patients than were usual at my practice, and even the assistance of a young locum had barely sufficed to stem the tide of the afflicted.

Holmes had been jubilant since his recent success, and had informed me that he expected no further cases to present themselves until after the festive season, when he expected to bring to a conclusion several matters which had been slowly maturing. As for me, I was glad to be able to spend time reading and regaining my strength.

My friend had mentioned his intention to spend the day bringing his index up to date and conducting a series of chemical experiments, so it was with some surprise that I looked up from my newspaper to see him staring fixedly out of the window.

"Clearly, something of importance is happening out there, to have captured your interest so completely," I said.

He shook his head without averting his gaze. "No, Watson, I was merely observing a rather sparse religious procession, no doubt parading as a reminder of the meaning of the forthcoming holiday."

"So your absent expression was because you were contemplating affairs of the cloth?"

"Not at all. I was contemplating misunderstandings."

"What can you mean, old fellow?"

He turned from the window and seated himself on the opposite side of the fireplace, holding up his hands to warm them near the flames.

"The procession was led by two men, carrying between them a sizeable banner portraying a cross."

I waited for him to elaborate, but he did not.

"I see nothing unusual in that." I concluded after a moment's consideration.

"Neither, apparently, do any of the faithful, anywhere in the world."

"Holmes, I confess to being totally confused."

"It is really quite simple. The cross is the recognized symbol of the device on which Our Saviour was crucified, even though that is not, in fact, the truth."

"That cannot be."

"But it is. You will recall that some research into the realms of religious history was necessary, when I undertook that affair in which the Archbishop of Canterbury was remotely connected, a few years ago."

"I remember that you forbade me to publish the details."

"Quite so."

"Be so kind then, as to explain yourself regarding your remark about the cross."

"Certainly. During that enquiry I was obliged to peruse the gospels, specifically the writings in the original Greek. I gained access to a copy by means of my slight acquaintance with a professor of antiquities at the British Museum. There I saw at once that the crucifixion instrument is described with the word *stauros,* which means a stake or a tree, but never a cross. Since those accounts are those of witnesses to the actual event, I am forced to the conclusion that the symbol used ever since is not the correct one."

"But," not for the first time, I was astounded by the breadth of my friend's knowledge, and by his conclusion, "this has always been taught, in Christian churches all over the world."

"And long before those churches existed, in the ancient world. For example, in the Egypt of the Pharaohs much the same symbol was called an *ankh.* That too had religious significance at the time."

I reflected that this was not the first of my friend's sudden revelations of this sort, and was about to present more arguments to what I considered to be a fantastical notion, when the loud ring of the door-bell intruded upon my thoughts. I rose and crossed the room to peer through the window, as he had done. Among the scant passers-by in Baker Street, an unfamiliar figure stood before our door.

"You may yet be presented with a further case before Christmas, Holmes."

As I returned to my chair, I saw that his eyes glittered. His abhorrence of inactivity was not new to me, and I felt that our intended respite had already faded from his mind.

"The caller may be here on another errand, to see you perhaps. We will soon find out, for I hear Mrs Hudson upon the stairs, leading a man with a heavy tread."

A moment later we rose as our landlady announced a middle-aged man of slightly above average height, wearing a suit of the boldest tweed I have ever seen. Attempting to make use of Holmes' methods, I noticed at once the faint lines around his eyes and mouth that suggested humour and a warm nature. His smile embraced us both as his eyes travelled from me to my friend.

"Good morning, gentlemen," he beamed. "I trust that your breakfast is over, and that I have not called too early. I have no desire to be an inconvenience."

"Not at all, dear sir." Holmes replied with a faint smile. "I am Sherlock Holmes and this is my friend and associate Doctor John Watson, whose assistance has often been of great value." He broke off, seeing that our landlady had remained at the door. "Yes, tea, Mrs Hudson, if you please."

Our visitor had removed his hat to reveal over-long grey hair that lent him a wild appearance. I guided him to the basket chair and we were soon all settled in our seats. The fellow did not wait to be questioned as Holmes clients often did, but launched at once into an informative tirade.

"Good sirs, I am Doctor Daniel De Witt Hall. You have doubtless already defined my accent as American, and indeed I am from West Virginia. I obtained my degree in the state of Ohio, before setting off to work abroad. After my commission was completed, I decided to live in London for a while, and arrived two weeks ago to take rooms in Burlescombe Place near Charing Cross Rail Station in anticipation of the arrival of my dear wife in time for Christmas."

He paused as Mrs Hudson knocked and entered the room bearing the tea-tray. Holmes, looking somewhat bemused in the face of our visitor's gushing introduction, waited until the door had closed behind her before making a quiet comment.

"And you are, I perceive, a mineralogist or geologist who has recently spent some little time in South Africa."

Mr Hall adopted a look of disbelief. "How ever did you know that, sir?" He paused for a moment to reflect. "I surely did not mention those things as yet. Why, this is fascinating. Are you a magician?"

I poured tea for us, noting Holmes' expression with amusement. This was not the first time he had been described thus.

"No, there is nothing magical about my work, Mr Hall, but much of it consists of observation. When I see that your face is tanned, though not enough to have been exposed to the hot sun for a long period, and the badge pinned to your coat is that of the American Geological Society, I remember that I have recently read in several newspapers of much activity in the diamond mines a few miles from Pretoria. To connect you with this was no great feat."

"Nevertheless, I find it astonishing."

Holmes sipped from his teacup and replaced it in its saucer. "It is no more than elementary, as I have often stated. If you would care to explain your difficulty to us, Mr Hall, but not of course until you have finished your tea, I will see what can be done to improve matters. Take a moment, if you wish, to put your thoughts in order and to ensure that you include even the smallest detail. There is no need to hurry."

We had all deposited our empty cups upon the tray, before our client seemed ready to begin. I noted that his expression had become uncertain.

"Now that I consider things," he said, "such as the serious crimes that must have been presented to you gentlemen in this room, my own problem suddenly seems trivial. I refrained from consulting Scotland Yard for the same reason."

I knew that being thought of as a second choice after the official force must have irked Holmes, but he did not show it. Instead, he encouraged our visitor to continue.

"Pray let me decide upon the importance of your situation, Mr Hall. As Watson will affirm, the most mundane circumstances frequently have unexpected depths."

I nodded my assent, and our client shifted in his chair, before beginning.

"Well, as I said, I arrived in your country two weeks ago. I was fortunate in finding accommodation almost immediately. It was as well that the rooms are furnished to an agreeable standard, since I had brought little more from Africa than my suitcase and the clothes I wore. I would have had more, but my house in Pretoria was burgled shortly before I left. Although little appeared to have been stolen, the robbers left considerable destruction behind them. When the letters began, I had been here scarcely three days."

Holmes leaned forward in his chair. "Pray describe them to us."

"At first I thought that there had been a mistake, for although they were addressed to me their content had no relevance. They were of a most scandalous and insulting nature, accusing me of acts that I would never contemplate. The first two I destroyed without a second thought, but when they continued to arrive, at irregular intervals and by both post and by hand, I retained them because it was by then clear to me that the sender was serious and that some action was required to set the matter right."

"I imagine that you have brought them with you?"

Mr Hall reached inside his coat and produced a handful of crumpled sheets which he handed to my friend with a flourish. "There, sir. You will, I am sure, understand my concern at once."

Holmes read each sheet, slowly nodding, before handing them to me. Torn from a cheap notebook, each of the ten pages contained but one line. I noted that the ink also was of poor quality and that, although the spelling was correct, the style of handwriting suggested that the author did not practice often. Also, the nib was worn sufficiently to cause the ink to spatter as the pen was returned from the inkwell. I perused each sheet in turn:

You are the lowest of men.

Your scandalous conduct has not gone unnoticed.

Have you no shame, sir?

Your outrageous deeds must not continue.

How many more poor women will you ruin, before your conscience restrains you?

You are no gentleman.

Where is your honour, sir?

If your true nature were revealed, your family would shun you.

How can you hold your head up, sir, in the company of ladies?

You can explain yourself, sir, in the reading room of the Charing Cross Hotel, at 7.30, tomorrow evening.

"I take it that this last message arrived this morning," Holmes said.

"Indeed, by the first post."

"And there is, of course, no truth whatsoever in these accusations?"

Mr Hall bristled visibly. "I should say not! I have not the slightest inkling of why I have been subjected to this persecution."

"Please do not take offence," I interjected. "It is necessary to establish the circumstances exactly, before embarking on an investigation."

Our client nodded his understanding, his expression reverting to its former benevolence.

"And you are quite certain that you know of no one who could be responsible for this?" Holmes enquired.

"I have not been in London long enough to make the acquaintance of anyone. It is a complete puzzle to me."

My friend adopted a thoughtful pose, his thin form tense in his chair. "Then it is almost certain that these events are connected to the time you spent in South Africa. The burglary that you mentioned is highly significant."

"But how can that be?"

"From the information you have given us, certain things can be deduced at once. For example, your journey to London was anticipated by someone you knew in Pretoria or in your place of work." Holmes paused as if something more had occurred to him. "Kindly tell us of the nature of your activities there."

"I was hired to locate and determine the quality of recent discoveries. New diamond fields promised to rival those of Kimberley, those extensive undertakings near the Vaal and Orange rivers."

"I had surmised as much. I believe that we are dealing here with a well-organised smuggling gang. Someone familiar with the mine and with yourself probably telegraphed accomplices in London, for how else would it come about that you were followed and your place of residence established? Further indications of their presence here are the proposed meeting at the Charing Cross Hotel, and that some of the letters were delivered by hand."

Mr Hall shook his head. "I taught mineralogy for years, in the state of Ohio, and I rode my students real hard, but I've yet to meet one who could analyse things as you do, Mr Holmes, even after all my instruction. I can think of no one in South Africa who could be involved in this though, but then I met so many people."

"That is unimportant for the moment," Holmes picked his cherrywood pipe from the rack but then, preoccupied with the matter in hand, laid it aside. "But at a later date I will suggest to Scotland Yard that they alert the South African authorities of possible smuggling operations in the area that you have described. It is clear that whoever began this sequence of events had some knowledge of you, Mr Hall."

"How is that, Mr Holmes?" our client asked.

"I, also, am unable to follow your reasoning," I confessed.

"It is simplicity itself," my friend explained. "Watson, you saw our client's response when I enquired as to the truthfulness of the accusations put forward in these letters. He was outraged that there could be any doubt of his innocence, because he is a man of honour to whom such conduct is unthinkable. His accuser is aware of this, and knows that his victim will go to great lengths to set the record straight. Hence his confident assumption that the meeting at the Charing Cross Hotel will take place tomorrow night. A man of less principle would have simply shrugged the matter off and continued on his way. These conclusions must have been sent from South Africa, since Mr Hall is unknown to the gang members in London, and it is therefore reasonable to assume that both the knowledge of his moral standards and the method of exploiting them originate there."

"You make it all sound so simple," our client remarked.

"It is merely an exercise in reasoning."

"Will you then, consent to accompany me to this rendezvous? It may be that we can apprehend this scoundrel, together with any accomplices who he may bring along, and hand them over to the police."

"Not I," Holmes replied, "nor Watson, for there is another aspect to this affair which must not be neglected. However, your encounter will be witnessed, and protection provided should it prove to be necessary. You may depend upon it, sir."

Mr De Witt Hall was effusive in his thanks, and enquired as to Holmes' fees. My friend explained that the work is its own reward, but that his clients were at liberty to defray any expenses that the investigation might produce. Appearing rather bemused at this our client left us, after receiving a repeated assurance that all would soon be well.

Looking down from our window, we watched as our visitor procured a hansom and was quickly lost to our sight. At my friend's suggestion we stood at an odd angle, presumably because he wished to ascertain whether Mr Hall was still attracting followers, without ourselves being observed while doing so.

"A peculiar business, Holmes," I remarked when we had resumed our seats near the fire.

He laughed shortly. "Not so, old fellow, surely you remember that we have faced this situation before. It is obvious that the letters and the proposed meeting have a single purpose – that of ensuring that his residence is unoccupied for enough time to enable a search. You mark my words, Watson, Mr Hall unknowingly brought something with him from South Africa, probably uncut diamonds, and the agents of the smuggling gang will go to any lengths to retrieve it."

"So you intend for us to observe his premises while he keeps his appointment?"

"Precisely. Are you with me?"

"As always," I smiled, feeling pleasure at his confidence in me. "But what of Mr De Witt Hall? Is he not in danger at the Charing Cross Hotel?"

Holmes shook his head and lit his pipe. "We can, I think, avoid such a situation. When luncheon is over, we will venture out into this cold afternoon long enough to send a telegram to Barker, the private enquiry agent who has proved useful from time to time. I will inform him as to the danger and, as he is not a man to be overcome easily, he will provide adequate protection for our client. I imagine that the true purpose of the meeting is to ascertain whether Mr Hall has already discovered the diamonds, if indeed that is what is involved here, and if so to force him to give them up. His tormentors seem to have covered the situation from every direction, which is what I would expect from a professional gang."

"When we set off Burlescombe Place then, I will ensure that my service revolver is in my pocket."

"Capital!" Holmes said as, with the time for luncheon approaching, we heard Mrs Hudson upon the stairs.

#

As I recall, there occurred but one more incident before Holmes and I set out for Burlescombe Place, the following evening.

We had just returned from the Post Office, the message to Barker despatched, and were about to resume our places around the fire.

"I see that the excessive chill has affected you, Watson," my friend observed. "Although dinner is some way off, I cannot think that a medicinal brandy would go amiss."

"That would be most welcome," I agreed.

Holmes picked up the decanter but froze as, once again, the door-bell rang unexpectedly.

"It seems that the Christmas season is to demand more activity from us than we had anticipated," he remarked as he abandoned the gesture.

I groaned inwardly. "Our respite has all but eluded us."

"Do not worry, Watson," he said pleasantly. "There will be time for everything."

Then the door swung open after a barely perceptible knock, and Mrs Hudson showed in a striking young woman wearing a costume of powder blue.

"Miss Agnes Coldford, to see Mr Holmes." Our landlady waited, in expectation of instructions to bring refreshment, I thought. Receiving none, she withdrew.

Holmes rose, as did I, and we wished the young lady good afternoon and Holmes introduced us before inviting her to sit. Her bonnet covered much of her head but the chestnut curls that had spilled out of the sides were of a good, rich colour. Had I been asked, I would have placed her age at more than twenty-five but not yet thirty and, I noted, she was tall and shapely. Her eyes, as I could make out when she drew nearer, were green, and seemed to possess an icy quality. This was belied by her facial appearance, which was that of an angel.

I made to offer her tea, coffee, or perhaps a brandy, although she showed no sign of exposure to the weather, but a glance from Holmes discontinued my intention. Surprised, I settled in my chair. For a moment our room was silent except for the whistling of the wind that had sprung up, and I waited in mild confusion for my friend to begin the interview.

"So, Miss Coldford," I saw his eyes glitter as he addressed her, but could not fathom the cause, "please be so good as to explain what has brought you here today. "I perceive that you arrived by carriage, since your cheeks are not reddened by the cold, and that you are anxious to impart something which you regard as important, but nothing more. If you will kindly elaborate, Doctor Watson and myself will endeavour to assist you in any way that we can."

"Thank you sirs," she answered in an unexpectedly submissive tone, "but my request is simple and possibly the most unusual that has ever been put to you."

Both Holmes and I leaned forward in our chairs, our curiosity aroused by this unusual statement.

"I find myself intrigued," he said. "Pray continue."

"I ask that you do nothing."

My expression doubtless revealed my puzzlement, but Holmes' countenance was unaltered.

"Do you refer to something that has already been presented to us?"

"Indeed. Earlier today I followed my stepfather, and observed him as he entered this house. I assume he has consulted you?"

"You must appreciate that I cannot discuss the affairs of any other visitor. Every case is, of necessity, kept confidential."

"I do, Mr Holmes, but there are hidden circumstances here. My step-father, Mr Daniel De Witt Hall, has no doubt spun a tale of robbery and persecution, in order to enlist your help?"

Holmes fixed her with a curious stare. "That is not unusual, in my profession."

She held up her hands, as if exasperated. "But it is untrue, I tell you. This is far from the first such occurrence, for he imagines many strange things. I have seen him tell many wild stories to people he hardly knows, and he is believed because, although absent-minded, he has a convincing way of relating them. I imagine he told you of stolen jewels, or gold, or that he is the subject of threatening visits or communications. Believe none of it, sirs! His mind is unstable. There are days when he fails to recognise me, though I am obliged to listen to his ramblings. If I can compensate you for your wasted time I will do so but, I beg of you, spend no more of it on these imagined fantasies. That is all I have to say, gentlemen. I felt I could not let you remain under such misapprehensions as my step-father often leaves behind him."

131

Holmes and I looked at each other, and I saw that he now wore a look of great surprise. From outside the sounds of passers-by, some with a liberal dose of Christmas spirit, reached us. The voices had not faded, when he asked our visitor:

"How did it come about, that you followed Mr Hall to Baker Street?"

"When I recognise that his mind is wandering, I often pursue him without his knowledge. I am forever afraid that her will step into the path of a carriage, or that he will lose his way."

"Has your step-father travelled abroad recently?" I enquired.

"Ah", she said, "you refer to the darkness of his skin. That came about from his falling asleep on a South Coast beach, earlier this year. The resulting sunburn was quite painful for him, and he complained for several days after."

"You have told us much that we were unaware of, Miss Coldford," Holmes acknowledged. "I see that we must now view the situation differently." He consulted his pocket-watch. "But now I see that my next appointment is imminent, so I must bid you good-day. Doctor Watson will accompany you to procure a cab in Baker Street."

"Please do not trouble yourself, Doctor," she said pleasantly. "I have an errand which I must fulfil, before returning to my home. Thank you, gentlemen, for your attention."

With that she rose abruptly, and left us. Holmes sprang from his chair, the moment we heard the front door close behind her. In an instant he was standing at the window, watching the street from an oblique angle with satisfaction written on his face.

"As I thought," he said.

"You have seen something of significance, out there?"

"Oh, certainly. Miss Coldford was delivered here by a private carriage, which waited for her throughout our interview. The driver, who has just met her to accompany her back to where their conveyance waits, is known to me."

"I, also, saw a falsehood in her revelations."

"Really, Watson? Pray elaborate."

"You will recall that I asked about her step-father's complexion," I began as he resumed his seat. "I enquired because Mr Hall's sunburn was akin to that suffered by myself and most of my regiment, during our time in Afghanistan. I cannot believe, taking into account the sunshine of an English summer and the little of it that we have been blessed with through the year, that he came by it within these shores. I consider that our client's explanation is by far the most likely."

Holmes clapped his hands delightedly. "Bravo, Watson. You improve constantly. Your observation was correct of course, but is far from all that can be discerned from Miss Coldford's visit. Tell me, old fellow, did Mr Daniel De Witt Hall strike you as at all absent-minded or in any way deficient of his senses?"

I shook my head. "Much to the contrary. The man seemed amiable, almost jovial at times and related his difficulty in a most clear and concise manner."

"That was my impression, precisely. Also, he presented the offending documents for our inspection, proving their existence. Had I mentioned this to Miss Coldford, she would doubtless have dismissed them as forgeries, or written by Mr Hall himself."

"So, her purpose here was to encourage us to abandon the case?"

"I suspected something of the sort from the moment she entered the room. "You see, Watson, I am already acquainted with her, although she is apparently unaware of it. Her real name is Miss Rebekah Dornay, a twice-convicted swindler and pickpocket. I could show you, from my index, the history of her life of crime as depicted by the newspapers. No, the chestnut wig did not deceive me and, of course, this clumsy attempt at distraction establishes a link with the criminal classes."

"You mentioned that you identified the man who met her, after she left."

"Indeed I did. He is Seth Malter, a known burglar and jewel thief who is also suspected of a recent murder. He was arrested some time ago, but escaped as he was being transported to court. I am sure that Inspector Lestrade will be delighted to see him."

#

The following evening we departed for Burlescombe place immediately after dinner. Darkness had long since fallen and the gas-lamps shone a ghostly sheen upon the pavements. I shivered in the bitterly cold air while Holmes despatched a telegram to Scotland Yard. Clearly, he expected an altercation.

Holmes dismissed the hansom near Charing Cross Railway Station, and we walked the short distance to the enclave which lay back from the main road. Burlescombe Place, we observed, comprised four Georgian houses surrounding a frost-covered lawned area. Three of these were lit and appeared to be private residences while the fourth, according to the engraved plate upon the door, was divided into two separate accommodations.

At Holmes' gesture, we approached the darkened house quietly.

"They are already here," he whispered. "I saw a flicker of light in a room above."

We were about to enter when we heard heavy footfalls behind us. Three roughs rushed towards us brandishing cudgels, and my friend at once drew his swordstick that was sheathed within his walking-cane.

"Those three were lounging near the entrance from the main road," he said with a calm that I did not share. "From the way we drew their attention, I suspected that they were lookouts. You are armed, Watson?"

"My service revolver is always with me."

"Excellent! Do not be afraid to use it, for I see that their weapons contain razor blades and nails."

Our assailants said nothing, but attacked immediately. The first, a huge man whose gold tooth glinted in the light of the nearby street-lamp, swung a vicious blow at Holmes' head. My friend barely avoided it and, as the man almost lost his balance from the expended force, lunged lightning-fast with his rapier. The cudgel fell to the ground, as its owner screamed and stared at his pierced wrist with disbelief. Blood flowed freely as he half-sank to his knees before an uppercut sent him sprawling backwards.

The remaining two thugs had concentrated on me, and the nearest received a bullet wound to his left thigh that caused him to fall in the path of his companion. The last attacker raised his weapon, but Holmes again thrust with his blade before I could get off a second shot, and his opponent held his hands against his bleeding ribcage as he fled.

"Some clearing up for Lestrade's men," Holmes indicated the two prone figures, "and there will be more to come. I fear that we have lost the element of surprise, however."

He took out a police whistle, and the shrill sound pierced the night.

We were both rather breathless after our encounters, but thankfully uninjured. Holmes opened the door before us to be confronted by a deserted staircase.

"Keep your weapon handy," he instructed me, "for we do not know the extent of our adversaries, nor if they are armed."

We climbed slowly, but stealth was no longer necessary. At the top of the stairs we were faced with two doors, the nearest of which was ajar with a faint light spilling onto the landing. Holmes stood to one side and pushed it fully open. The first thing that took my notice was that the room was in a state of considerable disarray, doubtlessly as a result of a search that had been conducted with no intention of concealing the intrusion.

A gas lamp had been lit but turned low, and in the shadows two figures faced us with pistols aimed.

"Good evening, Miss Rebekah Dornay," my friend said calmly. "I trust that you realise that a revolver of such small calibre is unlikely to incapacitate, at that distance?" He turned his attention to her companion. "And here we have Mr Seth Malter. No, Mr Malter, I am not surprised that you are involved in this affair, for you have included Miss Dornay in your misdeeds before, have you not? As soon as I realised that gems were the commodity in question, your name occurred to me immediately."

"Aren't you clever, Mr Holmes?" He asked sarcastically.

"You recognised me, when I came to your rooms?" Miss Dornay said with genuine surprise.

"Your picture has appeared in the newspapers, and your skill at disguise could perhaps be improved upon."

"If you want to live, Mr Holmes, you will tell your friend to lower his weapon and allow us to leave. We have two firearms against your single revolver."

Holmes peered from the nearby window then moved aside, surprising me by his obedience.

"I recommend that you both review your position, before leaving," he advised.

Miss Dornay crossed the room and looked out, as he had done.

"Seth!" she cried, "half of Scotland Yard is out there."

"Watch them," Malter said, indicating Holmes and myself as he strode quickly to join her. I saw the blood drain from his face. "Lestrade is with them. If he catches me, I'm done for. It'll be the hangman." He glanced around him hopelessly, as if looking for other means to escape. "I'm sorry, Beck, but it's my life if I'm caught."

With that he ran from the room, his boots clattering on the stairs. I went to the window and saw him emerge into the night with his pistol raised, only to be seized by two burly constables before he could fire. Inspector Lestrade himself speedily secured him with police handcuffs.

Miss Rebekah Dornay let her weapon fall to the floor and dropped her head to her chest. She could not meet our eyes.

"It is all up with me, Mr Holmes," she murmured as we left the house together and Lestrade's men closed in.

#

The following morning, Mrs Hudson barely had time to clear away the breakfast things before the door-bell rang.

"That will be Barker," Holmes informed me as we heard her answer.

Moments later our landlady announced the Surrey enquiry agent, who appeared little changed from when I had encountered him previously.

His stern countenance was unaltered in its expression as greetings were exchanged, and I concluded that the man was probably humourless. At Holmes' invitation he sat in the basket chair, placing his hat on a side-table. A ray of weak winter sunlight shone through the window, glinting for an instant on his grey-tinted spectacles and Masonic tie pin.

"It was as you suspected, Mr Holmes," he began after refusing refreshment. "Jude Gorvin."

"I was almost certain of it, since he is known to be an accomplice of Seth Malter in at least six jewel thefts that have taken place over the past three years."

"This Gorvin was the man who met our client last night at the Charing Cross Hotel?" I enquired.

"Indeed," Barker confirmed. "I sat at a table near to them, in order to overhear the conversation. Mr Hall I recognised from your description, and Gorvin was already known to me. He was quite charming at first, but grew steadily less so as Mr Hall insisted that he knew nothing of diamonds from South Africa."

"He spoke the truth," said Holmes, "The gems were inserted in a suitcase identical to Mr Hall's before they were exchanged under the guise of a burglary. Again, this suggests that someone close to him in South Africa is a member of the gang, for how would the appearance of his luggage be known to them otherwise?"

"You discovered the hiding-place, then?" Barker asked.

Muted sounds from outside reached us, in the moment that it took Holmes to answer. A horse galloped along Baker Street at an unusually fast pace, and someone shouted something that could have been 'Merry Christmas'.

"Watson and I returned to Mr Hall's premises after Lestrade's departure, last night. Miss Dornay and Seth Malter's search was extensive but not thorough and we found the diamonds, although in their uncut state they appeared less than attractive, concealed in the suitcase handle. On examining the stitching with my lens, its irregularity was apparent."

Barker nodded. "When your client continued to deny any knowledge of the jewels, the exchange became heated. Gorvin got to his feet and towered over Mr Hall in a most threatening manner. He had apparently forgotten that they were in a public place, for his threats became loud and unrestrained. At that point it appeared that a fight would break out and I thought it prudent to intervene, but it proved to be unnecessary."

"A constable had been summoned," I suggested.

Barker's taciturn expression lightened slightly. "Not at all, Doctor, and I could not have been more surprised. Mr Hall rose to face Gorvin and bristled like a bulldog in defiance. In quiet tones, he told the criminal how he had faced beasts and robbers while in South Africa, after which the threat he faced now was as nothing. I am convinced that your client would have given a quite adequate account of himself had the need arisen but Gorvin, seeing the attention he had drawn from the hotel staff and guests, thought it better for himself to withdraw. Needless to say, I followed him into the street and subdued him, before hauling him by the scruff of his neck to where I encountered a constable on his beat. I mentioned your name, Mr Holmes, and the officer immediately took charge and carted his prisoner away."

"Excellent, Barker, you have done well," Holmes acknowledged. "That I think, concludes this affair, for Mr Hall will be subjected to no more derogatory letters from an unknown source."

Barker rose at once, acknowledging that the interview was over. We all shook hands.

"As is usual," my friend continued, "you will receive my cheque by post in a few days. As for now, it remains only for Watson and myself to wish you the compliments of the season, together with a most contented and prosperous New Year."

The Adventure of the Murderous Gentleman

During the years of my long association with my friend Mr Sherlock Holmes, it was inevitable that we should meet individuals of strange, perhaps improbable, character. After a while it became almost normal to encounter, as I assisted him in some of his most unusual and bizarre cases, men who would stop at nothing to achieve their aims, whether the means to do so was by robbery, murder or other heinous acts. Apart from these, there was still another variety of criminal, though thankfully less common than the usual – I refer to those who kill their fellows for pleasure, to whom profit from their actions is a secondary attraction. Regarding these, one instance springs instantly to mind and, since my friend has recently permitted it, I will now set it onto paper so that the public will at last be aware of what took place.

I recall that the affair began one fine early summer morning, when Holmes and I returned to our Baker Street lodgings after an invigorating walk in Hyde Park. We entered the premises to be immediately confronted by Mrs Hudson, our landlady, who informed us that a client had called during our absence and now awaited us in our sitting-room.

Holmes preceded me on the stairs and we entered the room to find a clean-shaven gentleman of about fifty years of age, looking most unhappy as he sat stiffly in the basket chair. At the sight of us, he immediately rose to his feet.

"Mr Holmes, Doctor Watson." He approached us, extending his hand. "I have read of you both in the dailies. I do hope that I have acted correctly in coming here."

"That," my friend replied, "depends on your reason for seeking a consultation. Pray resume your seat and tell us what it is that is causing your evident distress."

"I had not realized that it was so obvious."

"I have seen despair written on many faces during my career as a consulting detective, and have long learned to recognise it. Hopefully we may be able to remedy your situation. Shall I call for tea?"

"Thank you, no. Your landlady has already made that kind offer."

"Then let us proceed. Let me assure you that you can rely on our absolute discretion, and request that you endeavour to omit not even the smallest detail."

When we were settled our client put his head in his hands briefly, again demonstrating his troubled state of mind. After a moment he looked at us with grieving eyes that seemed to me to contain also a hint of outrage, or anger.

"My name is Mr Chesney Lifford," he began. "You have probably already deduced from my accent that I am from the north of the country. After selling the tannery which had been in my family for generations, I moved to the capital six months ago. Shortly after I met a woman at a garden party, she was in her early twenties and appeared to find me interesting. Old fool that I am, I grew to care for her and we married not long after. Now I see that the only attraction for her was financial."

"That is a familiar story," I commented, "and I am truly sorry to hear that such an experience has befallen you."

Holmes' expression was now one of disinterest. "Are you certain, Mr Lifford, that you are seeking solace or assistance in the right place? I do not see how, as no crime has been committed, we can be of help."

"Please, there is more." Our client shook his head hopelessly. "I was struggling to accept that my wife had never loved me, and resolved yesterday morning to take a long walk to clear my mind of some of the anxiety that I felt. On returning home to Marylebone I encountered a fellow of extraordinary proportions awaiting me outside my house. I knew that Jeanette, my wife, would have left on her unexplained daily absence, and so the caller had received no attention. I enquired as to the reason for his visit, and he replied that it was a matter of life and death. Although I had no inkling of his meaning, my curiosity was aroused and I invited him in. When we were seated in my drawing-room and I had poured port for both of us, I asked him to explain. It is his reply, delivered in such a calm and matter-of-fact manner, that shook me to the very core. Even now, I cannot countenance it."

We leaned forward in our chairs, so that none of our client's painfully whispered words should escape us.

"Pray elaborate," Holmes said.

Mr Lifford hesitated, clearly collecting himself with difficulty. "This man introduced himself as Mr Harland Guild. He told me, quite without embarrassment, that his business was removing obstacles from the lives of those affected by circumstance. I found this puzzling, and as to what such a person would want with me I could not imagine, but he quickly enlightened me. He claimed that my wife had hired him to, as he put it, dispose of me. They had come to an agreement where she would pay him the sum of one hundred pounds, on inheriting my estate. My first thought was that this was some sort of jest but his expression, particularly his eyes, assured me otherwise. Also, although he displayed the manners of a gentleman, there was something insensitive about his speech. I was horrified and dumbfounded."

"If this was the case," I remarked, "then surely this man was working against himself by warning you of his intentions."

"Oh no, sir, the very opposite. You see, he went on to explain that his visit was to offer me a proposition. It was that, for twice the sum my wife had offered, he would turn his attentions to her and leave me in safety."

"He was willing to make your wife the victim, even though she had hired him?" Holmes queried with some astonishment.

"That is what he suggested. He explained that there is no personal element in his work, which he undertakes for his own pleasure and profit."

"The notion is outrageous, from beginning to end," I retorted.

"This man has come to my notice before, although he has never crossed my path." Holmes recalled. Scotland Yard have yet to prove anything against him. Several unexplained murders that could be laid at his door come to mind."

"Something that he mentioned might explain the difficulties of the official force," Mr Lifford suggested. "He assured me that my wife's demise would in no way reflect upon me, since he took pride in ensuring that each death had the appearance of an accident."

"Have you, in fact, notified Scotland Yard of these circumstances?"

"I have not. What could they do that they have not already done, since no crime has been committed?"

Holmes nodded. "Indeed, I could well imagine Lestrade or Gregson using those very words in response to your assertions."

"How did you respond to Mr Guild's proposition," I asked our client.

"I was so taken aback by his audacity and the nature of his suggestion that I found myself speechless. After a few minutes however, though still dismayed, I asked him to leave my house at once. He appeared oblivious to my disgust and anger, asking me if I was certain that my decision was the correct one. I fear that I was less than polite to him then, but he merely replied that we would meet again."

As he often did, Holmes lapsed into a thoughtful silence. After a few moments our client began to look uncomfortable, but I reassured him with a gesture. A heavy cart of some sort rumbled along Baker Street, the sound reaching us through the half-open window as my friend opened his eyes and addressed Mr Lifford.

"I will look into your case," he said. "Kindly furnish Doctor Watson with any further details that you consider to be helpful. I sympathise with you regarding your marital difficulties, but with those we cannot be of assistance. The problem of Mr Guild, however, is quite another matter."

I retrieved my notebook and committed to paper all that Mr Lifford was able to add. As I completed my task, Holmes again addressed our client.

"It is of paramount importance that you now follow my instructions exactly. Watson and myself will accompany you to your home in Marylebone, where you will gather enough clothing and personal items to sustain you for a sea voyage of several weeks. From there we will hire a carriage to convey us to Victoria Dock, where a journey will be arranged for you at one of the shipping offices. No, do not raise objections, Mr Lifford, but keep in mind that you are being pursued by one who is a merciless and experienced killer. By removing yourself from the capital you are ensuring your safety and simplifying my investigation also. As a further precaution, it may be as well to adopt a different name for the duration of your stay in the country of your destination."

"Very well, Mr Holmes. I am in your hands."

"Excellent." Holmes got to his feet and we retrieved our hats and coats. "Let us depart at once."

Transportation was secured immediately, and we left Baker Street with my friend alert at all times for observers or pursuers. We proceeded as Holmes had suggested, until we finally bade Mr Lifford farewell as he boarded the *S.S. Saturnalia* bound for Copenhagen.

"Hopefully," Holmes said then, "Mr Lifford is now beyond the reach of Mr Guild until he returns, by which time I have every expectation that this affair will be concluded. But for now, Watson, we will return to Baker Street for luncheon, since I perceive that you are already displaying a need of sustenance."

#

It did not surprise me that he was silent throughout our meal, for it was his custom to consider deeply the implications of a forthcoming case. Mrs Hudson had cleared away everything but the coffee cups, before he spoke again.

"I will endeavour to gather enough evidence to present to Scotland Yard. It would be as well I think, to place Mr Guild in Newgate for the rest of his life, even if he escapes the hangman."

"Undoubtedly. Did you not say, Holmes, that you had encountered this man before now?"

"Not directly. I will tell you that tale at a later date." He removed his napkin, and rose. "But this afternoon I must devote to discovering more about him and perhaps making a few arrangements. No, I will not require your company, Watson, but I would be obliged if you would mention to Mrs Hudson that I may be late for dinner."

With that he put on his hat and coat and left abruptly. As always on such occasions I felt somewhat put out at being excluded, but I told myself that by now I should have recognised his actions as one of his eccentricities. I made myself comfortable in my armchair, with the mid-day edition of *The London Post* and several accumulated medical journals near at hand.

As it happened, Holmes returned not long after our usual mealtime. We sat down at the table at once, I brimming with curiosity, and our landlady served a sizeable portion of roast goose. He ate with more enthusiasm than was usual for him, but his expression told me that his thoughts were far away. We had adjourned to our armchairs, when I could contain myself no longer.

"How did you fare this afternoon, Holmes? As you have no look of despondency about you, I feel safe in assuming that you have achieved some success."

He reached for the Persian slipper and began to fill his old briar. "I think it safe to say that my immediate preparations are complete. On leaving here I sought out the Irregulars, and bestowed upon them

147

the task of spreading throughout London that a certain Mr Verdon Dean, of Hackney, has need of the services of someone skilled in the removal of, shall we say, persons who represent an inconvenience to others, and requested that they act as go-betweens. After that, I arranged for temporary accommodation in rooms at Hackney and Limehouse. If we are fortunate, we may hear something this evening or tomorrow morning, but we must be patient." His expression changed and he suddenly sat up straight. "But I am assuming, old fellow, that you are with me on this. Forgive me for not asking your permission to include you."

"I will make arrangements for the locum who has replaced me at my practice during my spate of influenza to extend his stay," I smiled. "As always, I am with you."

We were well into an evening of reading and lively discussion when the door-bell rang. Holmes put down his glass of port and listened intently as our landlady answered.

"I heard no carriage arrive, so it is unlikely to be a new client," he concluded, "and by the tone of Mrs Hudson's voice I suspect that our caller is a messenger from the Irregulars. I am surprised at the speed of their accomplishment, and of the quickness of Mr Guild's response."

"As Mr Lifford is now unavailable to him, perhaps he is in need of work."

"Perhaps. I will go to save the young man from some of the scolding that he is doubtlessly enduring."

With that he leapt from his chair and descended the stairs quickly. I reflected that the gang of street Arabs to which the messenger belonged had been invaluable to Holmes over the years. He often mentioned that their presence went unnoticed in the streets of the capital, enabling them to see and hear much that was barred to others. I heard our landlady's high-pitched voice cease abruptly, discontinuing her unfavourable appraisal of our caller as my friend dismissed her kindly. From then on the conversation was conducted in hushed sentences, until the lad departed and the door closed.

"It went well," Holmes told me as he resumed his seat. "Mr Harland Guild is apparently well-known as a killman for hire among the London underworld. Wiggins sent that young fellow Jonah to tell me that our adversary is available, and I have replied that Mr Verdon Dean will meet him at the Hackney address tomorrow morning at ten."

I nodded. "But who is this Mr Verdon Dean, Holmes?"

"Have you not realised, Watson? It is I! Suitably disguised, we will present ourselves as partners in a building enterprise."

Our appearances were indeed altered considerably, by the time we procured a hansom outside our lodgings the following morning. Holmes now had grey hair and a drooping grey moustache, while my face was reddened and my acquired beard black and full. It was without surprise that I had seen that our reflections bore no resemblance to our usual selves, for I had witnessed my friend's skill with theatrical makeup on many previous occasions.

We arrived at a rather nondescript street in Hackney, well before the appointed time. The house that Holmes led me to was old but well preserved, and had apparently been the home of someone quite wealthy until recently. After we had settled ourselves in a well-decorated living-room, occupying stiff-backed chairs around a polished oval table, he proceeded to reiterate his instructions regarding the part I was to play. This continued for a while, but was suddenly interrupted by a discreet knocking of the street door.

"If you would be so good, Watson."

I made my way along the short corridor and opened the front door. A man of enormous size, his morning suit immaculate, stood smiling before me. I noted his innocent expression and that he used a perfumed oil on his unruly dark hair.

"Mr Verdon Dean?" He enquired in a pleasant and educated voice. "I received a message that you wished me to call. I am Mr Harland Guild."

"And I am Mr Dean's partner in our venture," I replied. "My name is Fergus Greystone. Mr Dean awaits us within."

We joined Holmes and polite introductions were made, although there was no shaking of hands, before we seated ourselves. After a few minutes of pleasant but pointless general discussion, during which our visitor did indeed display the manners of a gentleman, he paused to favour us with a charming smile.

"So, gentlemen, you are presumably aware of my profession or you would not have summoned me. You have but to state your difficulty for me to devise a way to remove it."

"The matter concerns a miser called Mr Benjamin Kyte," Holmes said in a hesitant voice that was quite unlike his own. "We have offered him a fair price for his hovel in Limehouse but he refuses to sell. Mr Greystone and myself have purchased every other habitation in Calders Row, to fulfil a contract to demolish and renew the entire thoroughfare, but with the present state of things we cannot proceed. There is a considerable sum involved in this, and we stand to lose much by the delay."

"So I would imagine. Have you ascertained with certainty that the removal of this man would leave the way clear for the progress of your venture?"

"We have made enquiries and come to an arrangement with the beneficiaries of Mr Kyte's will," said I. "He does not seem to be well thought of, even among his own people."

Mr Guild nodded. "I have encountered many such. For a consideration of one hundred and fifty pounds, I have no doubt that this problem could be solved quite soon."

"Very well," Holmes agreed, "but there must be no question of any connection to Mr Greystone or myself."

"Good heavens, sir!" Mr Guild's smile had become furtive, and I fancied that I saw a strange light in his eyes. "I am no amateur. My skill is considerable, and I believe that a list of my successes over at least the past ten years would surprise you. You need have no concerns on that score."

"But how to avoid the attentions of Scotland Yard? I understand that some of their detectives are most proficient, where murder is involved."

"We are not speaking of murder, but of accidents. When a body is found that has obviously suffered an accident, there is no investigation because there is no crime. The fact that I am walking the streets of London as a free man after so long testifies to this, does it not?"

Holmes and I glanced at each other, our faces carefully expressionless.

"When could such an event be arranged to take place?" I asked.

Our visitor shrugged his massive shoulders. "As soon as you would like. You have only to instruct me and, of course, to furnish my fee."

"Tomorrow, perhaps?" I suggested.

"There are various other arrangements that I must make," said Holmes, "but they should be completed by then."

"As you wish. At what time of day would be most convenient to you?"

"Let us say eleven o'clock"

"Then you have only to supply me with the details and the money, and you can consider our arrangement fulfilled after precisely that time."

Holmes produced a wad of banknotes and counted off the specified sum. I gave Mr Guild a slip of paper, written in a much-disguised hand, bearing the address of his victim. We rose to our feet as one.

"Should it have crossed your minds that I might abscond with your money, on that also you need have no concern. Such a dishonest act would cause my reputation in certain quarters irreparable damage, and could even bring about my ruination. That is your guarantee, gentlemen. You may depend upon me."

Holmes gave a little bow of acknowledgement. "Goodbye then, Mr Guild."

#

"There is more to discover, I think, about Mr Guild," Holmes remarked after we had returned to Baker Street and resumed our normal appearances. "I shall endeavour to learn more of the man this afternoon." He saw that I rubbed my irritated face. "Oh, I am sorry about that beard, Watson. You have my word that no further disguise will be necessary for you during the remainder of this affair. What did you make of our gentleman murderer?"

"His movements puzzled me," I remembered. "One shoulder was held lower than the other, and he walked with a pronounced limp, but not consistently. I am not skilled in the new science of curing disturbed minds, but I would say that he suffers also from some sort of mental derangement. His indifference, delight even, at the prospect of destroying his fellow-man strongly indicates this. His boasts of many victims I find horrifying. In addition, I noticed strange purplish marks in the corners of his eyes and at the tips of his ears."

"Bravo, old fellow!" Holmes leaned forward in his chair. "Your powers of observation increase still. It is those marks that have today put to rest a question that has been in my mind for a long time. I have not forgotten that I promised to tell you of my previous knowledge of Mr Guild." He glanced towards the clock that ticked away on the mantelpiece. "I believe that there is just sufficient time before luncheon."

"You mentioned that you had not actually met the fellow," I reminded him.

"Indeed, but you will recall Barker, the private agent who has been of some assistance on occasion. Some years ago he related to me an account which, on hearing Mr Lifford's description of Mr Guild, I remembered at once. The tale concerns the one and only time that I have ever had the slightest doubt in my belief of the invalidity of the supernatural."

"Pray elaborate. I am intrigued."

After a moment, Holmes continued. "At that time, the killings of a number of wealthy and notable individuals was the talk of London. Scotland Yard was close to arresting a suspect whose description matched that of Mr Guild closely, although his name was different. Suddenly the man was reported to have died, it was thought to have been because of a failing heart, and this was confirmed after an examination by a police doctor and another eminent practitioner. The corpse was set aside for a short while, to await any who might claim it, but before long it was found to have disappeared. Until now I agreed with the popular supposition that body-snatchers were responsible, although for a short time murders carried out in an identical fashion continued. What troubled me therefore, was the widespread inability to explain how this man could have risen from the dead to continue his crimes, when he had been twice certified as deceased. Naturally, there were rumours of witchcraft and the voodoo cults of Africa and the colonies and I confess, in the absence of a rational explanation, of allowing myself to doubt my conviction that these and all other supernatural practices are little more than fairy stories."

"Mr Guild, apparently, did not take the trouble to disguise his crimes as accidents, in those days."

"No, indeed. As far as I am aware, nothing more was heard from him until he approached Mr Lifford. Of course, there could be any number of other instances as yet undiscovered."

"What then, of today? You implied that the spots on Mr Guild's ears and near his eyes were significant."

Holmes nodded. "Since those times I have, as you know, conducted much research on a variety of subjects that could conceivably assist my work. Quite recently I read an account by an explorer who had witnessed a remarkable demonstration by a shaman in the jungles of South America. The man was feared among his tribe for his ability to induce apparent death to his chosen subjects, followed by their resurrection some time afterwards. The connection here, Watson, is that, if the traveller is to believed, the resurrected men and women, without exception, were permanently marked by purplish blotches such as we have seen today."

"So you believe that the drug, or whatever it may have been, used by the shaman was known to Mr Guild some years previously?"

"I am satisfied that it was, although how he came by it we may never discover. I was somewhat relieved to have my disbelief in all things mystical vindicated."

Before I could reply further, Mrs Hudson served our luncheon. After we had eaten, and with an apology, Holmes left before I could finish my coffee. He had assured me that he would return in time for dinner, so I resolved to visit my practice briefly to ensure that the locum was managing well.

#

Unexpectedly, my return was delayed. With the assistance of the locum, I was eventually able to cause an elderly lady, a patient of long-standing, to understand that the spreading paralysis that she was convinced afflicted her was nothing more than a touch of rheumatism.

Mrs Hudson was about to serve dinner, a well-filled chicken pie, shortly after my arrival at our lodgings. Holmes faced me across the table with an expression that told me at once that his afternoon had turned out to his satisfaction. As I awaited my dessert, he having refused any, I politely interrupted his discourse on the new science of fingerprinting to enquire as to his success.

"Later, Watson. I see that our landlady has put a light to the fire during our absence, which is as well since it had become a little chilly in here. When you have finished your meal we will repair to our armchairs and indulge ourselves in a glass of brandy. I will then tell you the essence of what has transpired since luncheon."

When we had taken our seats and Mrs Hudson had cleared away our plates, Holmes poured from the crystal decanter.

"There is more to Mr Guild than I had suspected," he began after we had taken our first sips of the harsh spirit. "On leaving Baker Street my first destination was a haunt of one of my informers who has spent much of his life on the fringes of the criminal underworld. There I learned much more about our adversary, including the reason for the cessation of his killings from shortly after his 'death' to his approach to Mr Lifford. You were quite correct in your assumption that his mental state is abnormal, since he is known to have spent some months in an asylum during his younger years. He was apparently able to obtain his release through the bribery of an unworldly but well-meaning uncle. From childhood, Mr Guild was always of unusually large stature with the temper of an enraged wolf. As he grew he became adept at hiding his true disposition, and took on the veneer of charm that we have seen. Afterwards I consulted several other of my scouts around the capital but, apart from confirmation, discovered nothing more."

"I formed the impression that you had more to tell, Holmes," I ventured.

"Indeed I have, but it will be more appropriate to disclose it to you in Limehouse tomorrow morning. I visited the house earlier to effect some minor but essential alterations, before dispatching a telegram to an old friend of some years ago. I expect his answer this evening."

I knew from long experience that to press him for further information would be futile. Therefore, when he abruptly began to discuss the latest headline emblazoned across the late edition of *The Standard*, I restrained my curiosity with difficulty. The clock showed almost nine-thirty when the door-bell rang. Holmes had left the room before the chimes died away.

Moments later he returned holding a yellow envelope that he had already torn open.

"Is it good news?" I enquired.

"Indeed." A satisfied smile crossed his face. "We can now proceed with confidence. The trap is set."

"Excellent. Tell me, does Mr Benjamin Kyte fully understand the risk to his safety?"

"Oh he does, Watson, he does."

"But who is he?"

A slow smile crossed his face. "Who else but myself?"

#

I felt an immediate sense of disgust as the hansom set us down in Calders Row. The terraced houses that lined both sides of the thoroughfare were, without exception, a depressing sight. The doors and window-frames had been starved of paint for many a year and the curtains, where any were in evidence, hung in filthy tatters. Birds, I noticed, had nested in some of the chimney-pots and on the roofs where slates had been displaced, while most walls bore cavities where mortar had long since crumbled away.

Holmes had become an aged grey man with a rasping voice and grim countenance, and I marvelled again at his skill at disguise. His thin form was bent and he hobbled uncertainly as we approached the house and he produced a key that opened the door with difficulty, the hinges protesting loudly.

"Welcome to the home of Mr Benjamin Kyte, Watson," he laughed. "The state of the place is disgusting, but I am supposed to be a miser. I give you my word, old fellow, that we will leave at the earliest moment possible."

We entered a dark and dismal room, heavy with dust and containing nothing but the remains of some furniture. The floor was tiled unevenly, and the windows, one at each end, were smeared to the extent that the light was much affected.

"Holmes, how could you…"

"It was necessary, I assure you." He guided me through the shadows. "Take great care while ascending these stairs. They are criminally dangerous and should have been replaced years ago. Keep to the left, Watson, against the wall."

We proceeded slowly, and I swear that I felt the entire staircase move beneath us. It was with some relief that I reached the top behind Holmes, who seemed unaffected by the risk to life and limb that we had undoubtedly taken. He opened the door confronting us, but neglected to close it after we had entered. I saw that the room contained nothing but an old table and chairs with a made-up bed against one wall. All appeared considerably cleaner than below, but the light was equally subdued.

"The door to the right, at the far end of the room, leads to a rear entrance," he explained as we stood near the doorway. "It is reached by means of a dark alley that runs behind the building. The door to our left, behind the table and chairs, conceals a large cupboard. I have removed the shelves and provided you with a seat and a spy-hole, so that you can bear witness to the proceedings for the sake of Scotland Yard."

"Holmes, you are exposing yourself to the greatest danger. That man is an experienced killer possessing tremendous strength. I know well your skill at defending yourself, but his extraordinary size is against you. His hands are almost twice the size of yours."

"Indeed, old friend, but I have a defence that I have not disclosed to you." He took something from his pocket. "Here is a police whistle. I want you to use it loudly, the instant Mr Guild makes any attempt to assault me."

I took it, in disbelief at this ineffectual proposal. "But this will not be heard outside the building, and in any case the street is empty. I have brought my service revolver, and you have my word that I will not hesitate to use it should you be attacked."

"As I undoubtedly will be, since this man has a curious pride in his profession. Promise me, Watson, that you will resort to your firearm only if the action I have recommended proves ineffective."

Reluctantly, I complied.

During the moment of silence that followed I heard movement elsewhere in the house. At first I imagined it to be the sort of sound that is usual in an aged structure, but when it was repeated I turned to Holmes.

"We are not alone here."

He nodded. "Pay it no attention. Everything is arranged."

"You mentioned, I believe, that there is more about all this that you wish me to know."

"Indeed there is," he inclined his head, "but I hear a heavy rapping on the front door. I will tell you afterwards, but by then much will have become evident to you."

At that he gestured that I should take my place in the cupboard, which I did immediately. I closed the door and sat upon the stool to look through the spy-hole. It gave an adequate view at precisely the correct height, and I had seen that it was not visible from outside. In the silence of this place I heard Holmes descending. I could make out his polite greeting of the visitor, and recognised the voice of Mr Guild. Except for Holmes' caution on the stairs, no more of what was said reached me until they entered the room and sat at the table. Through the spy-hole I could see that Mr Guild was dressed as immaculately as before but in more sober apparel.

Mr Guild placed his hat beside him on the table. "As I indicated just now, Mr Kyte, I am employed by the Northern and Cities Bank. We are currently enjoying a surplus in available funds as a result of several maturing investments, and are seeking to lend a proportion in such ways that will create maximum benefit to the recipients. It has come to our notice that your residence, although charming, is in need of some repair…"

"This has been so for years," Holmes interrupted in a trembling voice, "but I fear that my meagre finances would not support such a venture. For that reason, I have taken to using this room only. It is not ideal, but one becomes accustomed to one's limitations. A man must cut his cloth according to his pocket."

"That is my point exactly. I have here some explanatory notes that will reveal to you the most attractive rates of interest that would be applicable to a loan from us that would enable you to restore your home to its former glory. Pray read them now, and tell me of your conclusion."

Holmes fumbled in his waistcoat pocket and produced a set of pince-nez, which he held to his face. He lowered his head until it was almost touching the table, in order that he could begin his inspection. With his attention diverted, he could not see the danger. Mr Guild had poised a giant hand behind his neck, ready to deliver a blow with the force of a sledgehammer. As I watched, a cruel expression, that of a wild beast, came into the face of Mr Guild, and his eyes shone with a curious indifference. That Holmes was seconds away from death I had no doubt, and my first instinct was to reach for my service weapon. Then I remembered my promise to him and blew the whistle he had given me with all my might, my heart sinking with the futility of the gesture. The shrill sound was loud in the enclosed space and I had no faith in it, but then the door at the far end of the room, that which Holmes had explained as leading to a rear entrance, was flung open and I was astounded by what was revealed.

A spotted feline beast, like the leopards I had seen on the Asian continent, slowly entered the room. It stood hesitant, as if taking stock of the situation or choosing its prey. Its soulless eyes were fixed on Holmes and Mr Guild, as it lowered its body as if to spring.

Such was the shock that I experienced that my attention had been distracted from both men. Now I saw to my astonishment that Holmes displayed no fear but had become perfectly still. Mr Guild also had ceased in his intention, staring at the animal with bulging eyes and his mouth open in a silent scream. His arm dropped and he placed a hand on the table to force himself to his feet, his glance fixed as if hypnotised. For a moment he stood statue-still, before giving voice to a hideous cry of terror and dashing abruptly through the open door.

The cat followed him with its eyes, and then lay down to lick its paws. A tremendous crash which shook the building told me that Mr Guild had forgotten the instability of the staircase to his cost. A cloud of dust entered the room, to be curtailed immediately as Holmes rose and closed the door. I got to my feet and emerged from the cupboard, at the same moment that a man who was vaguely familiar to me appeared behind the animal. He was red-faced, with a mop of black hair and a long, untrimmed moustache. Other than the certainty that this was not our first meeting, I could recall nothing of him.

Holmes produced a cloth and wiped make-up from his face. The newcomer attached a leash to a collar around the neck of the beast, stroked its head affectionately, and spoke soothingly in a thickly-accented whisper.

"Good girl, Mabel. Just lie there for a minute or two." He then addressed me. "Do not be afraid, sir. I've had her since she was a cub. She's never attacked a living soul."

Nevertheless, I ventured no nearer until Holmes made the introduction.

"Watson, you may recall Mr Zamil, who we met during that affair in Warwickshire involving Lady Heminworth."

The memory came flooding back. "The circus-master, of course."

We shook hands.

"I am retired from the ring now, sir, but I could not leave behind some of my pets." Mr Zamil smiled proudly. "The circus goes on forever, but I am settled happily in Surrey."

"Allow me to wish you a long and contented respite."

He bowed in acknowledgement, and turned to Holmes.

My friend, who had stood with his back to the door, gave him a bulging envelope.

"As agreed, Mr Zamil. You will recall my assurance that you have committed no crime. Today you have served justice well, but I suggest that you do not delay in forgetting the incident."

"It shall be as you say, sir. I ask no questions. Goodbye, gentlemen." With that he left us, the feline trotting before him. It occurred to me to wonder how he proposed to return to his home.

As soon as we heard the outer door close, we emerged onto the landing. Dust swirled before us, but it had begun to settle. After a short while we could see that a sizeable portion of the balustrade was missing, and much of the staircase had become a gaping hole. Below, on the tiled floor of the living-room, lay the body of Mr Guild in a spreading pool of blood. I flinched as I saw that his fall had impaled him upon one of the broken stair-posts, but Holmes was unaffected by the scene.

"It could be thought of as fitting, I think, that his death should appear as accidental," he said as we returned to the room. "Nevertheless, I shall have to see Lestrade a little later, with some sort of explanation."

"You had indicated that our intention was to gain evidence against Mr Guild, and then inform Scotland Yard."

"Indeed, but I have observed before now that such situations often find their own conclusions."

"I would be grateful, Holmes, if you would explain the outcome of all this to me."

He scrubbed at his face, removing the last of his disguise. "Oh, it is all quite simple, Watson. During my foray of yesterday, I was able to discover more of Mr Guild than I have so far disclosed to you. To begin with, the interval between shortly after his supposed demise and his approach to Mr Lifford is explained by a visit to India. Whether this was to avoid further pursuit by the official force here, or with a view to continuing his criminal career there I have no means of knowing, but it is certain that he ventured into a forest at night and was attacked by a tiger."

"A terrible experience," I remarked. "I am surprised that he survived."

"Probably he would not have done, but for the intervention of a party of villagers who beat the beast off with sticks. You may have noticed the scars on his hands and neck that testify how close he came to death, as does his peculiar way of carrying himself. He eventually recovered, but the incident caused him to develop *ailurophobia* which, as you may know, is a morbid fear of felines. Every man has his Achilles heel, and on becoming aware of these facts I knew that, despite our adversary's physical advantages, I now had a way to defeat him. I was at a loss to find a way to gain the temporary use of a big cat, surely no zoo or similar establishment would allow it, and then Mr Zamil came to mind. He had no tiger, as I had hoped, but his pet cheetah filled the role admirably. His answer to my telegram assured me that the beast had been his pet from birth, and had no history of attack. This having been said, Watson, I confess to sharing your anxiety during its presence and your relief at its departure."

I heard him out, appalled. "But there was so much that could have altered the result of your plan. What if Mr Guild had responded differently?"

"From the description that I received, I was fairly certain of my ground. Had things turned out otherwise, I had a firearm concealed upon me. But my best line of defence, old friend, was yourself and your readiness to intervene on my behalf." He glanced around quickly. "There is nothing more to be done here. We can leave by the rear entrance, and then I suppose we must call at Scotland Yard on our way back to Baker Street, but afterwards I would be delighted if you would join me in sampling a rare cognac. It was a present from a grateful client and I have yet to open it."

The Adventure of The Resurrected Brother

In my declining years I feel a certain anxiety as I record a recent meeting with my friend Mr Sherlock Holmes, who has proved himself able to function much as he always did when a problem or unexplained incident attracts his interest.

My concern springs from the fact that, because of my advanced age, my memory has begun to fail me. It is still relatively easy to recall the many past mysteries, the solving of which gained my friend a well-deserved reputation, but of late it has become imperative to commit his recent exploits to paper while my recollections remain clear.

Much has changed since our days in Baker Street. Holmes and myself have survived a war the like of which the world has never before seen, a conflict in which flying machines and engines of destruction took a heavy toll of life. Poisonous gases and guns of hitherto unseen size brought about devastation greater than we could have imagined, and we came to realise that life could never again be the way it once was.

The year is now 1920, and almost two decades have passed since Holmes retired from his practice as the foremost consulting detective in the land. From then on Baker Street was behind us and our association was therefore dissolved. Yet that is not quite true. I took care to maintain correspondence with my friend, and he has on several occasions been kind enough to invite me to his Sussex cottage for a short visit. Moreover he has, sometimes reluctantly, related to me certain incidents in which he has chosen to involve himself since taking up residence in this most pleasant part of the country. After sharing a rather basic but satisfying meal we would sit, one at each side of the stone fireplace, enjoying our pipes as he enlightened me as to his activities, while daylight gave way to dusk and we felt an easy peace come upon us.

It was during one of these visits that I found myself again assisting Holmes, and some of the comradeship and thrill of adventure of former years returned, I like to think, to both our lives.

Since the cessation of hostilities, the hansom and other familiar conveyances have all but vanished, replaced by machines most often referred to as 'horseless carriages'. Holmes viewed these without interest, saying only that their advent would be the cause of considerable trouble in the years to come, and that he regretted the demise of the horse-drawn cab. As for myself, only the steam train remained as a vehicle for long journeys and short excursions were now difficult. So it was then that I resolved to learn to drive one of these noisy contraptions that blew out clouds of smoke, and that was accomplished with the purchase of a hardly-used Morris Cowley and a great deal of patience.

Spring had hardly given way to summer when I received a letter from my friend inviting me to join him for the coming weekend. Having mastered, as far as I could tell, my mechanical transportation, I set off for Sussex early one calm and sunny morning. At this hour I met only sparse traffic on the London streets and the capital was soon left behind. I had studied my map carefully but still, I confess, took several wrong turnings. The route I had chosen was one largely avoiding the main roads, for I was still unsure and had therefore resolved to confine myself to the leafy lanes and village streets as much as possible. Towards the end of my journey I came upon a fellow cranking the starting handle of what appeared to be a brand new Ford motor car near a roadside cottage, and from him I learned that I was within a few miles of Holmes' residence.

Finally I found my way to and entered the narrow track that led to my friend's home. The tall bushes to either side blotted out the sun and gave the impression of travelling through a tunnel as one does on a railway journey, but these suddenly fell away and I brought my vehicle to a halt in a quiet glade within sight of the cliffs and a calm sea. The engine came to rest, leaving only the cries of seagulls to disturb the silence. I approached the front door of the modest little building, which opened before I reached it, and to my delight beheld Holmes standing there puffing at his old briar.

"Good Morning, Watson," he said after removing his pipe. "I trust you had a pleasant journey with no mishaps?"

We shook hands, and I admitted, "I occasionally went off course."

"I would have been surprised had you said otherwise. We were accustomed to depending on the knowledge of the driver of whatever conveyance we used, once. It is very different now. But I am forgetting my manners. Come in, old fellow. It is too late for breakfast, but I assume you would not object to a mid-morning cup of coffee?"

"I would welcome it," I assured him.

We sat in the small sitting room. As Holmes prepared our beverage I could see, through a window to the rear of the house, gulls circling above the cliffs and the sun sparkling on the sea beyond. It was easy to understand why he had chosen such a place in which to spend his retirement, for the peace and tranquillity hereabouts were medicine to the nerves.

"Are you hungry?" he asked as he reappeared from the kitchen with a tray.

"Not especially. I find my appetite greatly reduced, of late."

"As do I. Not that mine ever matched yours, but the passing years bring many small changes."

"Indeed." We drank the strong brew and replaced our cups, and I asked him whether he passed his days here pleasurably.

"I cannot deny that it was strange at first," he replied. "I have mentioned before now how my adjustment from life in the capital to a more sedate existence was not as easy as I had expected. Still, my bees take up much of my time – I have fifteen hives now, all flourishing – and there have been the odd times when fellows from the village and surrounding properties have approached me with their little problems. I am glad to have been of some trifling assistance to them, and such instances serve as reassurance that age has not robbed me completely of my faculties."

"You do not miss the old days then, and Baker Street?"

He smiled, briefly. "This is not the first time that you have asked me that question. Until now I have answered that I do not, with little reservation." He paused thoughtfully, for an instant. "Now, however, I think that my feelings may be changing. I find that I am dwelling on our past adventures a great deal, of late."

"I recall that you often declared your intention to write monographs on various subjects, as a result of our encounters."

He sat back in his chair. "And doubtlessly I will, possibly during the coming winter. I have, however, been contemplating a return, probably of short duration, to London for some time."

"Something, I believe, has brought this to a head."

"You are as perceptive as ever, Watson. If your surmise is correct, then perhaps I can identify the cause."

He reached out and took an envelope from the sideboard and for me, a strange thing happened. As he turned back to face me I saw him for an instant as he was, at the height of our many adventures together. Then the image faded and I noted that his hair was streaked grey at the temples and his features appeared more hawk-like than ever. But as he slid the envelope across the small table that stood between us I saw in his eyes the same glitter, the same eagerness for the chase, that I recalled vividly from of old.

"See what you can make of this."

I peered at the envelope, not yet touching its surface. "It appears to be of good quality paper, and to be postmarked four days ago. It was apparently posted at a City of Westminster Post Office, suggesting that the sender may work in that district since it is not residential. I conclude also that the sender is not familiar with your career or movements."

"Your observations are correct, if a little obvious. The last, however, is not quite so. On what did you base it?"

"The envelope bears a Post Office rubber stamp, indicating that the letter was redirected after being delivered to a former address. It is seventeen years, since we left Baker Street."

Holmes clapped his hands. "Excellent, Watson! The years have not dulled your senses. Now kindly oblige me by extracting the letter from the envelope and reading it."

I obeyed, noting that the paper matched the envelope in colour and quality. The writing was clear but I discerned that the hand trembled slightly. I read it slowly, and then again.

My Dear Mr Sherlock Holmes,

I have heard much of you in previous years, but I am afraid that your present whereabouts is lost to me. I pray that this appeal reaches you, for if it does not I will surely go mad. This letter I have sent to an address that I know was formerly yours, and I am depending on the efficiency of our excellent Post Office to convey it to wherever you live now.

I beg you to communicate with me so that, if you will permit it, we can meet. I am in great need of an explanation of some recent experiences and, almost certainly, of your advice. I look forward greatly to hearing from you, if indeed you still live.

Yours, in hope and desperation,

Cordon Reeder.

Permanent Under-Secretary to the Minister of Military Expenditure.

"The fellow sounds in a state of excitement," I observed, "and he writes from the House of Commons."

"But the request is a personal one, not to be considered as from an official source."

"Quite." I studied his face intently. "Will you respond to it?"

He hesitated for a moment. "As I mentioned, I have been aware of a growing restlessness. Perhaps a short return to the capital will relieve it, so that I can give my bees my full attention."

"A capital notion. You must stay with me, of course."

"Pray do not take offence, Watson, but I think it better if I do not. I cannot predict the nature of Mr Reeder's problem, and therefore am unable to exclude the possibility of attendant danger. We are not the young men we once were, old friend, and I will not risk any harmful exposure to you."

"Nonsense!" I exclaimed eagerly. "We will assume the task together. Holmes, it will be like reliving the old days. If you wish to stay elsewhere, then so be it."

He rose abruptly and walked to the end of the room. I could not help but notice his slowness, compared to our former days. He turned then, and fixed me with a critical glare.

"Very well, but I must have your word of honour that, if I tell you at any time to desist, you will do so at once."

"You have it."

He nodded. "Then it remains, after you have spent a few days here, for me to arrange a room at the Langham Hotel. I will contact our client and conduct my investigation from there."

"Capital!" I said with some excitement. "But why must we wait? Your prospective client may be in a desperate state, as his letter suggests. Holmes, I am perfectly willing to postpone our planned excursions here, in favour of spending one night under your roof before we drive together to London to begin this unexpected, but very welcome adventure."

A slow, somewhat ironic smile crept across my friend's face. He gazed for a moment at the intricate pattern of the Persian carpet, then out of the window at the distant sea before he answered.

"It shall be as you say, old fellow."

#

Holmes appeared rather uneasy at first, as we sped through the lanes early the following morning. A low, overhanging branch brushed the roof of my vehicle and he looked up sharply, but after that he lit his pipe and became more settled. Unlike many times past when we travelled by train or hansom together, conversation was plentiful. He asked many questions about my new mode of transportation, enquiring both about its mechanical nature and my increasing mastery of its control. After a while he seemed satisfied and we reverted to re-living some of his exploits which I was privileged to share in our younger days. I was fortunate to find an establishment where I could purchase fuel, as it was running low by the time our journey was half completed and, on espying an inn nearby, we indulged ourselves by consuming an excellent lunch of roast pork. Presently we reached the outskirts of the capital, and from there I drove to the Langham Hotel where Holmes had telegraphed the previous evening during our walk through the local village. As he left me, carrying his scant luggage, I recalled that this place had featured in some of our earlier adventures and was gripped, for an instant, by a deep nostalgia.

Holmes had assured me that he would telegraph a reply to Mr Cordon Reeder during the morning, arranging an appointment for the following day or sooner. I was to meet my friend in the hotel lobby at four o'clock in any case, unless I received notification to the contrary.

I received no such message, and so presented myself punctually at four. Holmes, who like myself had effected a change of clothes, was waiting for me. After advising the receptionist to direct Mr Reeder to a table near the lobby, he led me there.

"Our appointment is for four-thirty, Watson. We have time for a brandy before our client arrives."

We sat near a pillar which held a gilt-framed mirror before which Holmes positioned himself carefully. Several tall leafy plants in enormous vases surrounded us, and there was a muted buzz of conversation from further off. A waiter appeared quickly and took our order. As we drank I noticed that Holmes fixed his gaze above me, no doubt to make deductions from the reflection of Mr Reeder before meeting him.

"He is late, Holmes," I said after consulting my timepiece.

"Not so. Unless I am mistaken he stands near the entrance that you yourself used. He is quite young, about twenty four or five I would say, with a rather uncertain disposition and hair that is very light in colour. He leans heavily on a cane and is dressed severely, in black as one would expect of a man in his position."

The man who approached our table had a pronounced limp and was indeed as my friend had described. He appeared rather cautious, as he looked at Holmes and then myself with uncertainty.

"Mr Sherlock Holmes?"

Holmes half-rose from his chair, indicating that Mr Reeder should sit with us. "I am he, and this is my associate Doctor John Watson, before whom you may speak as freely as to myself. But I perceive that you are somewhat overwrought, sir. Allow me to order you a brandy to calm your nerves."

"Thank you, no," our client replied. "It is true that I am perturbed by my predicament, but I cannot be away from the ministry a moment longer than is necessary."

"Very well, then. I should explain that I have been retired from my profession of consulting detective for some years, but have recently decided to return to it briefly. Pray tell us of your difficulties, so that we can see if it is possible to assist you."

"I am able to reward you generously, Mr Holmes."

"That will not be necessary. My fees were always calculated on a sliding scale, regardless of the means of the client."

"Then let me say how grateful I am to you for your response to my letter, and for your attention."

"It will be of no consequence, unless you furnish me with the facts."

Mr Reeder hesitated, as if doubtful that he would be believed.

"In the war I fought in France with the Fourth Army of the British Expeditionary Force," he began. "In some of the most bloody battles of the war."

"The Somme," I said. "Survivors I have spoken to describe it as a visit to hell."

Holmes gave me an irritated glance, but our client nodded. "That is indeed an accurate description. The memories will trouble me until the day I die."

"Undoubtedly," Holmes agreed. "Watson and myself saw action also, but not there. Is it from that experience that your problem arises?"

"It is true to say, I suppose, that it began on the battlefield. Half of our regiment were in the trenches, awaiting the order to charge. When at last it came my brother Jonathan and myself proceeded together with fixed bayonets, but on leaving the trench he stumbled. I reached out with my free hand to prevent him from falling, but not before he had toppled before me and suffered a hit that killed him instantly. Somehow, I and a few of our company survived, but I have been haunted for the past four years by the knowledge that it should be I, and not Jonathan who lies forever in that French field."

"You are not my first client to suffer from unnecessary guilt," Holmes recalled. "It would be quite a different matter, had you used him as a shield deliberately. But tell us, how does this most tragic event relate to your current troubles?"

Our client hesitated, and I saw from his expression that his conscience troubled him greatly.

"Two weeks ago, gentlemen, I was in my study at my home in Mayfair near midnight. I am unmarried and often work on routine ministry papers well into the early hours because I do not sleep well. My maid and valet do not live in the house and so I was quite alone when I received a telephone call at that ungodly hour. Imagine my horror and disbelief when the caller identified himself as my deceased brother."

I felt some astonishment at this extraordinary statement, but Holmes seemed unperturbed.

"Was the voice that of your brother?" he asked.

"As far as I could tell, it was. Pain and distress were evident."

"What did the caller say to you?"

"Only that he had not died on the battlefield, and wished to meet me."

"Did you arrange to do that?"

Our client fidgeted in his chair. "Jonathan, if indeed it was he, requested that I visit the Tailor's Arms, a public house on the Kings Road, at precisely five o'clock the following afternoon. He was most specific about the time."

"Doubtlessly that is significant."

"You kept the appointment, of course?" I ventured.

"Until the time of the meeting, I could think of nothing else. I arrived to find the road busy with traffic, which is usual for that time of day. The cab deposited me opposite the Tailor's Arms and I waited for a gap in the procession of vehicles to enable me to cross the road. After a few minutes I realised that Jonathan watched me from where he stood near the front of the building. When he saw that I had noticed him he turned away, and I frantically tried to force my way through the approaching cabs and omnibuses. When I finally crossed the road there was no sign of him. A group of loafers, who had been drinking noisily nearby had noticed nothing unusual, only a rather dilapidated soldier in a uniform that was the worse for wear. Hardly an uncommon sight to which you would pay much attention."

"Quite," Holmes said. "How did this man appear to you? Was he indeed your brother?"

"From the distance I was able to observe him, it seemed so. Part of his face was obscured by the collar of his greatcoat, and his stance was lop-sided, as if he were wounded."

"He did not shout anything that could have been a message or instruction to you?"

"Nothing. Afterwards I began to wonder if he existed only in my imagination, or if I had seen a ghost."

"I would suggest that you immediately dismiss that notion. Ghosts, and I have always doubted the existence of such, do not need to use telephones or arrange meetings, I am sure."

Mr Reeder nodded. "Of course, I did not seriously consider such an explanation. There is more to this, however. A week ago, at exactly the same time as before, I received a further telephone call. The voice was the same and I immediately began to ask why this person had left the scene of the meeting after observing my arrival. Everything I said was ignored, so that I felt I was speaking to someone who could not hear. The voice then took on a tone that was almost commanding, directing me to present myself at a hotel in Limehouse at ten o'clock that coming evening."

"That is an area best avoided after dark," I commented.

"Indeed it is, doctor, but I felt compelled to pursue this. I had begun to doubt that my brother still lived for I could not see how this was possible, but I had developed a strong curiosity which drove me. Also I had confided in a gentleman I know slightly from my work, who suggested I consult you. I regret now that I did not do so immediately."

"As I suspected from the moment I saw your occupation listed on your letter," Holmes said. "Brother Mycroft's hand is in this."

"He requested that I not mention him by name, but I see that it was unnecessary to do so."

"This is not the first time that he has furnished me with a puzzle. Pray continue."

"The venue in Limehouse was by no means a hotel. It was a half-derelict place where rooms were rented by the day, or even by the hour. Judging by the arrivals and departures that I witnessed as I approached the building, it was frequented by the lowest classes. On nearing the entrance a great brute of a man, reeling drunkenly, pushed his way past me. He then stopped and looked up, as if following the flight of a bird. I did likewise and was astounded to see my brother, or whoever it is who pretends to be him, gazing down at me from a tall unlit window. He shouted to me, and I was astounded because the voice was certainly that of Jonathan, and I confess to trembling as I listened."

"Did he make threats?" Holmes asked.

"No, he just shouted: *You killed me to save yourself. How can you live after that?*"

"Did you then seek to enter the building, to confront him?"

"A minute or two passed and the shock left me, then I rushed to the entrance with that intention. Before I could speak to the *concierge* two well-built men, extraordinarily so for Orientals, stepped from the shadows and manhandled me back into the street. I am ashamed to say that I found myself sitting in the gutter near that filthy establishment in complete confusion."

Holmes sat in a contemplative silence for a moment. "On both occasions," he pointed out, "your tormentor – for that is what he is – has ensured that you remain some distance from him. That immediately suggests that he fears that a closer encounter would reveal something to you that he would much rather keep hidden. Was that the last you heard of him?"

Our client shook his head. "No, but it was then that I decided to write to you. Last night as I prepared to retire, and at the exact time of the previous calls, I received yet another. This time the instruction was to meet tomorrow on Platform 2, Victoria Station, at mid-day exactly. May I prevail upon you gentlemen to accompany me?"

"In the clear light of day?" Holmes retorted. "You may depend upon it." He turned to me. "Watson?"

"As ever," I replied with enthusiasm.

"Then it is settled. Before you leave, Mr Reeder, there is one thing more that I must ask you. During your time in the trenches, was there anyone with whom you or your brother struck up a friendship, or even conducted regular conversations with?"

"There was Corporal Wendell Bright," our client remembered. "In fact, I can recall only he and Nurse Edith Merrow, who attended to me during my stay in hospital, from that terrible ordeal. I was invalided out, you see, half my left leg had been shot away."

"My military career had the same end," I told him. "Although my injuries were less severe."

Mr Reeder nodded absently, his expression vague. I could see that, for an instant, his mind had slipped back to the awful conflict in which he had participated, as mine sometimes did to Maiwand.

"Have you, Mr Reeder, consulted the official force on this matter?" Holmes asked then.

Our client's embarrassment was evident. "I confess that I have not. Apart from the tale being an unlikely one, it would almost certainly damage my standing in the Ministry if a police investigation of such events were connected to me."

"I understand your reluctance," Holmes said then. "I would be much in your debt if you would write down the addresses of Mr Wendell Bright and Nurse Merrow, and leave us your card, if you will. If you are in agreement we will join you outside Victoria Station, near the newspaper-seller's kiosk, at ten minutes before mid-day tomorrow."

"I cannot begin to express my gratitude, sirs."

"That is quite unnecessary," Holmes said. "We look forward to seeing you then, and perhaps to throwing some light upon these extraordinary circumstances."

#

The approach of mid-day found us among the crowd that filled the station. Mr Reeder met us as arranged and we proceeded at once to platform 2. Military uniforms were much in evidence, queueing among the waiting civilian passengers and in small groups that awaited later trains. Holmes' eyes were everywhere, scrutinizing the entire platform and often returning to the entrance. The babble of various conversations was constant, but temporarily blotted out as mighty engines appeared and came to rest before us. Several came and departed as we waited. It was as an express flashed through, exposing the opposite platform to our view, that our client suddenly stiffened and pointed suddenly:

"Look there!"

Holmes and I followed his direction. Separated from us by the tracks, the passengers opposite were equally numerous. Among the uniformed men and others hurrying to and fro, a strange figure stood near a stack of cages of racing pigeons. I glanced at Mr Reeder's ashen face and put out an arm to steady him.

"He is pointing in our direction, and shouting." Holmes observed.

"Yes, but I cannot hear."

"I read his lips, Watson. He said: 'You took my life. You are a coward and a murderer.'"

We watched as the figure turned away to leave the platform. He appeared to be a man of above average height, in the uniform of a private soldier. He stood and moved in a lop-sided manner and I could see, even from this distance, that his face was unnaturally pale.

I turned to speak to Holmes, but he was no longer there. Less than a minute later he appeared on the opposite platform, looking across at us, breathing hard and shrugging his shoulders hopelessly.

"Now that you have seen him more closely, can you be certain that this man is your brother?" I asked Mr Reeder.

Our client had been silent and still since his first sight of the figure, but now he struggled to regain himself. Both his appearance and his voice confirmed my opinion that he had suffered from the condition that had become known as 'shell-shock'.

"His face was full of pain, and his movements appeared to cause him some discomfort but yes, Doctor, I believe it was him."

Holmes returned soon after, the exertion of running having visibly taken its toll.

"He was nowhere to be seen," he said. "I observed everyone near the other entrance and on the steps."

"How can he have disappeared?"

"That would not have been difficult, among a crowd and with so many men in uniform. I suspect that his awkwardness of movement was part of the deception, and that he fled quite quickly."

"Is there anything more than can be done, Mr Holmes?" our client asked as we left the station.

Holmes appeared deep in thought. As we reached the bottom of the steps, he hesitated before replying. "I am entertaining a theory, Mr Reeder, based on what we know and what we have seen, but of course it is far from complete at this stage. What I am certain of is that your life is in danger, and that you must take all precautions from now until the hour when you can expect the next telephone call. Accordingly, Watson and I will now accompany you to your place of work, if it is your intention to go there. Have you any friends among your colleagues, who would be willing to safeguard your return home later?"

"Two of my fellow-workers will, I am sure, come to my aid. They are sturdily-built men, rugby players who are used to much physical activity."

"Excellent. We will arrange at a later date to meet at whatever venue your tormentor chooses. Never fear, we will put things to right."

Mr Reeder nodded. "My thanks to both of you gentlemen. I have every confidence that you will succeed. Are there other precautions that I should avail myself of?"

"I would recommend that you keep a revolver close by you, even at home. Possibly you have such a weapon retained from your army service. Above all do not venture from your home except when absolutely necessary, and never alone. Admit no strangers at any time."

"It shall be as you say."

"As for Watson and myself, we will continue our investigation. Several lines of enquiry suggest themselves, and these we must explore."

At Holmes' bidding I hailed a cab, and we presently arrived at Whitehall. His last words to our client, whose pallor had returned significantly, was to the effect that he should not relax his vigilance for any waking moment.

"What now, Holmes?" I enquired as the cab pulled away.

"Lunch, I think, old fellow. After which we will call upon Mr Wendell Bright."

#

Mr Bright, we saw from the information furnished by our client, lived in Hampstead. We arrived in a quiet tree-lined street in late afternoon. As the cab left us and disappeared around a corner I saw that Holmes was scrutinizing the tiny front garden.

"I fear that Mr Bright, like our client, did not emerge from the war unscathed."

"How can you possibly know that, Holmes? Have you met the man previously?"

"I have never set eyes on him," he assured me. "But between the gate and the entrance there are several patches of mud, and all but one bear footprints accompanied by the imprint of a stick or cane. Be so kind as to make use of that ornate door-knocker, and we will see if time has blunted my observation skills."

I did as he requested, and knew that his deduction was correct from the moment the door was opened. Mr Bright, although probably not much older than our client, had been aged considerably by his experiences. His hair was almost white and his face bore marks of prolonged strain. I noted that his movements were uncertain, and an instant later realised that the reason was obvious. The blank stare he gave us could only mean that the poor fellow was totally blind.

Holmes showed no surprise at this. "Corporal Wendell Bright?" he enquired.

The man's severe expression was at once relieved by a sad smile. "No one has addressed me as such for a good while, sir. Are you from the military?"

"Not at all, but my friend and myself are here on what is essentially a military matter. I am Sherlock Holmes, a consulting detective, and I am accompanied by my friend, Doctor John Watson."

"I have been told of you, but what can you want with me?"

"If you will permit it, I would like to discuss a war-time incident involving your comrade, Mr Cordon Reeder."

"Lieutenant Reeder!" Mr Bright exclaimed. "Yes, I remember him well. Won't you come in, gentlemen?"

We entered his home and I saw the cleanliness and tidiness with some surprise. I supposed he had someone who cared for his needs, but the ease with which he led us to his sitting-room caused me to realise that this was not necessarily so.

"I can sense that you gentlemen are surprised that I do not walk into obstacles," he said as if he had read my thoughts. "I have lived here since childhood, long before my parents passed away, and so I was familiar with everything before the war took my sight. I get few visitors of late, apart from my niece who helps me greatly. Please be seated and tell me more fully about Lieutenant Reeder's problem. I understand that he has done well for himself, since the war."

We sank into thickly cushioned armchairs and our host offered us tea, which we both declined.

"As we understand things," Holmes began, "Mr Reeder and his brother served together at the Battle of the Somme."

"That is correct. I spent many days next to them, freezing and starving in the trenches. Waiting to be ordered into action."

"Quite so. Can you recall the day that Mr Reeder was wounded, and his brother killed?"

Mr Bright fixed us with his sightless stare. "I will never forget it. The order came to leave the trench, to charge. Jonathan Reeder climbed out slightly before his brother and was immediately cut down. Cordon took his weight and lowered him gently to the ground hoping, I thought, that his brother still lived. I ran past them but I heard Cordon cry out and realised that he, too, was either wounded or dead."

"It could not have been then, that Jonathan Reeder shielded his brother?"

"I cannot see how. He had hardly regained his balance from the climb, before he was struck."

Holmes nodded. "It has been suggested that Cordon Reeder deliberately took shelter behind his brother's body."

"That is preposterous!" A tinge of angry red appeared on Mr Bright's cheeks. "As I have already said, Jonathan climbed out before his brother and had not yet stood up fully when he was hit. Cordon was still struggling for a foothold in the loose earth. To imply that there was cowardice involved is a disgrace, a slur on the man's name, and I will not have it!"

"Pray calm yourself, Mr Bright," Holmes said in his gentlest tone. "There is no danger of Mr Cordon Reeder being defamed. The suggestion was made by someone with a grudge against him, who most likely did not witness the event as you did."

"I would stand by my recollection, in any court in the land."

"Was the charge successful?" I asked Mr Bright.

"Not at all," he said after a moment. "I could never see the sense in the order, for we were rushing into a fusillade of enemy fire without a chance. To my surprise, I found myself very near the enemy lines, although how I got there unscathed I could not have explained, when I heard an explosion quite close and saw a brilliant flash. When I awoke in hospital I could no longer see, and they told me I never would again."

Holmes and I voiced our commiserations and Mr Bright related to us some of his earlier war experiences. After a while he seemed in better spirits, and we thanked him and left.

#

I had dinner with Holmes at the Langham Hotel, and we spent the evening together, inevitably re-living old times. By ten o'clock we were both showing signs of tiredness, and I rose from my chair to leave.

"Take care, Watson, as you drive back to your residence. It is perhaps rather a remote possibility, but be watchful that you are not observed or followed. More than ever in this new age, we must take care to anticipate risk. Good night, old fellow. I will see you here at nine sharp in the morning, when we will see what can be learned from a visit to Nurse Edith Merrow."

I was glad to find that my friend's caution was unnecessary. I drove through the streets of London unhindered, and was lost in sleep shortly after returning home.

At the appointed time next morning Holmes was waiting for me, resplendent in his grey tweed suit and soft felt hat, near the hotel entrance. We were bound for Hammersmith, he told me, but on arrival directed me to proceed all the way along the high street and beyond.

"How are you so certain, Holmes? You appear to have no map."

I drove more slowly, as a boy leading a cow crossed the road ahead. Out of the corner of my eye, I saw my friend smile.

"There is no mystery about that, Watson. I simply telephoned the lady earlier to ensure that she would be at home and prepared to receive us."

The road now became a wide track with farms and cottages on either side. Holmes peered before us and gave me directions.

"There! Turn by that great oak at the crossroads."

Shortly afterwards we found ourselves outside a charming stone cottage, with rhododendrons, geraniums and ivy evident in the small front garden and on the walls. As we alighted the front door opened, and a woman of about thirty welcomed us.

We entered a sitting room that was much as I expected. Dark beams ran the length of the ceiling, while copper warming pans from a distant age glinted upon the hearth. The lady, I have to say, would certainly have been handsome in her youth, but the rigours of her profession had hardened her stare and set her mouth in a straight line. I reflected that I had seen this effect upon the female countenance many times before, both in Maiwand and during the recent conflict.

Nurse Merrow proved to be a pleasant and cheerful hostess, offering us comfortable chairs around the fireplace and cups of Assam tea. Holmes surprised me by uncharacteristically confining himself to unrelated subjects and pleasantries, until the tea things were placed to one side.

"Now, you wanted to ask me about my service after the Battle of the Somme," she began before either my friend or myself spoke further. "Was there anyone in particular that you wished to enquire of?"

Holmes nodded. "Do you recall, among your patients, Lieutenant Cordon Reeder?"

Nurse Merrow smoothed her grey skirt as she tried to remember. "As I said when you telephoned I attended many patients, I could not hope to remember the number, but of course there are always some who remain in the mind for one reason or another. If I am thinking of the man you refer to, then he was a patient with a leg injury. Poor man, it was quite severe and I knew he would not walk again without the aid of a cane. He struck me as a brave man, both against his pain and, according to his comrades, on the battlefield. I believe he tried to save his brother, while under fire."

"So we believe. I take it that you have never heard anything to contradict that?"

She shook her head, brushing a stray lock of auburn hair back from her face. "I can recall no such thing. As far as I am aware, Lieutenant Reeder was a popular figure." She paused, with the air of someone to whom a sudden thought has just surfaced. "In fact, there was but one other patient, who I had almost forgotten, who was critical of him."

At once, Holmes leaned forward in his chair. "Pray, elaborate."

"A private, I think, also with a leg wound but not so serious as that of the Lieutenant. He used to relate humorous stories to the other patients, making them laugh despite their injuries. His impersonations of famous people were, as I recall, quite convincing, but it was he alone who berated Lieutenant Reeder. His comments were wounding, I would have said, on occasion."

"Do you remember the name of this man?" I asked.

She shook her head. "It was a few years ago, and there have been so many patients since."

"Was there anything of significance about him?" Holmes enquired.

"I believe he was of average height and rather pale, I think. But wait! I have it now. His name was Rufus Tiller."

"Do you know of his present whereabouts?"

"I regret that I cannot help you there."

Holmes got to his feet at once and I reflected that, as in the old days, he had lost interest in the lady from the instant that she had furnished the required information.

"My grateful thanks to you, Nurse Merrow. Your assistance has been most valuable."

The lady showed us out. She was a little bemused I thought, by our abrupt departure.

#

We had returned as far as Hammersmith High Street when Holmes instructed me to slow down.

"Ah," he said, peering out at the shops and houses. "Stop here, there's a good fellow."

I complied at once, and he scrambled from his seat to walk quickly away in the direction of the Post Office.

"Is everything all right, Holmes?" I asked when he reappeared.

He slid onto the leather seat and slammed the door. "That we shall know shortly. Bradstreet is still at the Yard, and I have requested that he conduct a search of their files for Rufus Tiller."

"You believe him to be posing as Mr Reeder's resurrected brother?"

"Possibly. At this stage that appears likely. Consider: according to Nurse Merrow he is pale and has sustained a leg injury, was skilled at impersonation and for some reason held our client in contempt. Did not the apparition we witnessed yesterday exhibit these features? Mark my words, Watson, the mystery here is not who is the villain but why he acts as he does."

Inspector Bradstreet had acted quickly. On our return to the Langham Hotel a telegram awaited Holmes.

"I asked Bradstreet to send a telegram rather than use the telephone," he remarked as he tore open the envelope, "since we could not be certain to be here at a given time." His eyes quickly scanned the sheet within. "Tiller is unknown at Scotland Yard, they have no record of him. We will now have lunch I think, Watson, before considering another source of information."

We repaired then to the dining room, where an excellent luncheon of roast lamb was served. Holmes ate his with little enthusiasm, as was his way when in the midst of a case, and leapt from his chair the moment his meal was finished.

"Enjoy your dessert, old fellow. I will forego mine and return soon in time for coffee."

He was as good as his word, reseating himself rather breathlessly as I finished my plums and custard. Moments later the coffee arrived and we drank our first cups before he would be drawn.

"Are you about to tell me where you have been, Holmes?" I enquired.

"Once again, to the nearest Post Office," he replied. "Since Tiller served with our client, the obvious place to discover facts about him is the Army Records Office. I dare say it is highly irregular, but during the war I assisted Major Simmonds on several occasions, and I am certain that he will wish to be of help to us now."

Holmes seemed to be in no hurry to finish his coffee. When he had done so, he ordered more. We left the dining-room shortly after and, at his suggestion, were about to repair to one of the sitting-rooms when a young man in the livery of the hotel approached us and handed him an envelope.

"Major Simmonds has been prompt," he murmured as he extracted the form. "This is excellent, he has been thorough."

"What does he tell us?"

"Suffice it to say that I now know considerably more about Tiller than previously. Before his army days he performed in half the music halls in the capital." He laughed, shortly. "Do you know, Watson, he called himself 'The Man of Many Faces'.

"A master of disguise? Sounds like our man, I would say."

"Indeed, but I am still curious as to the reason for his persecution of our client. We will, I think, pay a visit to Mr Cordon Reeder this evening, when he is most likely to have returned from his work."

We sat talking in the comfortable surroundings of one of the quiet rooms near the main entrance. Apart from an aged ex-military man who slept deeply throughout, we were quite alone. After an hour or so I felt the need of the afternoon rest that I now take frequently, and so we parted until dinner.

Holmes was good enough to allow me to use his room, where I slept for almost three hours, while he remained where he sat in deep contemplation. I confess to feeling awkward at dinner, having no evening clothes with me. He, in the same predicament, seemed unaffected. I enjoyed the roast chicken and what followed, but my friend barely touched his and was obviously anxious for us to be on our way.

Mr Reeder, I remembered, lived in Mayfair. I drove slowly as we entered the area, conscious of the homes of the very rich that surrounded us. I reflected that little seemed to have changed since we were here years ago, as younger men.

"The next turn to the left will bring us to Regal Mews, I think. Our client's residence is number eighteen."

I brought my vehicle to a halt in front of an imposing structure. Tall chimneys reached towards the darkening sky, and the house appeared to be of sturdy construction with a sprawling lawn before it. We approached by means of a paved path and Holmes rapped upon the door with his cane. After several minutes the silence within remained. He raised his cane to knock again but stopped suddenly, as if somehow warned that something was amiss. We exchanged cautious glances before he gripped the ornate door-handle and turned it slowly. The door opened easily.

"All is not well here, Watson," he whispered as we stepped into a darkened room.

I noticed that the heavy curtains were fully drawn, and we hesitated to allow our eyes to adjust to the shadows. The door to the corridor leading to the next room was open and my friend gestured to indicate that we should be silent and still. I strained to hear, but there was no sound and no movement anywhere. After a short while I sensed that Holmes was running his hand over the wall to our left, at about shoulder height. I heard a loud *click!* and light flooded through the room.

"As I thought," he said, "electric light. I noticed the cables fitted to the wall outside. The house appears empty, and I am curious to discover why it was left unlocked."

"Considering Mr Reeder's current problem, and his fears, it is hard to imagine such an oversight."

"Precisely. This parlour holds nothing out of the ordinary, but let us see what the sitting-room has to offer."

He led the way along the short corridor, again pressing a switch to illuminate the next room. As the electric chandelier came to life we both came to an immediate halt, for the bodies of two men lay sprawled before us. One of them was that of our client.

We approached carefully, disturbing nothing. I observed their condition carefully.

"Both men have sustained gunshot wounds to the head. I would say that death occurred about twelve hours ago," I concluded.

Holmes said nothing, so that I turned to him to ensure that he had heard. He wore an expression which utterly surprised me, one that I can recall seeing rarely in all the years of our association. His eyes held a hint of sadness and when he spoke it was with deep regret.

"I should have foreseen this, Watson. In my younger days I would never have committed such an error. I am indeed older, but it is uncertain if I have become wiser."

"You cannot blame yourself, Holmes. You advised Mr Reeder to avail himself of protection, and judging by this fellow's physique I would say that he was one of the rugby players that he spoke of. Also, his right hand was in the act of withdrawing a revolver from his pocket, so the attack must have been sudden."

"I have said before now that it is you who are the detective rather than I," he said grimly. "That appears not to have changed."

With that he opened a door at the other side of the room which led into a small study. His gait appeared weary as he entered, and moments later I heard him speak into a telephone.

"Are you all right, Holmes?" I asked as he returned.

"I have telephoned Scotland Yard, and Bradstreet will be arriving soon," he replied, ignoring my question. "Before then, we have the opportunity to conduct our own examination. I would be obliged if you would look out from the front window, and alert me at the first sight of him."

I obeyed, and Inspector Bradstreet, accompanied by two burly constables, arrived in less than half an hour. During this time, only the sound of Holmes' movements had disturbed the silence of the house. I admitted the men from the official force, and showed them to the sitting-room where my friend stood near the bodies.

"Good evening, Inspector," Holmes said solemnly. "As I explained during our telephone conversation, these men are Mr Cordon Reeder, about who I had spoken to you before, and a companion who is as yet unknown. The rear door of the building has been forced and I believe the murderer awaited them as they entered the house before striking and then leaving the same way." He pointed to an armchair in a corner. "From beneath that chair I retrieved – without touching it, never fear – a six-shot revolver of recent manufacture. With the aid of my lens I discovered a clear thumbprint on the handle. Doubtlessly you will be able to make something of it. This was a crime of passion not profit, for what criminal in his senses would leave his weapon for examination if he wished to remain free?"

The inspector, who had not said a word other than to return Holmes' greeting, wore a bemused look. Holmes was not usually so forthcoming so quickly, and I attributed this changed behaviour to the shock and regret he had suffered at the discovery of our dead client.

"Thank you, Mr Holmes," the Scotland Yard man said after a moment. "We will begin our own investigation. Much has changed since the war, you know, and our capabilities have increased somewhat. Nevertheless, I would be grateful for the benefit of any other observations you may have made."

Holmes nodded and proceeded to list his impressions. As of old Bradstreet listened eagerly and took notes. The constables were silent but paid close attention until they were ordered to search the upper floor. When the conversation was over, we left to return to the hotel.

"I will not detain you, Watson," my friend said as we arrived at the entrance. "When I learn anything further I will communicate with you."

At that he alighted and I, feeling rather snubbed, again drove my vehicle home. It was apparent to me that his failure to prevent Mr Reeder's death had affected him deeply, and I recalled that this had happened before. This was before the war when we were younger men, and I resolved to remind him of this with the object of dismissing his fears about his powers diminishing with age.

That night I slept fitfully, hoping that my friend would not let his disappointment cause him to return to Sussex prematurely. Also, I wondered whether Inspector Bradstreet would further consult Holmes, or keep him informed as to the progress of the case. The early sun shone through my bedroom window and I decided not to delay rising. I had washed, shaved and dressed, and was at the point of finishing my last piece of breakfast toast, when a telegram arrived.

The message was short:

Come at once.

Holmes.

It was still early when I alighted outside the Langham Hotel. Holmes and Bradstreet were near the reception area deep in conversation, and my friend saw me at once.

"Watson," he began when greetings had been exchanged, "Bradstreet here has been busy since last night. According to the records at the Yard, the owner of the thumbprint on the weapon at Mr Reeder's house was one Paul Durwin, who resides in Clapham."

"He is known to us from several convictions for petty theft," the inspector volunteered. "A visit to him should establish whether he owns the revolver and is therefore our killer, or if he has some other explanation. I thought you gentlemen might care to accompany me, for old time's sake."

"We would indeed." Holmes sounded much improved from the previous evening. I concurred also.

"I have a police vehicle waiting around the corner."

Presently, we found ourselves in a narrow street of old and rather decrepit houses. Bradstreet identified the number of the one we sought and, after instructing the police driver to wait, climbed out ahead of us.

"Are you armed, Watson?" Holmes enquired as we caught up with the inspector and crossed the street.

"I have my hand on my service weapon at this moment."

"Excellent. I doubt if you will need it, but it is as well to be prepared."

The inspector approached a door that was in dire need of a coat of paint and rapped upon it.

We inclined our heads to listen but there was only silence within. He raised his fist again, but lowered it as we heard movement. Then the door opened to reveal a dishevelled man whose pale face grew more so as he beheld us.

At once his eyes fell to the floor and I saw utter resignation in his face when he lifted his head.

"Come in, gentlemen," he said in a voice we could barely hear. Without any other word spoken we entered, and I felt that our visit had been anticipated.

We filed into a parlour that was clean but sparsely furnished. Our host let himself fall into the only armchair and we stood around him.

"Are you Paul Durwin?" Bradstreet asked him.

He shook his head.

"Or, more often, Rufus Tiller?" Holmes enquired.

"I cannot deny it."

Bradstreet studied the man carefully for a moment. "We have identified you as the owner of a gun that killed two men in Mayfair yesterday. How do you explain this?"

"I killed them. There is no other explanation."

Holmes and Bradstreet exchanged glances.

"Then I must arrest you for the murder of Mr Cordon Reeder and Mr Robert Arlen." Bradstreet produced a pair of police handcuffs. And snapped them on Tiller's wrist. He remained still and indifferent.

"Must we go immediately?" he asked then.

Bradstreet looked at him curiously. "What do you mean?"

"I would like the full circumstances known, so that whatever accounts and memories of me remain shall not depict me as a criminal. My actions were fired, not from greed or a desire for unlawful possession, but from revenge. A revenge that sprang from love."

Bradstreet looked perplexed, and I saw Holmes raise his eyebrows. I remembered that he had said that the mystery here was the reason behind all that had occurred.

"Surely, Bradstreet, we can afford a few minutes," Holmes ventured.

"It's irregular, but seeing as it's you, Mr Holmes. I suppose there's no harm in it."

"Very well," Holmes said to Tiller. "You have a chance to tell your story. Pray be concise, and speak the truth."

Tiller, with Bradstreet standing beside him, sat back in his chair. There was a moment of complete silence, and then he seemed to collect his thoughts.

"It began, if there was a beginning, in the trenches at the Battle of the Somme. For days we waited for orders, for the call to action, but none came. We stood in a pool of mud for days and nights, we all ate and slept where we were. In those long lines of men, I found myself next to Cordon Reeder and his brother, Jonathan. There were no exchanges between us but I heard much of their conversation, and it was in this way that I learned of the brother's devotion to each other. When Jonathan died I was no more than a few yards away, and like Lieutenant Reeder I suffered a leg wound during the assault."

"You witnessed the elder Reeder's death?" Holmes interrupted.

"It happened before my eyes."

"Is there then, any truth in your accusation that Cordon Reeder positioned his brother to shield himself?"

A crafty smile crept across Tiller's face."No, that was an invention of mine, intended to drive him to the point of madness, as I will explain. I spent my recovery in the same field hospital ward as Cordon Reeder, and it was there that I first saw Nurse Lily Crowther." His eyes flitted across our faces, and I had the impression that he was feeling some embarrassment. Seeing no sympathy, he continued: "Until the moment when I first saw her I had little interest in women, always having lived with my widowed mother, but to be confronted with such an angel changed my life in an instant. She was the sweetest girl I could ever have imagined, and I looked forward with all my heart to the occasions when   she dressed my wounds or enquired as to my condition. I began to think of her as mine, and turned my head away when she treated the other soldiers." Here he paused, and I could see that the memory was painful to him. "Can you imagine then, my disappointment when I realised that she had eyes only for Cordon Reeder? As the weeks passed, it became obvious to us all. Some of the others laughed and congratulated him on his 'conquest', but to me every smile she gave him was a dagger in my heart."

The reason for his animosity towards our client, as described by Nurse Edith Merrow, now became clear. Holmes' expression suggested that his thoughts were similar.

"Do you mean to tell us," Inspector Bradstreet asked with some incredulity, "that your actions and crimes in all this were because of *a woman?*"

Tiller looked at him in a strange way. "That would not be an inaccurate assessment, but there is more. You see, to me she was becoming my whole life. I imagined us together, and this eclipsed everything that had gone before. The time came for my discharge from the hospital and, unfit to render further service to my country, I resumed my former life. My mother passed away but I hardly noticed her absence, because Nurse Crowther still filled my mind. Unable to keep myself informed about her life, I read the newspapers avidly to keep track of Cordon Reeder. The news that I dreaded, that they had married, never appeared but I saw that he was progressing in government circles. Then came the Spanish Flu epidemic of 1918. At that time he led a committee that was set up to combat the disease, and made the final decision to despatch a contingent of specially-trained nurses to a badly infected hospital in Manchester. This was strongly opposed by most of his colleagues for many reasons, but he would have his way. Quite recently I discovered that most of those poor nurses died, and that among them was my beloved Lily. This news caused me such melancholia that I wanted nothing else but to die. Several times I found myself on the brink of taking my own life, as the only way of seeing her again. Then one day it came into my mind that the cause of her death was Cordon Reeder, because he had the final say in placing her in peril."

"Did it not occur to you," Holmes asked him, "that Mr Reeder was probably unaware that Miss Crowther was in the Group? After all, unless I have misunderstood you, he had no further contact with her after leaving the hospital."

Tiller shrugged his shoulders. "That did not seem to matter. All that I could see was that he was responsible for her death, and that I could not leave this life without making him pay. It struck me as fitting that, using my skills at disguise learned long ago, I should use the guilt he carried about causing the death of a brother that he loved, to avenge the death he had caused of someone that I, myself, adored."

"Enough of this," Bradstreet said impatiently. "If you are confessing, then get on with it."

Tiller glanced at him, but continued as if hadn't heard. "I had a plan. I intended to appear as Jonathan Reeder unexpectedly and with increasing frequency. Cordon Reeder had always held doubts in his mind about his brother's death, and I wished to intensify them. Had I not been prevented, a week or two would have seen him fit for the mad-house." He scowled, looking directly at my friend. "But after Victoria Station, my task became more difficult. I recognised you, Mr Holmes, and remembered your reputation of old. I could not risk failure, and leaving my Lily unavenged was now more likely, so I decided to abandon my plan and act at once. I forced my way into Cordon Reeder's home, only to find it empty. I therefore resolved to await his return and then to shoot him, which I did a short time later. I did not expect him to have a companion, but when this other man appeared and attempted to retaliate, I had no choice but to kill him also. I cannot remember now, but I believe I dropped my weapon to the floor as I left. That was of no importance, and neither was my fate." He rose to his feet. "You see then, gentlemen, why your arrival, although sooner than expected, came as no surprise."

"I have seldom heard such a story of a man deceiving himself so much, and certainly not to the point of murder," Bradstreet commented. "The best you can hope for, my lad, is to spend the rest of your days in an asylum. Apart from that, it's the hangman I'm sure."

"Yet there is something pitiful about this account," I said.

"Don't waste your sympathy, Doctor. The streets of London will be safer, without the likes of him. Who knows who he might have taken a fancy to next?"

Holmes nodded. "This is far from the first time that I have seen a man ruined by his obsession with a woman, even when she is unaware of it. I think, Bradstreet, that you should take him now as he appears to have come to the end of his tale."

The inspector began to move towards the door with Tiller, held to him by the handcuffs, at his side.

"Thank you for your assistance, gentlemen, it was quite like in our younger days."

The words were hardly out of Bradstreet's mouth when Tiller, passing the sideboard, quickly wrenched open a drawer with his free hand. Something flashed and at first I thought that Bradstreet, now spattered with blood, was injured, but then Tiller sank to his knees pulling the inspector down with him.

"Watson!" Holmes cried, and I responded at once. I knelt beside Tiller and loosened his collar but it was quickly apparent that he was beyond my help.

I stood up and shook my head. "I can do nothing for him. He plunged a fork from the cutlery drawer deep into his neck. The rapid loss of so much blood suggests that he has severed the jugular."

Bradstreet removed the handcuff from Tiller's lifeless hand. "He has saved the hangman a job, I expect. This is not the way I would have chosen for this affair to end, though."

"It was not our decision, inspector," Holmes replied impassively. "I take it that you would like Watson and myself to visit you at the Yard tomorrow, to add to your report."

"I would be obliged."

With that, the inspector went to arrange for the removal of the body. Holmes and I left the premises in poor spirits, for tragedy was abundant in this case. My surprise was therefore considerable when he, rather than descending into a dark mood as of old, suddenly smiled and placed his hand upon my shoulder.

"I think, old fellow, that we are in dire need of something to cheer us up. What do you say to a drink in that tavern that I see on the corner, followed by luncheon at Simpson's?"

"At this moment, I can think of nothing better," I replied with enthusiasm.

#

It was as I replaced my empty glass upon the worn table, that I asked my friend the question to which I dreaded the answer.

"Has it crossed your mind, Holmes, that you could easily re-establish yourself as a consulting detective, perhaps with even more success than before?"

For a moment, it seemed like an age, he appeared to consider. Then a slow smile spread across his face.

"Dear old Watson, it is clear to me that you would like nothing better than for us to resume our activities, and I will confess that a part of me is in accordance. But consider, old fellow, that we are now in a new age. The London we knew has gone forever. Now we see around us machines instead of horse-drawn hansoms, Scotland Yard appears more efficient to the point where my assistance will soon be unnecessary and you and I no longer have the energy of youth. Then there is the certainty that nothing will ever be the same since that terrible war. Witness the increasing strangeness of everyday behaviour and even little things, such as the abominable noise that is now recognised as music, and this becomes clear. We are out of our element. You may recall that I have said, on more than one occasion in Baker Street, that you are a fixed point in a changing world. I should have realised then, I now see, that I am also. No, my conclusion, and I gave the matter some thought before you mentioned it, is exactly the opposite. "

I knew of course that my friend was correct, as usual. Nevertheless, my heart sank. Then he looked me in the eye and smiled warmly, and his words restored me instantly.

"But, and make no mistake here, old friend, what I have said by no means precludes our opportunities to meet more often, and re-live our adventures many times before your fireside or mine. And who knows what strange events will present themselves, even in our twilight years, to cause us once more to set off together in pursuit of explanation?"

The Adventure of the Paternal Ghost

It is well known to readers of my accounts of the extraordinary cases of my friend Mr Sherlock Holmes that he preferred, and indeed conducted some of his most memorable investigations into, problems of an unusual or singular nature. Before now, I have committed many of these to paper so that those who have interest might appreciate the deductive genius of the man who was, at that time, London's only consulting detective. My following recollections will illustrate this further.

#

Holmes' jubilant mood at breakfast one fine spring morning did not surprise me. Over the previous few days he had seen the successful conclusion of the Market Street scandal, the affair of Mrs Juliette Kerr and the thwarting of the attempted ruination of Mr Percy Fellingham.

"You really have succeeded to a remarkable extent, Holmes," I remarked, although he had not mentioned his triumphs.

"I would believe that you had taken to reading my mind, Watson, were I not aware that my facial expression had probably betrayed my thoughts. But you are correct, I am pleased immensely by the outcome of our activities."

"I contributed little enough, but I hope I was of some small assistance."

"Nonsense, my dear fellow, you were instrumental in at least two instances, to my arriving at the correct conclusion in the most trying of circumstances. You cannot imagine how many times I have asked myself where I would be, without my Boswell."

I felt my face begin to flush, with both embarrassment and pride. "You are most kind, Holmes."

Before he could say anything more our landlady knocked and entered, to ask if we required more coffee and to clear away our empty plates. We both declined and she left us, carrying a laden tray. Moments later the door-bell rang and after a short conversation below, Mrs Hudson reappeared to usher a rather bewildered man of about forty years into our presence.

"Mr Cedric Topham, to see Mr Holmes," she announced, before closing the door softly as she left.

Our visitor paused, glancing from Holmes to myself. In this brief interval, I decided to use my friend's methods to scrutinise the fellow and see what information I could glean.

He was a tall man, though not so tall as Holmes, in his middle years and dressed in a fashionable morning-coat. His face had a lop-sided appearance, an effect which I quickly realised was produced because his hair was combed in such a way as to be piled to one side of his head. His expression struck me as glum and his voice, when first he spoke, held a note of grief or of fear.

"Good morning, gentlemen," he began uncertainly. "Which of you, pray, is Mr Sherlock Holmes?"

Holmes was before him in two strides, extending his hand and dismissing the man's dilemma.

"It is I that you seek. Allow me to introduce Doctor John Watson. His assistance in my work has been invaluable, and you may be assured that he is the soul of discretion."

"I am indebted to you for granting me an interview without an appointment."

"You have, in fact, called at an opportune time. I have no cases requiring my immediate attention, and Doctor Watson is not due to return to his practice until the end of the week." He guided Mr Topham to the hearth. "But I see that something is indeed troubling you. Allow me to relieve you of your hat and coat and then take the basket chair, so that we can see what can be done."

When we all three were settled, Holmes enquired if the young man would like tea.

"Thank you, no, Mr Holmes. I am not inclined to eat or drink at all just now. My burden of worry is so great, that I feel no desire to do so."

"I would not recommend such a course," said I. "Lack of nourishment can have nothing but a detrimental effect, regardless of your present circumstances."

Holmes nodded his agreement. "Pray elaborate, and we will assist you in any way we can."

"I am not sure that anyone can help. Scotland Yard would probably think me mad."

"They are not noted for their imagination. Continue, please."

Our client swallowed heavily. "I am being haunted, hounded by a ghost."

I expected my friend to immediately assure our client that, based on much experience, he had formed the impression that no such things existed, and so it surprised me when his expression remained unaltered.

"Is this apparition of someone with whom you were acquainted?"

"It is that of my father."

Holmes and I glanced briefly at each other, and I wondered if he could be thinking, as I was, that this was a situation that we had not before encountered.

For a moment or two there was silence, except for the faint noise of our landlady rattling crockery in the kitchen, and that of the hooves of passing horses along Baker Street.

"It would be best, I think, if you were to begin at the beginning," Holmes said then. "Kindly be as specific as you can, even to the smallest detail."

Mr Topham hesitated, obviously with some embarrassment.

"It is normal, thankfully, that parents should love their offspring," he began. "But in our house the opposite was true. I can recall no instance when my father favoured me with a smile, much less a kind word. Unlike him, my mother was not cruel but indifferent, and I have long since formed the opinion that I entered this world unbidden."

"I am exceedingly sorry to learn this," I interrupted, earning myself an immediate scowl of impatience from Holmes.

"My father seemed always to be irritated by any number of things, my presence among them, as I grew from a child to a man. Gradually his disposition became worse, as he was consumed on occasion by violent rages that worsened year by year. About six months ago these became both more frequent and more intense, to the point where I was obliged to forcibly restrain him to protect my mother."

"It came about that he injured her?" Holmes asked.

"Indeed. I returned home one day – I should mention that I am unmarried and live still with my parents for convenience sake – to find her covered in blood. My father stood over her with a fire-iron, raving like the madman he had become. A neighbour, alarmed by the screams and calls for help, had summoned a constable who arrived minutes after me. Together we disarmed my father, and he was put in handcuffs. As he was being led away he screamed at me hysterically, threatening to kill me when he was released."

"Did he, in fact, attempt this?" Holmes enquired seriously.

"He could not, because he was committed to an asylum by the local court. This did not surprise me, since my mother died from her injuries not long after his arrest. Some weeks later, news was brought to me that he too had died, from pneumonia, doubtlessly contracted in the place of his detention. I spoke at length with the bearer of these tidings and learned that the body had already been buried for fear of contagion. I asked the messenger whether my father had mentioned me as his end approached, and the man's hesitant reply is with me still. He said he looked forward to seeing me in hell."

"A dreadful story," I acknowledged. "You have my sympathy, sir."

Mr Topham expressed his thanks, as Holmes appeared to be considering the matter.

"You have said that your father's ghost has appeared to you. Kindly tell us how that came about."

"It must be four weeks ago – I must apologise for my inaccuracy, my mind has been in turmoil – since I appealed to my employer, who is a kindly man, for a few days of rest. He was aware of the effect that the death of my parents has had upon me and allowed me three days without pay. I decided that a long walk would help to clear my head, and so the first day found me ambling beside the Serpentine. Eventually I sat upon a bench, occupying myself with nothing more than watching the sunlight play upon the surface of the water, when I chanced to glance towards the opposite bank where a group of elderly people appeared to be listening to a lecture from a man who made much use of gestures to illustrate his talk. Standing alone and a short way apart from the group was a man who seemed to be staring in my direction. I was shocked, and racked with disbelief, when I saw that it was my father! A dizzy spell overcame me briefly, but immediately it passed I got to my feet and made off towards where I could cross to the other bank. When I arrived at the spot the lecture was continuing, but of my father there was no sign. I imagine that he retreated into the nearby trees and left the scene from there."

Holmes leaned his thin body forward in his chair. "Why are you so certain that this man was your father? From such a distance, would not recognition be difficult?"

"I am blessed with long-sightedness," Mr Topham struggled with the recollection, "but even so I could not see his features clearly. It was more his stance, the way he held himself, and his general appearance that convinced me."

"You identified this man as a ghost, but was there any reason that he could not have simply resembled your father? After all, those who claim to have seen such apparitions invariably describe their form as transparent and the encounters as taking place at night."

"No, Mr Holmes, he looked to be as solid as you or I. However, that is not the end of it. The following day I discovered a piece of tattered parchment on the floor of my hallway. It had not arrived by post since there was neither envelope nor stamp upon it. I have brought it for your inspection."

With that, he reached into the pocket of his morning-coat and withdrew a discoloured fragment of paper. My friend took it and examined it with his lens.

"This paper is not ancient, it has simply been made to appear so by the application of heat. The message reads: *the madness that engulfed me awaits you also. your time is short.* Is this in your father's hand, Mr Topham?"

Our client nodded. "I have seen no example of it for many years, but to the best of my recollection, it is. Also, he was never much of a scholar. You will have noticed the absence of capital letters."

"Indeed. An unusual ghost, who writes letters, wouldn't you say?"

"I suppose my assumption was fanciful."

"It was exactly the conclusion you were intended to reach. Has anything else occurred?"

"Subsequently, there were two more letters."

Again, he took them from his pocket and passed them to Holmes, who examined them as he had the first.

"Their intent is the same. *you cannot escape your fate,* and *your destiny is in your own hands.* The content seems to suggest that you should contemplate suicide. Evidently, the object of all this is your demise. Who would benefit from that?"

"There is no one." He looked perplexed at the notion. "I have no friends and few remaining relatives."

"And there has been nothing more?"

"There has. Since the letters I have been accosted by a man who I remember from my youth. He was once our greengrocer and was apparently unaware of my father's death, which he said could not be as he had recently seen him in Paddington High Street. When I insisted that my father had passed on, he gave me a peculiar look and excused himself."

"Did this man elaborate, or converse with 'your father'?"

"No, he saw him on the edge of a crowd, on the opposite side of the street."

"From a distance, as you did?"

"It must have been."

Holmes folded his hands in his lap, but I saw by the glitter in his grey eyes that he had become interested.

"What action did you take then?"

Our client fell silent for a moment. "I needed, you understand, to know the truth of this. I acted in a way of which I am not proud, and that I would not normally consider."

"You had your father's body exhumed?"

"I did," he said in a dull voice, "but not legally. I know how long it takes for the wheels of the law to turn, so I resorted to the only other way there was."

"Grave robbers?"

He hung his head. "Two of them. We went to St Michael's churchyard, late one night. They must have been experienced, for they made short work of it."

"What did you discover?" I asked then.

"I jumped down into the opened grave and prised the lid from the coffin with my own hands. It was empty."

"Someone has put themselves to a great deal of trouble to convince you that your father has risen from the grave," said Holmes. "But that notion is easily disproved. Before you return to Paddington, your singing, and your employment as a gentleman's barber, I would be grateful if you would inform us as to anything more which you consider might be helpful to our investigation. In particular, anything of your father's history."

Mr Topham appeared astonished. "Mr Holmes, I am aware that I mentioned that my father was supposedly seen in Paddington, but I did not state that I reside there. Neither did I mention my profession or the fact that I am a gifted tenor. You amaze me, sir."

"There is really no mystery about it." A quick smile passed across Holmes' face. "When I see affixed to your morning-coat a button bearing an insignia that I recognise, that of the Paddington Hairdressers Choral Society, and then notice marks of the habitual use of scissors on your thumb and forefinger, what else am I to conclude? As you will now realise, it was simplicity itself."

"As you explain it, yes, but I would never have thought of such things."

"It is my business to do so."

"Of course. As to my father, I have already explained his rejection of me. That is why, having no parental guidance, I had to find my own place in the world. Our local barber, who both my father and myself patronised, kindly took me on as an apprentice. I progressed, and have been a partner in his establishment for about three years." He paused, realising perhaps that he had digressed. "I recall that I asked my father several times, over the years, about his occupation. My mother, it seemed, had always been kept in ignorance of it. My father's only reply to such an enquiry was a vague reference to a government post of some secrecy, which was also offered as an explanation for his frequent long absences from home."

I underlined this in my notebook, in which I had been recording the essence of the conversation throughout, knowing that Holmes might wish to refer to it later.

"Did your family ever experience financial difficulty?" he asked.

Our visitor shook his head. "Not that I recall. I cannot say with certainty that my father's income was sufficient, though. I once overheard a conversation between my parents, during which it was mentioned that my uncle, Mr Albert Topham, was a contributor to our household. This did not surprise me, since I knew already that our house was bequeathed to us by him."

"He is a man of some means, then?"

"I do not believe he was at the time when he invited us to live with him, during my childhood. Like myself he was unmarried, and after a few years became determined to make his fortune in the South African gold fields. He left us, with the provision that we should pay a modest rent during his absence, to subsequently inform us that he had transferred the deeds to my father. I also discovered that he sent a goodly sum regularly, to assist in our maintenance. I regret to say that we have heard nothing from him for some time so that we had begun to wonder if, as he has mentioned in his letters from time to time, he could at last be coming home."

"Most interesting," Holmes acknowledged. "Mr Topham, it will greatly assist us if you would provide a likeness of your father. A photographic portrait, perhaps?"

"I regret that I cannot, for the only image of him that I know of is the portrait that hangs in the hallway of what is now my home. It seemed a strange variation of his usual character when he sat for it, and I wondered if it was commissioned because he wished, out of envy, his image to be displayed with that of his brother."

"A possibility, of course," Holmes nodded. "If it is convenient, Doctor Watson and I will now accompany you to your residence, where we can view these portraits. It is of paramount importance that we are able to recognise this 'ghost', should we encounter him."

"But certainly, you are both most welcome."

A hansom was procured without difficulty. I said little during the journey, but Holmes and Mr Topham conducted a conversation that mostly consisted of our client's account of the further indifferences of his father and his jealousy of his brother's success. It seemed to me that Mr Albert Topham's generosity had passed largely unnoticed by his brother.

I took to gazing out at the passing scene, although the monotone of our client's voice was still clearly audible to me. I watched St Mary's Hospital pass by, and Paddington Green Police Station of considerable reputation. Our driver turned into a tree-lined lane before we reached the High Street, and we soon found ourselves confronted by tall iron gates standing open. In the paved courtyard I asked that the hansom should wait for us, as we alighted.

217

The house was smaller than I expected from Mr Topham's description. It was a square structure of grey stone that had crumbled in places, without wings or extension. We were met by an attractive young girl in the uniform of a maid and our client explained that, apart from the elderly cook, she was his only servant. As we had refused refreshments, he led us immediately to a low oak-beamed passage where three portraits were displayed. We stood back to obtain a better view, and I saw that Holmes was examining the portraits carefully.

He stood before a picture of a grim-faced man, dark-haired and with eyes that appeared, even on canvas, as rather empty.

"The plaque reads 'Mr Jeremiah Topham'," he said to our client. "He was your father, I presume?"

"He was. It is an excellent likeness."

"And the other, in the frame decorated with gold leaf?"

"My uncle, Albert, who, to the best of my knowledge, still resides in the Transvaal."

The image was that of a heavier man with a jovial expression. The resemblance to our client and his father was nevertheless evident.

Holmes moved a few feet along the passage, to where a smaller frame held the painted countenance of a man with some similarities to the others.

"Another uncle?" I asked.

"That is my nephew, Mr Benjamin Stokehouse," Mr Topham said. "He is the son of my elder sister. Sadly, both she and her husband succumbed to a local influenza epidemic."

218

"But Mr Stokehouse still lives?" Holmes enquired.

"Indeed he does, although he also is often ill and prone to chest infections. He was fortunate in that his investments enabled him to retire quite early. For most of his life he has suffered from severe bronchitis."

"Does he live in London?"

"He does as far as I am aware, since I see little of him. It will not surprise you to learn that he and my father disagreed about many things, which is probably why he is almost a stranger to me." He looked at Holmes with some surprise. "Surely, he cannot be connected to your investigation?"

"You will recall that I mentioned the importance of even minor details, at the outset."

"Of course. I have his address in Notting Hill, somewhere in my study. Please step this way, gentlemen, and I will find it for you."

We left shortly afterwards. Holmes requested our driver to stop once so that a telegram could be despatched, during our return to Baker Street.

"To Lestrade?" I asked as he resumed his seat on reappearing from the Post Office.

"To Mycroft," he corrected me. "But now, a luncheon of Mrs Hudson's rainbow trout awaits us, I think."

Holmes ate with unusual enthusiasm, though his preoccupation with the new enquiry was evident. He refused dessert as he often did, leaping to his feet the moment our coffee cups were empty.

"I will be with you in an instant," I said, rising from the table.

"There is no need to inconvenience yourself, Watson. I do not anticipate that I shall be away for long. Should Mrs Hudson be out, pray be so good as to receive Mycroft's reply for me. It may arrive before my return."

I barely had time to reply in the affirmative, before he had seized his hat and coat and departed. It occurred to me then that I had once more allowed my unread medical journals to accumulate, so I settled myself in my chair and began to read. No more than two hours had passed however, before I heard my friend's familiar tread upon the stairs. He shouted a greeting as he entered, and poured two glasses of port from the decanter immediately after shedding his outer garments.

"Have we heard from my brother?" he asked as he lowered himself into his chair.

I took a sip, and placed my glass upon a side-table. "Not as yet. Your mood suggests that your afternoon was successful."

"It was, though I perceive from your tone that you are slightly aggrieved that I did not request your company. The lady who I consulted is wary of another presence when acting as my informant, so it was for the best that I saw her alone. All that I learned was not unexpected."

"Who is this lady, Holmes?"

"You have heard me speak of her before now. She is an actress currently performing at the Lyceum Theatre, with Henry Irving. Her name is Miss Gloriana Roland."

"I recall your previous mentions of her. But what was your purpose in visiting her today?"

His reply was delayed, as he took a long draught of his drink. I heard the shouts of a newspaper-seller, announcing the mid-day edition, from somewhere along Baker Street.

"My purpose, Watson, was the same as that of sending a wire to Mycroft, earlier. I am trying to separate the truth of Mr Jeremiah Topham from his lies. Miss Roland, though a successful actress, is something of a busybody, and is aware of all that occurs within the theatrical profession in the capital. She is certain that no one of her acquaintance has been hired to impersonate a dead man, or to equip another to do so."

"So we are seeking someone who has learned his skills, if he has any, elsewhere." I smiled in anticipation of Holmes' response to what I was about to say next. "Unless of course, we are at last involved in the pursuit of a genuine ghost."

He scowled, predictably. "You are aware of my opinions and deductions on that score. It did, however, occur to me at once that our client might be completely unaware of his father having an identical twin brother." He considered for a moment. "It is unlikely, but I will ask this of Mr Benjamin Stokehouse, who I intend to interview soon. As a member of the family, he is sure to know the answer."

Before I could reply, the door-bell rang and we heard our landlady at the front door. Minutes later, a yellow envelope was in Holmes' hands.

He extracted the form and glanced at it briefly. "It is as I suspected. Mr Jeremiah Topham is unknown in Whitehall."

"Then what was his occupation? How can his absences be truly explained?

"That we will doubtlessly discover shortly."

He would say no more of the subject, but took up his violin to play a mournful tune that suddenly erupted into a fast pace and then a shrill crescendo. I suspected it to be his own composition, and when I looked up from my reading it was to see that his eyes remained closed and his face held an expression of rapturous delight, as if the strains were a comfort to his soul.

Our dinner proved to be one of Mrs Hudson's steak and mushroom pies. I ate mine with relish but, not unexpectedly, Holmes merely sampled his portion before toying with the remains. He requested that our landlady provide an extra pot of coffee, which he consumed before I had begun mine. As we repaired to our armchairs he was already contemplating the steps we should take to bring about a conclusion to this puzzling case, and I had resigned myself to an evening of little conversation between long silences, when the peal of the door-bell brought him out of his thoughts.

"Are you expecting anyone?" I asked.

He wore the look of a man emerging from a deep sleep. "I have no appointments."

"It could be an emergency. Fortunately, I have re-stocked my medical bag." I rose and peered through the window, as we heard the front door open.

"It is another telegram. The boy has just left. A new client, perhaps?"

"We will know in a moment. Mrs Hudson is on her way."

With that he got to his feet and took the envelope from her at our sitting-room door. By the time he resumed his seat the form was open and he read it without expression, before passing it to me.

Mr Holmes. Help me. He attempted to take my life.

Topham.

Holmes now wore a furious look, but his anger was against himself.

"I should have foreseen this, Watson. How many times have I emphasised the danger of making assumptions? Yet I assumed that this 'ghost' would go no further than attempting to terrify our client by his random appearances." He stood up quickly. "Bah! I would have expected more of an amateur."

#

Our driver was promised an extra half-sovereign if he could get us to Paddington quickly, and so we found ourselves before Mr Topham's door before the light began to fade.

Holmes raised his stick, but the door opened immediately.

"Mr Holmes, Doctor Watson! Thank God!" Our client stood aside unsteadily to allow us to enter. I saw that his face was skinned along one side, with blood seeping onto his collar. His clothes were torn and his hand badly bruised. He limped slightly as he led us to a comfortable sitting-room with new furniture. He did not forget his manners.

"First, can I offer you gentlemen something? The cook is still here. It was she who I sent to despatch the telegram."

Holmes brushed the kind suggestion aside. "No, thank you, Mr Topham. Doctor Watson will attend to your injuries, as you relate to me the circumstances in which you came by them."

At that I took bandages and ointment from my medical bag and began to attend to him. It was soon apparent that the smeared blood worsened the appearance of the wounds. The cook, a pleasant middle-aged lady called Mrs Cranmore, supplied hot water and towels. Despite Holmes' request, my patient said little during my ministrations so that I concluded that he had suffered a severe shock. I resolved to leave an adequate amount of laudanum with him, on our departure.

"Has the pain lessened?" I enquired when I had dressed the last of his wounds.

"Yes, thank you, Doctor," he replied in a shaky voice. "I am a little unsteady, but I believe I have come to no serious harm."

"Nevertheless," I handed him the medication. "You must not exert yourself for the next few days and should take this regularly. Your facial abrasions should heal quickly. They are not serious."

"Are you able, now, to explain to us?" Holmes enquired with some impatience.

Mr Topham nodded. "There is very little to it. My maid reported that, as she left here at the end of her duties, a man began to follow her. She immediately retraced her steps and advised me of her fear, whereupon I accompanied her to her home."

"Did you, yourself, notice any pursuit as you walked with her?"

"There was none, I am certain of it. She lives with her parents in a cottage near the railway station, less than a quarter of a mile distant, and we hardly saw a soul. In fact she apologised as we arrived, saying that she must have imagined the incident and that she was sorry to have caused me so much trouble. I saw her safely inside and returned."

"Has the girl mentioned similar incidents, previously?"

"Never, but she is of a nervous disposition, and I confess that I believed her fears were imaginary. I thought it would do no harm to accompany her to dispel her anxiety."

"Most commendable," I murmured.

"I had walked almost halfway back, to a place where two lanes meet to form a crossroads, when a cart appeared. It was driven at a fast pace, and it overtook me and swerved into my path. I was knocked off my feet and landed in a thorn bush, where I received these injuries. By the time I disentangled myself the cart was disappearing among the trees along the lane ahead, but I had already seen the driver's face."

"It was the man that you have identified as your father's ghost, of course," Holmes concluded.

"I am quite certain of it. He wore a wide-brimmed hat, but I am in no doubt."

"Further proof, if any were necessary, that it is a man we are dealing with."

Our client shook his head. "Yet the coffin was empty, and the resemblance was clear to me. What does this mean, Mr Holmes?"

"Simply that you are being persecuted for reasons as yet unknown to us." My friend spent a moment in consideration. "If you are feeling somewhat recovered, Doctor Watson and I will leave you now. On our way back to Baker Street I will telegraph Inspector Lestrade of Scotland Yard, requesting that he assign a constable to remain outside your home until tomorrow, when I expect to have brought these events to their conclusion. I suggest that you ensure that all the doors and windows of this house are locked until the officer arrives. I also recommend a glass of brandy, to still your nerves and cause your trembling to cease." He glanced at me for a sign of approval, which I gave, before remembering: "Is Mrs Cranmore on the premises still?"

"She will have left by now. Her husband invariably arrives to collect her."

"Excellent. Goodnight then, Mr Topham. I would be obliged if you would visit us at Baker Street at, say, four o'clock tomorrow afternoon, if that is convenient. I will confirm this by wire."

Appearing somewhat bemused, our client assented, and we left.

There was little conversation between us in the hansom, as Holmes had lapsed into a silent reverie. It was now late evening and, as we resettled ourselves in our armchairs, I knew that he would wish to retire soon, since he had inferred that there was work to be done on the morrow. He had, I recalled, twice suggested that this affair would be over soon.

"Holmes," I began as we filled our last pipes of the day, "how can you be sure that Mr Topham's problem will be solved so quickly?"

He blew out a cloud of aromatic smoke and leaned back in his chair. "Consider - our client's father, Mr Jeremiah Topham is deceased, I am in no doubt of that, and his uncle, Mr Albert Topham, still resides in South Africa."

"So we are given to understand."

"Then who else, who is related to our client and therefore is likely to be able to tell us more, remains?"

"Mr Topham mentioned a nephew," I said after a moment's recollection.

"He did indeed. Mr Benjamin Stokehouse lives in Notting Hill. If the truth of this business is as I suspect, then he will provide us with confirmation in the morning."

#

Holmes' irritation as I consumed my breakfast was evident. He had taken no more than two cups of coffee, refusing anything more substantial as he often did when the end of a case was in sight.

"I do think, Watson, that you could eat a little faster without inviting indigestion," he scowled.

"Have a care, old fellow. I will be finished in a moment."

I gulped down the last of my coffee and rose, to find my hat and coat immediately thrust at me. A few minutes later we halted a passing cab and Holmes shouted our destination to the driver.

In Notting Hill we left the hansom in a quiet street of terraced houses. The residence of Mr Benjamin Stokehouse proved to be elderly, bearing signs of much repair.

The door opened to reveal a thick-set man who I judged to be about fifty years of age, evidently intending to leave the premises since he was about to put on his hat.

"Mr Benjamin Stokehouse?" Holmes asked.

"I am, sir," the man's difficulty in breathing was immediately obvious. "Who are you, and to what do I owe this pleasure?"

"My name is Sherlock Holmes, and this is my associate Doctor John Watson. I am a consulting detective, investigating some curious incidents involving Mr Jeremiah Topham."

Mr Stokehouse stared at us blankly, then nodded. "Yes, I believe I have heard of you. But, Mr Holmes, I fear that you have had a wasted journey. You see, my grandfather, scoundrel that he was, died several months ago. Tell me sir, if it is not breaking a confidence to do so, who it is who is so unaware of this as to hire you."

"My client is Mr Cedric Topham."

"Cedric? Why, I have not seen my uncle for many a year. We are not a family who are close, in fact I discovered my grandfather's death through a third party." He ceased speaking abruptly, to succumb to a fit of coughing. When it had subsided, he turned back to us, gasping. "What is troubling him?"

"He claims that he is being haunted."

"A joke, surely." He laughed, with some effort, briefly. "I do not remember him as being so fanciful."

"He has seen his father, since the burial."

"Ridiculous! Have I not just stated that the man is dead?" Mr Stokehouse removed his hat as he retreated over the threshold. "Come in, sirs. Clearly there is something amiss here, and it is probably as well to discuss it."

Shortly afterwards we found ourselves in a sitting-room panelled in dark wood. We refused our host's offer of sherry and seated ourselves in worn but comfortable chairs.

"Your uncle is quite certain that he has seen his father several times," Holmes repeated. "He was concerned enough to cause the grave to be opened, only to find the coffin empty."

Mr Stokehouse struggled noisily to breathe. "If this were some sort of trick, I can see no purpose in it. However, I would not put such a scheme out of the question. My grandfather, as my mother often stated, was an only child and an absolute blackguard who thought nothing of beating her and his wife for the least of reasons. Uncle Cedric, I understand, did not fare well either."

"No indeed. Shortly before he died, your grandfather cursed your uncle."

"That is no surprise to me. I was appalled at his treatment of my grandmother. My father had long held the suspicion that there was another woman, possibly a lady of the night, involved."

"Certainly our client described his father's long absences from home," I remembered.

"There were many." With difficulty, he attempted to breathe evenly. "I am striving to recollect more of my grandfather that might explain his apparent resurrection, but the fact is that he was estranged from me for a number of years." His thoughtful expression cleared suddenly. "There is one man who may be able to assist you. I recall my mother mentioning him several times. He is my grandfather's solicitor whose name, if my memory serves me well, is Mr Bradwood Kitterly."

Holmes' face lit up immediately, but Mr Stokehouse appeared not to notice. He related to us several minor incidents of his grandfather's misdeeds towards members of the family, before we took our leave.

"I'll wager that the name of that solicitor had some significance for you," I said, watching Holmes' face as he raised his stick to summon a cab.

"You improve constantly, Watson. Mr Kitterly and I are certainly known to each other. He has the distinction of obtaining the release of scores of blackguards and scoundrels from their rightful imprisonment, by exploiting contradictions in our ill-conceived laws. His other methods include the production of false witnesses, and possibly the blackmail of those who would otherwise furnish truthful testimony. There are few methods of deceit unknown and yet to be practised by him, I think."

"I am astounded that you or Scotland Yard have not caused him to be disbarred, at the very least."

"Ah, but he is clever. One day he will make an error, sufficiently for Gregson, Lestrade or myself to pounce, and the wheels of justice will turn more smoothly afterwards."

We ate a scant luncheon at a coffee-house on the outskirts of Kensington. The premises of Mr Bradwood Kitterly, Holmes confided, were a short walk away. So it was that less than ten minutes had passed, before we found ourselves before a stone-faced middle-aged woman who sat before a typewriting machine in a tiny office.

"Is Mr Kitterly expecting either of you gentlemen?" She asked in response to Holmes' request.

"That I would doubt. Kindly present my card to your employer."

She took it from where he had placed it on her desk, and made her inspection. "You are a consulting detective?" she retorted, with a disapproving glare.

"That is my profession."

She hesitated for so long that I became convinced that she would find a reason to dismiss us, but then she glanced at the door at the back of the room and nodded. "Very well, I will see whether Mr Kitterly has time."

She rose and turned abruptly, to strut away and knock at the door. After a moment, a faint voice bade her enter the room beyond.

"Impertinent woman," I commented.

Holmes smiled. "She is exactly the sort that I would have expected Mr Kitterly to employ. I would be surprised indeed to learn that she knows the true nature of his business."

"He is so shrewd, to be able to deceive his secretary?"

"Much more so. His respectable appearance is vital to his activities."

She reappeared in the doorway frowning, possibly because her employer's decision was unexpected.

"Mr Kitterly will see you now, gentlemen," she announced in a regretful tone.

Holmes granted her an undeserved smile as we passed, and she closed the door behind us. We were now in a room at least twice the size of the other, lined with leather-bound books on both sides. Behind the well-polished desk sat a small man wearing a grey coat over a white shirt with a wing collar. His appearance was mild, even benign, but his eyes held the look of a cunning fox.

"Ah, Mr Sherlock Holmes and Doctor Watson." His voice was perfectly calm, but the welcoming smile had the artificial quality of that of a horse-racing tout. "We have crossed swords before, but never actually met."

He did not rise or offer his hand, but gestured that we should take the chairs at the front of the desk. We did so and he smiled wistfully, while waiting for Holmes to explain himself.

"You are indeed known to me," my friend confirmed. "On three occasions you have deflected the arm of the law from justly punishing those whom my investigations have exposed. I am aware of your activities, sir, as you are aware of mine."

Mr Kitterly's expression did not alter. "Come, come now, Mr Holmes, our system of law is not perfect. There are bound to be instances when innocent men, and sometimes women, become entangled in crime simply because they are unfortunate enough to be nearby when such acts are committed. I consider it my duty to help these luckless souls for justice, as you know, is always depicted as a statue wearing a blindfold."

"A fact of which you have invariably taken advantage," Holmes replied dryly.

Perhaps I imagined it, but I thought that the solicitor's smile had narrowed.

"Much as I would be delighted to discuss such matters with you gentlemen for the remainder of the afternoon," he replied, "my curiosity compels me to enquire the reason for your presence here. Please be brief, as there are currently many demands upon my time."

"We are here to ask how you arranged for the father of my client, Mr Cedric Topham, to appear to return from the grave. I have assured him of a rational explanation, but he is quite distressed, nevertheless."

The smile narrowed further. "I am neither a surgeon nor a magician, Mr Holmes. Mr Jeremiah Topham was a client and friend for many years. I attended his funeral and, always in my experience, the dead remain so."

"Except when they *seem* to return, of course. How did you achieve such a deception?"

"I really cannot....."

"I should emphasise," Holmes interrupted, "that needless further investigation would prove most irksome to me. Delay in settling this matter would doubtlessly result in a review of my files, and who knows what forgotten uncompleted affairs I may discover? For example, the three instances that I mentioned, The Calderware swindle, the Mossington land scandal and the unfortunate investments of Mr Fergus Dooley have never, in the eyes of Scotland Yard, been satisfactorily concluded. Until now, I have withheld the essence of these crimes for my own reasons, but they are weighing with increasing heaviness upon my conscience."

Mr Kitterly, suddenly in obvious discomfort, shifted in his chair. "I would have nothing to fear from such disclosures, naturally. I had no inkling that these events remain unfinished. Nevertheless, I do see your difficulty in the case of Mr Topham and, coincidentally, I was presented with a most curious proposition in connection with his father. I will explain it to you in detail, and you will surely see that I have broken no law."

"He is as deceitful as any man I have encountered," I remarked a short while later as we searched for a cab.

Holmes nodded. "He knows that nothing as yet can be proved against him, although he all but admitted the hiring of someone to falsify the handwriting of our client's father. However, it is now within my grasp to bring this affair to a satisfactory conclusion. As you see, Watson, a hansom has just deposited its fare near the corner. If we are quick we will procure it before that rather stout gentleman who has emerged from the tailor's shop and then, after a pause to despatch telegrams to Lestrade and our client, it will convey us back to our lodgings. I will be surprised if all has not become clear by the time Mrs Hudson is ready to serve our dinner."

As it was, we had been in our rooms long enough for our landlady to serve tea before clearing away the cups, when our visitors arrived within a few minutes of each other. Inspector Lestrade was accompanied by a man who, I saw at once, bore a striking resemblance to the portrait of Mr Jeremiah Topham that was displayed at our client's house in Paddington. The 'ghost', as Holmes had insisted from the beginning, was indeed a man of flesh and blood.

No sooner had introductions been completed and our guests settled in their seats, than the door-bell rang once more. A few minutes passed before Mrs Hudson announced Mr Cedric Topham, and our client stepped into the room. As he caught sight of Inspector Lestrade's companion he halted in mid-stride, expressions of confusion and outrage competing for dominance across his features.

"Who are you, sir?" he demanded of the stranger. "You are not my father, you have not so many years behind you but, by God, you resemble him greatly." He turned to my friend. "Do you have an explanation, Mr Holmes?"

Holmes rose and approached him. "Calm yourself, Mr Topham. Everything will be made clear to you presently. Allow me to introduce Inspector Lestrade of Scotland Yard. This gentleman who is so like your late father in appearance is Mr Matthew Borwood."

Mr Topham's puzzlement was not appeased. "But who....."

"You will recall your father's frequent absences from his home and his wife. This will come as something of a shock to you, but the fact is that he had a second family. The mother of Mr Borwood is deceased, she was a serving girl who raised him, mostly alone." He paused to allow our client to absorb the shock. "Pray come and sit over here, the chairs are all taken but the sofa is comfortable." He turned to address all three of our guests. "Before we begin, would anyone care for tea?"

Everyone declined, and after we were all seated Holmes waited as a heavy cart rumbled along Baker Street. When the vibrations had ceased, he began:

First, Mr Topham, I should make it clear that Mr Borwood impersonated your father under the threat of blackmail. Theatrical make-up was applied to cause him to appear older, and it was arranged that you should become aware of him always at a distance. His only crime in this was in agreeing, although again under threat, to drive that cart last night with intent to injure you."

"That is not so!" Mr Borwood cried. "I intended only to cause you to be afraid."

"That is something that has to be decided, hence the presence of the inspector."

Our client glared angrily at Mr Borwood.

Lestrade nodded, and spoke harshly to his prisoner before Holmes continued.

"The perpetrator of this deception knew of your family circumstances and took measures to convince you that your father still lived. He had his body exhumed and disposed of secretly, anticipating that you would seek confirmation that such a resurrection had taken place."

"Why?" asked our client when Holmes paused in his narrative. "What possible purpose lies behind all this?"

"The answer to that lies with your uncle, Mr Albert Topham, who recently died in South Africa. I see from your shocked expression that you were unaware of his passing. You will perhaps be equally surprised to learn that he had amassed a considerable fortune to which your father was the heir." Holmes paused again, probably to allow our client to absorb his words. "All of which, upon *his* death, becomes yours."

"So someone, who knew of this, sought to substitute this man," he again glanced contemptuously at Mr Borwood, "in place of my father to receive my inheritance? I see the reason for the cart now, it was feared that I would discover the scheme and raise objections, as I most certainly would have. Doubtlessly, it was intended that I should be murdered."

"No, no!" Mr Borwood shouted. "The persecution was to be intensified until you were certified as mad, by a doctor who would be paid to do so. You were intended to be committed to an asylum until the legacy was settled. Then, when there was no chance of your interference, measures were to be taken to bring about your release." He looked frantically around him, searching for a sympathetic face. "That is the truth, I swear. It was meant that you should regain your

236

freedom, never knowing what had been taken from you. You would have been unharmed; *he gave me his word.*"

"About whom are you speaking?" Lestrade enquired gruffly. "There is someone else behind this, I can see."

"Someone Mr Topham knows well, as did his father," Holmes said quietly.

"But *who*?" Our client asked in exasperation.

"None other than Mr Bradwood Kitterly."

Mr Topham appeared more astounded than he had a few moments before, when he had learned of his uncle's death and his inheritance. "Our family solicitor? Surely not. The very idea is ridiculous. He and my father were friends for many years."

"Quite so. They shared an intimacy that gave Mr Kitterly a position of power over your family, although they did not realise it. It does not surprise me that he proved unworthy of their trust, since he has a long history of crime that Scotland Yard has been unable to prove until now."

Lestrade affirmed this with a murmur, and Holmes turned his attention to Mr Borwood.

"Mr Kitterly has long been a great asset to the criminal classes, and will continue to use his position to be so," my friend adopted the air of someone who has just received a revelation, "unless of course you are prepared to give evidence that will convict him?"

Mr Borwood stared at the carpet, saying nothing.

237

"You have stated that he was blackmailing you to secure your obedience," my friend persisted. "Pray be so kind as to explain how this was possible."

He raised his head and looked directly at Holmes, and for the first time I saw anger in his face.

"Mr Kitterly *made* it possible. He said that I had murdered a man in a drunken brawl. He showed me the evidence he had manufactured and told me of the false witnesses he has arranged. Were it against someone else I, myself, would have been convinced."

"The scoundrel!" said I.

Holmes turned to the inspector. "What do you say, Lestrade? Has Mr Borwood committed any crime, apart from driving the cart last night?"

"Nothing I would call serious," the little detective replied.

"Then, Mr Borwood, will you assist us in bringing this man who is a disgrace to his profession to justice. You alone can do this."

Mr Borwood looked at each of us in turn, his expression one of anxiety. Then he summoned some inner strength and smiled for the first time.

"Yes," he said. "Yes, I will do it."

"Capital!" Holmes sat back in his chair. "Watson, be a good fellow and ask Mrs Hudson to bring us refreshments. There is no reason why we should not fortify ourselves as we discuss this further."

The Adventure of the Tinkers Arms

More than three decades has passed, since Mr Sherlock Holmes began his career as a consulting detective. As I have recorded before now, I have been privileged to accompany him on many of his cases and often witnessed his extraordinary powers of reasoning and deduction. Since then times have changed, as they inevitably do for us all – our dear Queen has been succeeded by His Majesty King Edward VII who has himself been succeeded by His Majesty King George V, the hansom cab has been largely replaced by mechanically driven vehicles and, of course, my friend and myself have advanced in years. Overshadowing all of these things is the outbreak of a war with Imperial Germany that Holmes has long predicted, a conflict of such horror as we could never have imagined.

He and I, now considered too old to serve our country, were able to meet less frequently since his retirement. Nevertheless, Holmes abilities showed no signs of diminishing, at least none that I could detect, and there were still occasions when our friend Inspector Hopkins saw fit to enlist his assistance to solve some cases that had puzzled the best of the official force.

Holmes had recently been recalled to the capital from his Sussex retirement by his brother, for reasons he would not disclose to me except to say that the matter was now concluded. Our September reunion was by arrangement, and after a great deal of reminiscing we discussed at length the news of the first Battle of Marne and the common expectation (shared by neither of us) that the war would be over by Christmas.

"At least," said Holmes, "the German retreat will serve to save Paris, for now."

I was about to reply when a police coach came to a halt as we left the Langham Hotel, a scene of some of Holmes' past adventures and our current rendezvous point, as he was staying there for the duration of this visit.

"It's Hopkins," I observed. "He has seen us and is approaching. How could he have known of your presence in London? Perhaps his passing is by chance."

Holmes shook his head. "I think not. Suffice it to say that my recent business with Mycroft had a connection with Scotland Yard. I would not put it past my brother to recommend my services if the official force appeared to be in need of them. Perhaps he's even involved in whatever Hopkins is bringing to us."

The inspector, looking a little older than when I had last encountered him, greeted us with great enthusiasm. After much shaking of hands and asking after the health of both my friend and myself, he appeared slightly at a loss for words. I noted that his vehicle had waited.

"Come, Hopkins," Holmes said then, "let us not continue this pretence that our meeting was accidental. I'm in London for but a short time, but I'm prepared to assist you, should that be necessary."

The official detective nodded wearily. "I would appreciate that, Mr Holmes."

"Perhaps you would care to join Watson and myself in my room, where we can discuss this as we avail ourselves of some strong coffee."

"Thank you sir, but I would prefer it if you gentlemen would accompany me now, if you would be so good. For reasons not made clear to me, the victim appears to be of some importance."

Holmes glanced at me, and I assented. The prospect of yet another adventure together, as in days gone by, warmed my heart. I confess to feeling extreme nostalgia.

"Very well, Hopkins, where are we bound?" my friend enquired as we crossed the street to board our transport.

The inspector signalled to the driver, who acknowledged and set the horses off at a fast trot as soon as we were settled.

"An inn - The Tinkers Arms on the Commercial Road," was the delayed reply. "Do you know it?"

"I've heard mention of it before."

"I've also heard of that place." I interjected. "It has been a hostelry since the 1600s."

"A very old establishment indeed, Doctor." Hopkins agreed.

Holmes gestured for Hopkins to continue with his elaboration.

"A man was found dead in bed, in a locked room. He had checked in last night. The innkeeper had noted that the fellow had remained in his room all night and today as well. Finally at mid-morning, he became concerned, and when there was no answer, he summoned the police. For some reason that I've yet to ascertain, the Assistant Commissioner had the local constable on the beat keeping an eye on the place, and he immediately sent word to the Yard. At the Assistant Commissioner's direction, I took four constables and, acting on the assurance of the innkeeper that the man was still inside but not answering repeated calls, we broke down the door."

We raced through the streets of London, clogged with late afternoon traffic, until we came upon the Commercial Road. It still seemed strange to me to encounter mechanical vehicles among the traditional horse-drawn carriages and coaches, which were now disappearing from the roads at a rate which I found to be alarming. This thoroughfare too, was changing – not yet safe, but not as dangerous as it had once been in the days of The Ripper. It crossed my mind that the London that Holmes and I had known for so long was giving way to a new era.

"What do you know of the victim?" Holmes asked Hopkins, breaking the silence that had settled upon us.

The inspector produced his notebook. "According to items found in the dead man's pockets, he is - or was - Doctor George Higgins. He's British, but seems to have been resident in Germany for some time, and returned here only yesterday by way of the ship *Rheda* which docked at the Isle of Dogs. As far as I could tell, the man was strangled or suffocated." Here he glanced at me quickly, "Yet there were no marks on the body. Perhaps you would be good enough to confirm that, Doctor Watson?"

I nodded. "Of course."

"No marks?" Holmes repeated.

"The police doctor who attended found none."

"Very well. When we arrive we'll see what can be learned."

The inspector nodded. "I would like to hear your conclusions, gentlemen."

By my estimation it was no more than a quarter of an hour later when we came to rest outside a long low building with a thatched roof. The discoloured walls were badly in need of whitewash, and the structure was strengthened by buttresses in several places. My impression was of a building in its decline and several centuries old.

We alighted and entered through a low doorway edged with black beams. The innkeeper, a portly fellow with a sombre expression, made to approach until Hopkins held up a hand.

"We will speak to you later, Mr Berry. For now, we must again see the room."

"A moment." interrupted Holmes. He turned to the innkeeper. "You summoned the police?"

The man nodded. "I did."

"What made you suspicious that something was amiss?"

"At first it didn't seem unusual for him – the doctor – to be in his room for so long, and it's none of our business if a guest chooses to stay in like that. They sometimes do. But finally, when a night and much of the day had passed, I became concerned."

"Who is employed here? Is there a Mrs Berry?"

"No sir. Just me and a couple of girls in the kitchen. I don't make enough to hire any additional help."

Holmes nodded. "How were you certain that Doctor Higgins was still in his room? Couldn't he have gone out and locked the door behind him?"

Berry shook his head. "There are only two ways out of the building – by way of the rear door, which is always kept locked, and through the front which is readily visible, as you see, from both the kitchen and the reception area. That's how I knew he was still here."

"But why summon the police? Could you not have opened the door yourself and verified whether he was there without breaking it down?"

"There is only one key to the room, you see, and he had it with him." He glanced at Hopkins. "The inspector saw it, it was on one of the tables, where he must have left it after locking himself in, and...."

"Yes?"

"And before he killed himself. The glass on the table – well, we've seen this kind of thing here before. I knew enough to summon the police before disturbing the room."

I glanced at Holmes, and then Hopkins. Until now there had been no mention of a glass, but perhaps this was part of what Hopkins wanted us to examine without benefit of his own opinions.

The landlord looked from one to the other of us, as if seeking some sort of approval for his actions, but Holmes simply said, "We shall speak with you again, Mr Berry. Now, if you will excuse us?"

Berry nodded and bowed his head as he moved aside to allow us to pass. I had expected to climb the short flight of rather rickety stairs that confronted us, but instead the inspector ushered us to one side of them and down a short corridor beneath. That the door had been forced was clearly evident, and I could sense Holmes' silent groan as he saw the plentiful signs of the police investigation within the small shabby room. With Hopkins and myself beside him, he stood on the threshold in silence, his eyes taking in every detail of what lay before us.

"See what you can learn from the body," he then instructed me.

I approached the magnificent and ancient four-poster bed that I could well imagine to have been part of the original fittings of the place, while my friend produced his lens and proceeded to examine the scuffed wooden floor while the inspector looked on.

Not long after, Holmes got to his feet. Shaking his head, he looked at our friend reproachfully.

"Dear me, Hopkins, after all these years you still haven't learned to restrain your men. A herd of cattle could have been no more successful in destroying whatever evidence this room contained. Had you called me in earlier, I could have learned so much more."

The inspector looked downcast. "I'm sorry, Mr Holmes, I...."

"No matter," Holmes turned away abruptly and approached the bed. To my surprise he didn't immediately focus his attention on the body, but took out a handkerchief and collected a sample of liquid dregs from the glass standing on the night-table that had been mentioned by Mister Berry. He then folded the scrap of cloth carefully and returned it to his pocket before pausing to sniff the air. I also became aware of a curious medicinal smell. I leaned over to the nearly empty glass, recognising the strong odours of port and opium. Then I looked back towards the dead man.

I shortly concluded my examination. "He has been dead for nearly twenty-four hours," I announced. "Probably not long after he checked in last night. Whatever the possible effect of the substance in the glass, I can confirm that this man died of suffocation, rather than strangulation,"

"Not opium poisoning?" asked Holmes.

I shook my head. "It may have been a factor in knocking him out so that he could be murdered without resistance, but it isn't what killed him. There are no signs of an opium overdose, in spite of Mister Berry's theory."

"There is one other factor to consider," said Holmes. I paused to allow him to speak, but he motioned that I should continue.

"As I have already stated, this man died of suffocation. Something has been pressed against him – it is as if a pillow were held to his face and upper chest. Observe how his nightshirt is flattened. Also, his features, particularly the nose, have been flattened somewhat as well."

"And yet," Holmes noted, "the pillow shows no signs of being used for such a purpose – no indentations from the facial features or dried spittle, for instance, and nothing else in the room could have been used for such a purpose."

"In any case," added Hopkins, "the room was locked. No one could have entered to smother him because the sole key had been withdrawn from inside the door." He pointed, and we saw that it lay on a small mahogany table in a corner.

"And this is the only key?" Holmes asked.

"The innkeeper assures me so."

Holmes took a step back. "So it would appear that an external cause for this man's demise is unlikely. That being so, we are left with…"

He left his observation unfinished, and turned to rap upon the walls with his knuckles. Beginning at the side of the bed, he progressed around the room past the single window until he arrived at the opposite side. His face bore no expression as he finished, but a moment later he turned to the four-poster itself. He stretched his body until he could almost reach to where the supporting posts met the canopy. He then leaned into the space beneath, directly above the body and from where he could inspect the underside of the canopy, before straightening himself once more into an upright position. The ghost of a smile appeared on his lips, and was gone in an instant.

Near the window, which he had already examined, he turned to face us. For a few minutes he was still and appeared deep in thought. The only sound was the murmur of activity from the bar-room in another part of the building.

"This window cannot be opened," Holmes declared. Centuries of old paint and repairs have sealed it forever."

"We had already ascertained that," responded Hopkins.

Holmes then went through the dead man's personal effects, meagre as they were. The small leather case contained a change of linen, a toothbrush and tooth powder, and little else. Holmes satisfied himself that there were no secret compartments or spaces within the case.

"Did Doctor Higgins have other personal effects of any significance?" he asked.

Hopkins shook his head. "No. His pockets contained a few coins, a handkerchief, and his notecase, which held only a pound or two and a bit of German money. Nothing more." He then took a step closer. "Have you discovered anything? My men and I have already carried out most of the inspections that you have yourself, but as always I thought it best to let you proceed with your own methods. There is nothing to be found, is there?"

"Oh yes, Inspector," Holmes replied. "There was much to be found. I know how the murder was committed, but I will not disclose my findings without enough proof for you to use in court. I also intend to find out the circumstances leading to this man's death. When I've discovered something of his prior activities in Germany, I believe all will be much clearer. You may expect an arrest to result from this incident, and I should be able to conclude my investigation within no more than a day or two. Now, before we leave, a few more words with the innkeeper, I think."

"The glass on the table," continued Holmes when we found the man in the bar. "Do you think Doctor Higgins used it to kill himself?"

Berry nodded. "It wouldn't be the first time that a guest here has taken his own life. It's thoughtless, sirs, choosing that way to depart, leaving us to deal with the remains."

"Did he show any indications of what he planned?"

"None. He checked in last night, saying something about just having arrived in London by ship, and went immediately to his room. He didn't come out, nor have any visitors, and we didn't see him again."

"He went to his room with the only key? Why is there no other? Surely to have one made would be more economical than the necessary repairs following breaking down the door?"

Berry lowered his gaze. "The other was lost long ago. I just never got around to having another made. Money is always a bit tight, you see...."

Holmes nodded, and then said, "You have two girls who work in the kitchen. Are they here now? They are? Excellent. We may learn something from a quick word with them." He abruptly turned and vanished into the rear of the building, giving no indication that the inspector or I were invited or required.

Hopkins had only time to ask Berry one other question – how long had he owned the inn – and to hear the response "Fifteen years." - before Holmes returned. He seemed satisfied, and we departed soon after.

The inspector appeared a little disappointed during the return journey, but Holmes was of an unusually light-hearted disposition. We parted company with Hopkins outside the Langham, he having received an assurance that a message concerning our progress would reach him at Scotland Yard very soon.

"What do you say to having something to eat?" My friend asked. "As you know, the roast beef here is excellent."

Although I lived just a stone's throw away at the eastern end of Queen Anne Street, I agreed at once, and we enjoyed a sumptuous meal together. Holmes said nothing more about the Tinkers Arms until we had drunk the last of our coffee.

"I miss my chemical table in our old lodgings," he remarked then. "Is it possible that Barts would allow me to use their facilities, do you think?"

I thought back to our visit to the inn. "You wish to analyse the sample you took, to confirm that it contains opium?"

"And port, and anything else that might be present. That is my intention."

"I would imagine that even if your reputation is insufficient, my familiarity with many of the staff there would serve as a guarantee of your admission."

"Thank you, old friend. If you are agreeable then, we will proceed there at once."

On our arrival, he remarked that the laboratory section of the hospital had changed little, except for some expansion, in the years since he had seen it last. Having gained permission, he began his experiment while I chatted amiably with old friends, some of whom introduced me to more recent members of staff. Thus, it didn't seem long before Holmes reappeared, and we made our farewells.

"Did the analysis turn out as you hoped?" I asked him as we descended the steps.

"The result was exactly as I expected. It was a strong solution of opium. Mister Berry made a mistake by leaving it on the table and then claiming there is only one key."

"You believe the innkeeper administered the drug?"

"I know it. You will recall that I said there was one other factor to consider. Did you notice nothing during our search of the room?"

I thought for a moment, and then I understood. "The opium was in the glass, which may or may not have already been in the room or brought by the doctor, but there was no bottle or container for the opium to be found. How, if the opium belonged to Doctor Higgins and he intended to drink it, did he bring it into the room?"

"Excellent, Watson." Holmes raised his walking-cane, and a cab came to a halt in response. "You will recall that Berry stated that once the doctor checked in and went to his room, he was seen no more. I confirmed this with the two girls in the kitchen – neither of whom seemed to be very likely to lie convincingly. Mister Berry was emphatic that there were no visitors, so his story has painted a scene where Doctor Higgins was absolutely alone in his room, locked in with the sole key, and with a glass of opium-laced port – all meant to imply that he killed himself. But there was no bottle. That was Berry's mistake."

"Yes," I said. "That, and the key."

"Exactly. It's absurd that he wouldn't have a duplicate key – in fact I suspect that most of the keys there are interchangeable in those ancient locks. By trying to convey that the doctor killed himself in a locked room, yet forgetting to leave a bottle to hold the port or the opium before it was poured into a glass, Berry has destroyed the credibility of his tale."

"I think that you had some sort of suspicion before we ever arrived, that all wouldn't be what it seemed. You seemed to have already heard of The Tinkers Arms when Hopkins first mentioned the place."

"Perhaps. We may be able to verify my suspicions at our next stop."

I was curious, but I knew from of old that to press Holmes on his intentions would avail me nothing. He would explain when he felt that the time was right. Meanwhile, our driver was swerving around other carriages and the numerous and unfamiliar horseless vehicles, at a rate that I found alarming. When we entered St James Square, I was not sorry to alight.

I saw that Holmes was aware of my plight - possibly my colour had faded. His expression was one of faint amusement.

"Why are we here?" I asked him as we entered through massive double doors.

"I need facts to confirm my theory."

"About the Tinkers Arms?"

"Precisely."

We approached a bespectacled librarian who informed us that my old friend, Lomax, wasn't working that day. I had hoped that he would make quick work of Holmes' questions, but my friend was prepared to carry out the research himself. The librarian directed us to a section devoted to local history. It occurred to me that I might pass the time in the medical section, but Holmes seemed - as he sometimes did - to read my mind.

"No, stay with me. This will not take long."

He was quite correct. By the time I had taken a seat at a nearby reading-table, he had scanned the shelves and selected a thick and well-worn volume. I did not interrupt as he seated himself and quickly turned the pages, soon to find the information he sought and to pore over it briefly. Presently he closed the book and got to his feet.

"That, I think, will suffice."

"You have found something of relevance?"

"I confirmed my supposition."

As we looked for a cab outside in St James Square, I quickly reviewed all that I had learned in Holmes' company. It all appeared to me as a series of facts which I couldn't yet associate with that which I knew must have occurred.

"How do we proceed now?" I asked as one of the few horse-drawn vehicles nearby came to a halt before us.

"At this moment, we cannot," he replied. "I've solved part of this mystery, but my conclusions are valueless without confirmation. This I will attempt to arrange during the evening, from my room in the hotel. As for you Watson, I suggest you use this hansom to return to your home. I'll see you in the morning as before, and I expect us to learn much then. Enjoy your dinner, and kindly convey my respects to Mrs Watson."

With that he turned away abruptly, doubtlessly to seek his own conveyance to return to the Langham. As the driver urged the horse into a brisk trot, I felt some relief at travelling at a more sedate and familiar pace. The London we had known was fading before our eyes, and I understood that neither Holmes nor I would fit comfortably into the altered times ahead. I recalled that he had described me, several times during our years in Baker Street, as 'the one fixed point in a changing age'.

My wife was, as always, glad to see me. She raised no objections when I explained that I must meet Holmes again the following day, saying only that I should be careful and make allowances for being no longer young.

I had intended call upon Holmes in his room the next morning, but as I alighted from the hansom I saw that he waited near the main entrance to the hotel.

"Did you succeed in making your arrangements?" I asked him when greetings had been exchanged.

"I did indeed. In his reply, Mycroft indicated that he'd expected my telegram. We have an appointment in," he consulted his pocket-watch, "a little more than half an hour from now."

"I recall that you saw his hand in this from the beginning."

"It occurred to me that many of his agents must be concerned with the war. If he did involve us yesterday, it's because he's short-handed. If he confirms my suspicions about Doctor George Higgins, then only one piece of the puzzle remains." He considered for a moment. "If you can restrain yourself, say as little as possible in my brother's presence."

We arrived at Whitehall not long after, to be escorted to a room much different to that I remembered from previous occasions. Gone was Mycroft's former grand office and voluminous desk. His current wartime sanctum was much smaller, rather drab with two tiny but heavily-curtained windows.

"Sherlock! Doctor Watson!" He welcomed us in a most uncharacteristic manner. I hadn't thought him capable of such joviality. "It has been too long since your last visit. I think you will find these chairs comfortable. Do sit down."

As we complied, settling ourselves around a small conference table, I reflected that his corpulence appeared greater than before. Like his brother, his hair now had more than a suggestion of grey, but beyond those things his appearance had changed little.

"Mycroft, I believe you know why we are here," Holmes began. "No, I think we will forego tea, thank you."

The elder Holmes leaned back in his chair. "Ah, yes of course. I was keeping an eye on this situation, and when Higgins was murdered, and as I knew you were still in the capital, I thought you might be able to advise Inspector Hopkins. How goes the investigation, may I ask?"

"As you know, I had returned to the capital at your bidding," my friend answered obliquely, "and concluded that other little matter that was presented to me. Vindley has already been arrested.

He will be tried *in camera* and will do no more harm, but my participation in this affair doesn't mean that I'm at your disposal to correct every other difficulty that your department might encounter. You will recall that I have now retired, and it baffles me that you have not done so yourself."

"But if I did, Sherlock, what would I do with my remaining days? I myself can only spend so long at the Diogenes Club every day before boredom sets in. You, I know, find that state of mind as abhorrent as I do myself."

"Very well. But I cannot proceed with this, unless I am better informed."

Mycroft nodded, suddenly becoming as serious as I ever remembered him. "I wanted you to initially investigate without any preconceived notions, but now I will tell you what I can. As for discretion, I don't have to mention to you both……"

The stony silence lasted for a few moments, before the question was brushed aside. This wasn't the first time that Holmes and I had been questioned as to our trustworthiness, however lightly, and I thought it inconceivable that Mycroft could still find it necessary to do so. It was most likely, I concluded, that he was conforming to long-familiar and inflexible regulations.

"Who was this man, Doctor George Higgins?" Holmes asked then.

Mycroft hesitated, perhaps deciding how much to divulge. "Higgins has held a senior post in a Berlin hospital for many years. Many of his patients held a high rank in the Kaiser's armed forces, and he was able to supply us with much that he learned from them. He was an expert at interrogation, you see - top of his class in training, and spoke their language fluently. Until now, none of the

Germans had the slightest suspicion of the true reason for his occasionally odd and out-of-place questions, skilfully hidden among queries about medical conditions. Much to my great regret he was recently discovered, however. We don't how that came about, but he fled Germany by steamship and hid himself within the Tinker's Arms on arrival here to await contact.

"We're not sure why he chose there, instead of coming straight to me for protection. When we learned where he was, we felt that he had some specific reason for going there, and that we should see what was happening instead of immediately intruding. Then he was murdered, and since we already had the place under observation, the Assistant Commissioner was able to step in quickly. It was at that point, Sherlock, that I brought you in. The war has left my department rather short-handed."

"And will be more so, I fear" said Holmes, "before this conflict ceases."

"I knew of course that you would suspect that I was somehow involved. If you hadn't wired me asking for an appointment, I would have reached out to you." He adjusted his bulk in his chair, causing the leather to squeak. "It has occurred to Scotland Yard, I hope, that the innkeeper at The Tinkers Arms is undoubtedly an agent of the Kaiser."

"Perhaps not, as yet," my friend said, "but I certainly intend to point it out to Hopkins. The evidence suggests that it is most likely Doctor Higgins met his end in that supposedly locked room at the hands of the innkeeper. This will become increasingly apparent, I think, and more will be revealed before this affair is concluded."

"I look forward to hearing of the man's arrest, and also to your report, Sherlock." Mycroft struggled to his feet and glanced at the casement clock that ticked away behind us. "But now I have a meeting with the Home Secretary to attend, so I will bid you gentlemen good-day."

As we walked along Whitehall a few minutes later, I could tell that Holmes' displeasure had not lessened.

"My report!" he repeated, scowling. "Sometimes, I believe that my brother believes that I'm one of his lackeys."

"He is a clever and devious man, Holmes, such as his occupation requires, but it cannot be denied that he takes advantage of your kinship."

Holmes shrugged, dismissing the subject. "Nevertheless, this affair must be finished. Then I shall return for a short rest in Sussex with my bees." He looked around. "Raise your cane to summon the cab that has just appeared near the corner, and we'll repair to the Langham for an early luncheon. On the way, I'll need to stop at a Post Office to despatch a telegram to Hopkins."

"To advise him about the innkeeper?"

"No. Simply to suggest that he withdraw any of his men who might still be lingering at the Tinkers Arms - although it would still be as well to have him and a constable or two there but less obviously in evidence by tonight. You may care to inform Mrs Watson that you won't be home until the early hours - if you intend to see this through with me."

I smiled. "As ever."

"I knew my Watson would not have changed."

In accordance with Holmes' instructions I found myself crouched behind a bush near the inn later, an hour before midnight approached. Here, I couldn't be seen from the road, but there had been little traffic in any case during the last hour. The lights of the inn had been extinguished, one by one, and the place had been in complete darkness for some little time. I moved to relieve the cramp in my legs, causing an owl to be disturbed from its nearby roost. Startled by its outraged cry, I kept to what shadows I could as I approached the building cautiously.

Holmes had explained earlier his intention to stay overnight in The Tinkers Arms. In disguise he would, if it were possible, occupy the same room as the murdered doctor. He seemed certain that this would bring about the conclusion of this affair but, apart from arranging to admit me through the locked door at the rear of the building, he would say no more.

I moved with stealth, entering a sheltered passage and then moving through the near-blackness to the rear of the inn. As I neared the door it swung open noiselessly, to reveal a tall grey-haired man with a drooping moustache. Had I not expected Holmes, I wouldn't have recognised him, as he led me along the short corridor and into the room where Doctor Higgins had died. Moving silently, he lit a dark lantern. Then, in the faint light, I saw that he held a finger to his lips. "Remain still as much as possible," he whispered. "I do not expect a long wait."

"For who?" I said almost soundlessly. "The innkeeper?"

"The same. When I hinted to him that I was a colleague of Doctor Higgins, following behind him from Germany, he showed me to this room at once."

"Then we will discover how the doctor met his death?"

"That is what I am anticipating. Did you notice that the room door has been quickly repaired? And once again there is supposedly but one key, which I have in my possession. When Berry pressed a glass of port on me before I retired, I accepted it, and it stands untouched on the night-table. You will see, if your eyes have adjusted to the poor light, that I've rearranged the pillow as a substitute for my body."

As we waited, he proceeded to restore his normal appearance, making no noise. No more conversation passed between us, and our vigil continued. It wasn't as long as others I've shared with him, and after some little time during which the silence was disturbed only by the occasional cry of a night-bird, we heard a far-off clock strike the midnight hour.

Soon after, I saw a faint glow pass along the foot of the door and we heard the muted sounds of someone ascending the stairs. Beside me, Holmes stiffened like a hunting hound that has espied its prey. A few minutes of silence elapsed before a strange vibration filled the room. Surprised, I looked around but could see nothing to account for it. As the noise increased, Holmes gripped my arm.

"There!" he said excitedly. "Do you see?"

I was about to whisper that I had failed to understand what it was that he had alluded to, when the faint light revealed to me that the canopy of the bed was descending. It continued to do so as we watched, emitting a harsh scraping noise before finally coming to rest flat upon the sheets.

"You would have been smothered," I said in a low voice as the sound ceased.

"Indeed, as was Doctor Higgins and others long before him," Holmes replied.

I saw that the canopy had been forced down by a thick spiral pole of hard wood, which when retracted was hidden near the ceiling. The pole extended down by several feet.

"Berry operates it from the room above. We must now act quickly, before he reverses the mechanism."

With that, Holmes crossed the room to the night-table. Setting aside the lamp and the glass of port, he then quietly lifted and laid the table onto the top of lowered canopy. After several more moments had passed – long enough to be assured that the occupant of the bed would certainly be dead - the canopy began to ascend, but more slowly because of the additional and unbalanced weight. In the silence that resumed, we could hear the grunts and oaths of Mr Berry, and the loud creaking of ancient wood as he attempted to turn the screw and restore the canopy to its usual height. The night-table was carried upwards until it met the ceiling, when the mechanism jammed, whereupon Holmes threw open the door and left the room hurriedly. I followed, and seconds later saw him as he opened the rear door by which I had entered the building previously. He stepped outside, and then the shrill tone of his police whistle split the silence. When he reappeared, it was in the company of Inspector Hopkins and two burly constables who, at Holmes' direction, rushed past us to hurry up the narrow staircase. The inn shook with their steps.

Immediately after the constables' heavy tread upon the stairs came a surprised shout, followed by angry curses, mostly in German. Berry was then half-dragged downstairs and into the dead doctor's room where we waited to confront him. His face was reddened with effort from his struggle with his captors.

"What is this?" Hopkins demanded of him, pointing to the disabled canopy.

"A device that kills enemies of the Kaiser," was the innkeeper's reply, in a voice quite unlike that which he had used previously. He now spoke in educated tones, precise and cold.

"Yes, a killing machine if I ever saw one," the official detective agreed. "It's the hangman for you, and no mistake. What do you have to say for yourself?"

"I'll say nothing except that your little victory here tonight, yours and Mr Holmes', is worthless against the might of my homeland. Doctor Higgins is gone, and so is the information that he carried to England."

Holmes gave him a steely look. "Possibly a list of German agents operating here? Ah, I see from your smile that I'm correct. An unfortunate, but not insurmountable problem. But, tell us, why did he come here first?"

"Because I was on the list," answered Berry – or whatever his true name was – "and he was arrogant enough to believe that he could implicate me further before reporting to his superiors. But he had not been careful enough. He had inadvertently made his intentions known, to one who he believed was a colleague but was actually working for us, before leaving Germany. So it was, that I had been notified and was waiting for him." He stood straighter, as if about to salute. "So you see, there is nothing left to say. You have me, but you lose."

Hopkins scowled. "Take him away, Cranwell."

The constables complied at once, forcefully, with the former innkeeper uttering oaths of increasing severity in two languages as he was bundled out of the room.

"Doubtlessly he has accomplices, near at hand," Holmes said, "but Mycroft's people are certain to get him to reveal them, as well as the names on the doctor's lost list if he knows them."

"Always supposing that Scotland Yard doesn't do so first," Hopkins remarked with a quick smile. I had no doubt that whomever made the attempt would be successful. (And in fact, they were.)

Suddenly, weariness pressed hard upon me, and I could hardly stifle a yawn.

"Forgive me for keeping you away from your bed," Holmes said.

"The police coaches that I ordered should be arriving soon," Hopkins volunteered. "Permit me to offer you transportation to your hotel, Mr Holmes, and you to your home, Doctor. A good night's work was done here, I think."

So it was that Holmes and I stood before the darkened Langham in the early hours. As I lived so close, I'd dismissed the driver who offered to carry me the short distance on to Queen Anne Street. The streets were silent and deserted, save for the occasional appearance of a constable on his beat.

"Holmes, I had the impression that you already knew what we were dealing with, almost from the start – from the time Hopkins told us the name of the inn. Tell me - was that so?"

In the meagre illumination of the street-lamp, my friend nodded.

"You are correct. Once we arrived in the doctor's room, my suspicions were verified. There were a number of indicators. You will recall that I examined the bed-posts after viewing Doctor Higgins' body. That was because I'd noticed that the varnish had worn away near their highest point. At first I thought that was because its application was insufficient, but when I saw similar marks on all four posts I realised that it was from a common cause."

"The scraping noise, as the canopy descended," I ventured.

"Precisely. As you know, I took a sample of the liquid remaining in the glass from which Doctor Higgins had evidently drunk, for analysis. The resulting identification of opium told me that it was intended that he should be incapable of rising from the bed. The innkeeper was therefore certain that his victim couldn't avoid a rather unpleasant death."

"I see," I said hesitantly, "but why was it necessary for us to visit the library, in St James Square?"

Holmes acknowledged the greeting of a passing constable, who evidently recognised him. "That was a long shot, to gain final confirmation of my understanding of the situation. The volume that I consulted was a historical record of unexplained events in various London locations. I discovered that there was an unsubstantiated account of a murderous device at an inn during the sixteenth century. It was installed by a Spanish family who purchased the inn, their intention being to cause the death of various naval commanders who habitually stayed there after their ships had docked. This, I believe, was in preparation for the forthcoming Armada."

"Monstrous!" I retorted.

"Quite. There were several other instances recorded over the following centuries, as certain individuals came to know the purpose of the device and used it for their own ends. It had long been rumoured that The Tinkers Arms was the inn in question, and the victims all died in the same manner as Doctor Higgins. When his death was described to us, I remembered that the inn has a dark history." He shook his head slightly, as if disbelieving of the cruelty of men to each other. "But now, Watson, it's quite late, and you can be back in your home within just a few minutes. Goodnight my friend, and don't look so crestfallen. I'll call on you in the morning before I leave, and I am certain that with this war continuing, we will share more adventures before too much time has passed."

The Adventure of the Troubled Wife

During my long association with my friend, Mr Sherlock Holmes, I often witnessed his acute evaluation of the circumstances surrounding a case, before he brought it to a successful conclusion. Many of these investigations were of conventional crimes, but as time wore on he became increasingly inclined towards situations of a strange or unusual nature, such as I have received his permission to relate here.

It was not long after the capture of Colonel Sebastian Moran, that we returned to our lodgings one morning after an exhilarating walk in The Regents Park. Holmes, having newly resumed his Baker Street activities, was in high spirits.

"I do not think it will be long, Holmes, before more clients present themselves here. Scotland Yard is aware of your return, and the newspapers will ensure that word spreads quickly."

Divesting himself of his hat and coat, he answered cheerfully. "More so than you apparently expect, old fellow. Surely you cannot have missed the young woman on the far side of the street, as we set out? Or if you did, her presence near the corner on our return did not escape your notice, surely?"

"I confess to being aware of her only just now. You believe then, that she will bring you a new problem?"

"Her behaviour suggests it, but we shall see." He had been about to settle himself in his armchair, but instead he crossed the room to peer down from the window. "Ah, it seems my surmise was correct. She has made her decision and is approaching our front door."

The door-bell rang and was almost immediately answered by our landlady, who showed the woman into our sitting-room.

"Mrs Ellen Cooper, to see Mr Holmes."

"Thank you, Mrs Hudson." As she withdrew, my friend gave our visitor a curious look, but made no comment except to welcome her with rather less enthusiasm than was his usual practice.

Mrs Cooper was an imposing figure. Quite tall and slim, she wore a costume of dark green with a matching hat. I would have said she was in her early thirties, and it seemed to me that her most prominent features were hair of a rich auburn and a wide, sensuous mouth.

When we were all seated and introductions had been made, I offered her refreshment which she politely refused, stating that she was anxious to confide in us.

"I see that you have experienced some anxiety of late," Holmes said. "Very well. Take a few moments to place your thoughts in order, and then relate your experience from the beginning. Include even the smallest detail, for they are often significant. There is no need to hurry."

"Thank you," she began. "I hope you will not think that I have wasted your time, for the fear that blights my life haunts me in a dream."

I glanced at my friend, wondering if he would dismiss her at once or recommend that she should consult a priest, but he simply nodded, his expression unaltered.

"Nevertheless, pray continue."

She glanced at me, then back to Holmes, and attempted to quell her restless fingers.

"In my dream, it is midnight. I am taken to a place where I am surrounded by fearsome images, grim statues that, I somehow know, would wish me great harm were they alive. I am forced to lie upon a long table and I cannot see clearly, as great black birds swoop down on me from above. You see, gentlemen, I have had a morbid fear of birds since childhood, when my father enjoyed the sport of falconry. He took me to a display, probably to arouse my interest in such things, but one of the hawks attacked me for a reason that was never discovered."

"Forgive me," I interrupted, "but did the creature leave marks upon you?"

"Mercifully no. It plucked the hat from my head and pecked my skull until I bled. The wounds healed, and any remaining scars are hidden beneath my hair."

"Do the birds attack in silence?" Holmes asked then.

"Not at all. Their cries are deafening, screeches that chill my blood."

"Yet they have not actually pierced you in any way, nor shed blood as in your childhood experience?"

"No. I awake in my bed convinced that my dream is reality even in the cold light of morning, but I have no wounds. This does not diminish the effect on me, however. The horror of it persists."

We sat without speaking for several moments, the only sounds reaching us through the half-open window. The cries of newspaper sellers, the voice of someone prophesying doom should we fail to repent, and that of a woman selling apples, floated up to us.

"Does this occur every night?" Holmes enquired.

She shook her head. "No, there is no pattern to it that I can see. Over the past three weeks I have dreamed of this on two nights together, then single nights spaced apart irregularly. On one occasion there were three together, I think."

"Does your husband not confirm that you have remained in the bed-chamber throughout the night?"

"He and I have been separated for almost three months now, sirs. He knows nothing of this."

"May I ask why you are apart?"

Her head went down, and her gaze fell to the floor. "I long for a child. He thinks only of his business."

"I am exceedingly sorry to learn of this. What, in fact, is his profession?"

"He sells houses, usually to foreigners who wish to live here."

"I see. Has it occurred to you that he might be responsible in some way for your difficulties? This has to be the work of someone who is familiar to your aversion to birds, you understand."

Mrs Cooper nodded. "I have thought of this, of course, but I cannot see how."

"Tell us please," I said then, "of the method used to prevent you from rising from the table."

"I am strapped down, by my arms."

"And are there no marks from this, visible on awakening?"

"None. In the dream, a man with a white beard binds my arms with thick cloth, before securing the straps."

"Thank you." I murmured thoughtfully, "That is quite clear."

"Have you sought medical assistance on this matter?" Holmes asked.

"It was my first thought to do so," she replied. "Doctor Pressingham dismissed the dream as nothing more than fanciful, and prescribed a sleeping draught."

"I perceive that you are not excessively rich, but are you expecting to receive a large sum of money in the near future? An inheritance or legacy, perhaps?"

Our client looked surprised at the question. "Nothing of the sort, as far as I am aware."

"Have you lived at your current residence for long?"

"About six months." She considered for a moment. "Yes, it was about three months before my husband left that we bought the house."

Holmes got to his feet. "That, I think, is all I need to know for now. Thank you, Mrs Cooper, for presenting us with a most unusual case. One thing I must ask of you, and that is that you despatch a telegram to this address immediately or soon after rising, the next and all subsequent mornings after you experience the dream. Kindly give your address, and any other details that you believe may be necessary, to Doctor Watson. I have no doubt that you will hear from us before long."

With that he surprised me, by turning abruptly and crossing the room to the window without a word of farewell. I thought this most discourteous, and resisted the urge to apologise for Holmes as I escorted the lady downstairs and procured for her a hansom.

He had not moved by the time I re-entered our sitting-room.

"Holmes," I called, waiting until he had half-turned towards me before continuing, "it is most unlike you to treat a lady so." Then a sudden thought struck me. "Did you approach the window so hurriedly, in order to determine whether our client had been followed here?"

He shook his head. "No, Watson, that is not it at all. But you may take it that I am accepting this case for no other reason than to satisfy my curiosity as to its actual nature."

"I can see the mystery here. We are unsure even, if there are known criminals involved."

"Are we, old fellow?" He replied, and would say no more on the subject.

We heard nothing the following day, but the morning after brought the message that told us that Mrs Cooper had again been troubled by the nightmare. When the breakfast things had been cleared away, Holmes took to his armchair and remained there for some time in deep thought.

When I returned from my practice in the early afternoon, he was replacing some volumes of his index to the overburdened bookshelves.

"You have been adding to your scrapbooks, then?"

"No, consulting them. It was necessary, I felt."

"Have you made any progress?"

"Only in recognising the necessity of watching our client's house tonight," he said slowly. "The visitations, if we may call them that, occur randomly and not in accordance with a pattern. Now that there has been another, it is as likely as not that it will be repeated tonight. If that fails to happen, I will keep guard for the next few nights. You are looking tired, Watson, so I will not expect you to accompany me."

"If I can be of service, I will of course go with you," said I, slightly affronted. "I can sleep for a short while in my room until dinner-time. It will be sufficient."

He smiled faintly, as he reached for the tobacco in the Persian slipper, but there was something cold in his expression. "I thought I knew my Watson."

It was half an hour before midnight when our hansom halted beneath a great old oak further along the street in Clerkenwell, near the address that Mrs Cooper had given us. Holmes had explained to the driver, who he had used previously, that waiting and the possible following of a carriage would certainly be involved, and that the fare would be increased accordingly.

Nothing came of our vigil, and we returned to Baker Street after almost three hours. However, on repeating our observation at the same time the following evening, we were rewarded by the appearance, not long after midnight, of a one-horse carriage driven by a man wearing a broad-brimmed hat and a dark cloak. As it came to rest near Mrs Cooper's door, a small man with a white beard wearing a tall top hat jumped to the pavement and promptly let himself into her home.

"Holmes!" I whispered. "Mrs Cooper mentioned a man with a white beard."

"She did indeed. We may now be able to see to where she is taken."

"It was no dream, then?"

In the meagre light from a distant street-lamp, I saw him shake his head. "I never thought that it was."

Moments later the white-bearded man reappeared, guiding Mrs Cooper as one would a blind person. She wore a coat over long night-clothes and moved mechanically, her gaze fixed and spellbound. They boarded the carriage and set off, and my friend waited until they were out of sight before rapping with his stick as a signal to our driver. We moved slowly, ever conscious that we might be noticed at this hour on these deserted roads. Our driver was clearly experienced in such stealth, waiting until the carriage was about to turn the corners ahead before proceeding along each street that we came upon.

Our surroundings deteriorated considerably, within a short while. The terraced residences were replaced by decrepit shops, and then by warehouses in dimly-lit thoroughfares. We found ourselves in a street that boasted two taverns, one on each side. Each was in darkness, but from one of the doorways a figure emerged, staggering uncertainly. It crossed the street at a ragged run, constantly fighting for balance and directly in our path. I heard our driver exclaim as the horse reared in fright, and it took some little time to calm it. The drunken figure had disappeared by the time we were able to continue, and as we turned the next corner I was surprised to see the carriage we were pursuing only then increasing its pace ahead.

Holmes made a satisfied sound, which told me he had learned something, and he shouted to our driver: "The carriage is slowing down. There is no need to disguise our presence now. You may overtake and return us to Baker Street."

Our driver shook the reins, and the horse broke into a trot. As we passed our quarry we could see that it was now empty. I looked at Holmes, who answered my question before it was asked.

"You saw, Watson, that the carriage was not as far ahead as would have been expected, despite the slight delay in our progress caused by our drunken friend back there. That was because it also had come to a halt, though which of those warehouses Mrs Cooper was taken into I cannot yet tell."

"Should we not make some attempt to rescue her?" I asked urgently.

"I am not inclined to do so now. You will recall that, although she has suffered repeated frights, she has come to no physical harm. There is more to this, I think."

The following morning the expected telegram arrived, and Holmes announced that he intended to make use of the details previously supplied by Mrs Cooper, and visit her husband in Soho. I had anticipated my need for the time to accompany him, and had therefore arranged for Michaelson, who was new to the profession, to act as locum and add to his experience. As soon as the breakfast things had been cleared away, Holmes reached for his coat and his ear-flapped travelling cap.

"A hansom has just delivered a fare just across the street," he said after a glance from the window. "If we hurry, we will catch it."

We were soon on our way. The streets were busier at this hour, slowing our progress, and causing Holmes to show signs of impatience.

"I would prefer to find Mr Cooper at home, rather than to arrive at his premises after he has left to conduct his business," he said.

I consulted my pocket-watch. "We may still be in time."

Holmes nodded but said nothing more until the hansom deposited us in a street of two-storey terraced houses that looked as if they might once have been the work-places of doctors or solicitors before becoming residential.

"Number seventeen, the address that Mrs Cooper gave us, is over there," I pointed out.

We crossed to the other side of the street and Holmes rapped upon the door with his stick. Presently it was answered by a hunched-up elderly man in butler's attire, with the eyes of a bloodhound.

My friend wished him good morning. "We are here to see Mr Uriah Cooper," he announced. "My name is Sherlock Holmes, and this is my associate Doctor John Watson."

"I regret that Mr Cooper is not at home, sir."

"Has he left then, for his employment?"

The man hesitated, which was its own answer.

"Kindly tell him that the matter is urgent, and concerns his wife," Holmes insisted.

After staring fixedly at us for several moments, the butler appeared to make up his mind.

"Very well, Gentlemen. Please step inside."

We entered a hall that smelled of polish, and was hung with a portrait of our Queen and another of a stern-looking looking man in old-fashioned dress. An ancestor, I presumed.

The butler disappeared awkwardly down a corridor.

After a while a young man with the air of one who is in a great hurry emerged from the passage. I saw that he was tall, but not of Holmes' height, and that he apparently regarded us as one would a servant.

"Jenkins tells me that you are here on my wife's behalf," he began at once. "You may tell her that the divorce will proceed regardless. I expect to receive documents to that effect soon, which I will sign and forward to her representatives. Is there anything else, gentlemen?"

"Because she wishes for a child?" I said with some exasperation.

"Child, be damned. I will not be associated with anyone of such kin. She should have been honest with me from the beginning."

His remarks confounded me, but before I could reply I was silenced by a warning glance from Holmes.

"That is not the purpose of our visit," he told Mr Cooper. "I am a consulting detective and we are investigating your wife's repeated abductions and subsequent torment."

Our host raised his eyebrows. "What is this nonsense? Something she has invented to delay things, I'll be bound. If you seek to accuse me of anything, you should know that I returned from

France only yesterday. Whatever she complains of, I had no part in it."

"I understand that you sell houses to foreign residents."

"I do indeed, and I am quite sure that Monsieur Etienne Broullade, a prominent Paris businessman, will be prepared to swear that I was in his company almost constantly, during the past four days."

Holmes nodded, and changed his approach. "Are you aware of your wife's excessive fear of birds?"

Mr Cooper looked surprised at the question, but laughed harshly. "More of her foolishness. I have noticed her avoid sparrows and pigeons, during our walks in St James Park. I found her actions embarrassing."

"You did not think to enquire the reason?" I asked.

"Why would that be necessary? She has her habits, as has everyone else. I did not concern myself with her strange little ways when we were together, and I certainly will not trouble to do so now." He pulled a pocket-watch from his waistcoat. "But, although this has been somewhat entertaining, I must conclude it now. I have a client waiting, and a carriage will arrive for me very soon. Good-day to you, gentlemen."

He turned abruptly and disappeared the way he had come. The butler was at once beside us to promptly show us out.

"Odious fellow," I remarked when we had walked away from the house.

"I perceive that there is some mystery to you, Watson, as to Mr Cooper's explanation of his estrangement from his wife. All will be clear to you eventually but I can say now, with utmost conviction, that they deserve each other."

His tone, which I was familiar with, told me that it would avail me nothing if I attempted to extract an explanation from him. Accordingly, I remained silent. Moments later, he surprised me by answering one of my unspoken questions.

"I am satisfied that he is not concerned in our client's predicament."

"How then, do we proceed?"

"Come, Watson, is it not obvious? Who else is likely to be aware of our client's aversion to birds?"

"A sibling, perhaps?"

"She has none."

Not thinking to ask how he knew, I considered briefly. He hailed a passing cab. "Ha! She consulted her doctor."

"Precisely. We shall see if Doctor Pressingham is willing to shed any light on this."

The physician, as it turned out, proved to be a small man who was at first very guarded.

"You will appreciate, gentlemen," he said from across his desk, "that I am not at liberty to discuss my patients' ailments."

"As I doctor myself, I understand of course," I replied. "But in general terms, surely."

As I spoke, I noticed that Holmes was unusually quiet, his eyes roving around the room. When they settled upon Doctor

Pressingham, I could have sworn that a fleeting smile was on his lips.

"I believe that Mrs Cooper is suffering from delusions," the physician said. He rubbed his unshaven face. "I prescribed a sleeping draught, in the hope that she would rest sufficiently deeply to overcome these fantasies, but I am sorry to learn that this treatment has been unsuccessful. Clearly, it will be necessary to further examine the lady and define her ailment more precisely. I must make a note of it."

He took up a pencil and scribbled something on a pad, and to my surprise I saw that Holmes stared at me, inclining his head. There was no mistaking the signal: it was time to leave.

We got to our feet and I thanked Doctor Pressingham. He gave a little bow in return and we left.

"He is about to begin his surgery," I concluded as we passed through the waiting-room that was quickly filling with coughing and bandaged patients. "Rather late, I would have thought."

"But not surprising," Holmes said as we reached the street. "You must have observed how tired he appeared, and that he was unshaven. The man has been up most of the night."

"I am not unfamiliar with his situation," I reflected. "One call after another, during the night, is exhausting. That is surely the cause of his weariness."

The smile returned to Holmes' face for an instant. "Perhaps. But now I think we will return to Baker Street for the late luncheon that I see you are anticipating."

A hansom waited further along the street, and we procured it at once. My friend did not prove to be very communicative during the journey, but I felt disposed to interrupt his thoughts to satisfy myself on certain points.

"Holmes," I began, "your behaviour in the presence of Doctor Pressingham puzzled me."

He turned from the window. "How so, old fellow?"

"You were unusually hesitant. I cannot think that this was simply because you thought it better that I converse with one of the same profession."

"Not for the first time you underestimate yourself, Watson. However, on this occasion I knew that you would ask appropriate questions while I observed the Doctor and the contents of his surgery."

"And did you learn anything, from your inspection?"

"Exactly what, by now, I expected to learn. But look, we are almost at our door, and I recall that Mrs Hudson has a fine roast chicken for us."

The meal was fine indeed, and we ate mostly in companionable silence. When we had consumed dessert and our coffee cups were empty, I enquired as to our next excursion.

"I think the time has come for us to examine the warehouse of last night," he announced. "Although I expect that there will be less for us to see than there would have been previously."

Again we boarded a hansom, and my friend instructed the driver to follow the route of the night before, which he explained. After we alighted and our conveyance had left us, I saw that there were in fact four warehouses in a row, each securely locked. Holmes paraded before them briefly and then stood before that which he had selected.

"Are you certain that this is the one?" I asked him. "Or are we to try each in turn until we succeed."

He gave me a disdainful look. "My dear fellow, you surely know my methods better than that." After a moment he stood back and pointed to the entrance doors that were set into the much larger gates. "Observe, the lock of the door on the extreme left is corroded to the extent that it would be impossible to release without forcing the mechanism, while the next door has grass and weeds that would prevent its movement. The lock of the third door is in similar condition to the first, and so we are left with the fourth entrance. A further indication is the smear of oil on the relatively new lock."

"As always, you make it appear so simple," I said, feeling rather foolish at my failure to notice.

We looked up and down the short street, to ensure that it was deserted. A cat, sitting atop a dustbin, watched us with disapproving eyes, but we were otherwise unseen.

Holmes produced his pick-lock, and in minutes I was pulling the door open. We stepped into the half-light of the cavernous space before us, and were immediately halted by the odious smell and a cacophony of noise.

"What is this place, Holmes?" I said, confused.

"Exactly what I had surmised. You will recall that Mrs Cooper related that she actually *heard* the birds that threatened to attack her. Before you is the explanation of that, and of the remainder of her description of the place of her torment."

My eyes had become adjusted to the poor light. The place appeared to be one of storage for fairground or circus accessories, long abandoned judging by the profusion of dust and cobwebs. Along one wall were several tall cages, one of them having toppled onto its side. Within them a number of large black crows were imprisoned. The noise from their cries for release, and probably for food, was an assault upon the ears, and the stench from their droppings tainted the air. Along the walls were the remains of statues with roguish and evil expressions, not of stone but of some sort of imitation material such as you would expect in a theatrical production. Many were smashed almost beyond recognition.

In the centre of the expanse was a full-sized billiard table, with straps affixed to the sides. Clearly the place of Mrs Cooper's restraint.

"There, Watson!" Holmes pointed into the shadowy void above us, and I followed his direction.

A number of pulleys hung from the ceiling, their chains swaying slightly. These were the method of lowering hideous likenesses of predatory birds, made more so by the addition of grotesque colouring, to within a few feet of the table beneath.

"That must have been a disturbing spectacle," I observed. "Horrifying, to say the least of it".

Holmes nodded. "Indeed. Imagine how they would appear if presented with the accompaniment of the cries of those poor caged creatures, to a woman drugged and mesmerised."

"Is that what happened to Mrs Cooper?"

"Undoubtedly. It also appears that our pursuit last night was detected, since some effort has been made to clear out this place. There was insufficient time, I imagine, to complete the task."

I looked around us, at the scene of the lady's torment. "But why, Holmes? What is the purpose of this? Who is behind it?"

He crossed the room and began to release the captive birds, after unfastening, by means of a long pole, the single skylight to open for them a path to freedom. When the last one had flown, he restored the window to its former position before answering.

"As to who is behind this I can name but one, and there certainly is another. Regarding why, I have as yet only a suspicion. Here is a partial explanation."

Before he began, we made our way back to the street. We were, I think, both glad to breathe clean air again, and to be out of that depressing place. Before my friend could continue, I presented my own deduction.

"So, Doctor Pressingham is concerned here, either alone or with an accomplice."

"Excellent, Watson. Kindly explain your chain of reasoning."

"This place has been cleared overnight, no doubt with the intention of impeding our investigation. For one or two men this would be a task of several hours, and rather wearying."

"Quite so."

"And we noticed Doctor Pressingham's tired condition."

"Indeed, and you are correct, although this could have been from one or more summons to his patient's bedside through the night as you suggested. But when coupled with my observations of the certificates on his surgery wall, and the fact that he supplied our client with 'a sleeping draught' his guilt appears more likely."

"What did you see there?"

"Along with his qualification of medical competence, there was a similar diploma indicating that he is proficient in mesmerism. You see how this explains the condition of Mrs Cooper, at the times she was abducted. The effects of the preparation taken before retiring would have been enhanced by hypnotic means to induce her dream-like state of unreality."

"That seems likely, but it is not conclusive, surely?"

"Not at all, but it became so when I observed the tiny white hairs adhering to the sides of the doctor's face. Evidently, in his depleted state he had not taken sufficient care in removing his disguise."

"The white beard!" I shook my head. "But what can he hope to gain by this?"

"Not he, but they. You will recall that there was a coachman assisting. I have my own suspicions regarding his identity, or at least of several probabilities."

Sometime later, we retired to our usual chairs after an excellent dinner. I began to read one of the medical journals that had long awaited my attention, expecting to pass the evening quietly. Holmes, however continually displayed signs of restlessness, until he finally lowered his newspaper while shaking his head.

"It is of no use, Watson. I cannot settle."

"Something troubles you, then?"

"I have given some thought to how this case should proceed. There are several sources that could provide useful information, and I cannot sit here when I could be consulting them. Do not let me disturb you, old fellow, for I do not require your company on this occasion. Most probably it will be late when I return, but I will share with you what I have learned at breakfast."

With that he rose abruptly, took up his hat and coat and was gone. Feeling somewhat disconcerted, I poured myself a glass of brandy and continued reading.

I retired later than was my usual practice and lay awake for some time, but I did not hear Holmes return. I had almost finished a hearty breakfast next morning, by the time he appeared.

He waved away his own meal, and requested that Mrs Hudson bring a large pot of coffee. As I finally laid down my knife and fork, I thought him deep in his own thoughts and unforthcoming.

"Well, Holmes, were your enquiries of last night successful?" I asked when I could bear his silence no longer. "Do we now know the reason for the doctor's actions?"

He met my gaze unsmiling. "I believe that I am now conversant with much of what surrounds the situation. Certainly, Doctor Pressingham, though not innocent, is as much a victim as our client."

I prepared myself to listen to a possibly long narrative, but Holmes had barely begun when I heard a carriage come to rest outside our door. Listening, we heard our landlady speak briefly before admitting someone, and then quick footsteps ascended the stairs.

"You have another client, I believe."

"I think not. The footfalls are familiar."

My doubts that he could so easily have ascertained this were dispelled, immediately Mrs Hudson entered our room.

"Mrs Ellen Cooper, to see Mr Holmes," she announced as before.

"Pray come in, Mrs Cooper," Holmes called, at the same time surprising me by gesturing to our landlady to withdraw without offering our visitor refreshment. "I perceive from your anxious state that there has been a recent development in your situation."

She sat at my invitation, and recovered herself after a few minutes.

"There has indeed," she said then. "No more than an hour ago, I was accosted, no, attacked, while walking along Clerkenwell High Street. An elderly, white-bearded man attempted to abduct me."

Holmes and I exchanged glances.

"Did you recognise your assailant?" Holmes asked.

"I did not," she answered thoughtfully, "but after a few moments I experienced the strangest feeling that I knew him from my past. I was, however, unable to remember, and quickly dismissed the notion."

"If this was an attempted abduction, as you surmised, I would expect that there was some method of conveyance at hand?"

"Why, yes, a carriage waited not far off. I found this to be odd though, since the white-bearded man seemed not to be in a hurry to force me into it. He seemed to have more interest in speaking to the small crowd that had gathered around us. I was appalled when he accused me of approaching him for immoral purposes, but before I could speak in my own defence he fled to the waiting coach and was promptly driven away."

"Most curious," I commented.

Holmes did not appear to experience the confusion that I felt.

"What occurred immediately after this man left?" he enquired.

"The crowd, about five men, I think, were unanimous in their condemnation of me. One would have thought that the man's accusations were the truth. Then a constable appeared and they rushed to him, with the result that I was taken to the local police station where I was charged. It was only with the intervention of Jordan, my brother and a well-known businessman, that I was released on bail."

Holmes looked up sharply. "Were the 'witnesses' gone by then? Pray think carefully before you answer, as it is of the first importance."

She shifted in her chair. "Yes, I am quite certain that I was alone except for Inspector Radcliffe, when I requested him to summon my brother who guaranteed that I would attend court when the trial takes place."

"Excellent. First I must tell you, Mrs Cooper, that you need have no further fears of torments during the night such as you have experienced recently. Doctor Watson and I have ensured that your enemies are unlikely to continue with this. The outrage of this morning was another attempt to achieve the same result and I believe, having identified this, that we can soon bring this affair to a satisfactory close."

"You have now deduced the reason for all this, Holmes?" I said with some surprise.

He nodded. "Is it not obvious, when you have recognised the common factor of each event?"

"Obvious?" she repeated. "I confess to being confused. What is the purpose of these people? What have they against me?"

"Their purpose, unless I am very much mistaken, is to remove you from your residence for some little time."

Mrs Cooper and I stared at him without comprehension.

"Consider the likely outcome of each of their schemes," he continued. "After repeated ordeals over several nights would not the effects upon you, together with your account of the experiences, cause you to be thought either insane or on the verge of such a condition? Sooner or later, it is almost certain that you would be committed to an asylum or a private clinic. As for the events of this morning, will you not be imprisoned if found guilty? In each case, your premises would be left empty."

Her expression became puzzled. "But I keep nothing valuable there. If their intention is to enter in my absence, then for what purpose? I think, Mr Holmes, that you may be in error."

"It may not be valuables that they seek." My friend, unusually, showed no sign of offence. "That, I intend to confirm shortly. You have stated that none of those speaking against you were present at your release so, since they were certainly hired to play the part of accusers, they will have reported that you were detained. Therefore your house will, according to their understanding, be empty tonight. I suggest that you pack enough clothes for, say, three days, and take up residence in a distant hotel, or stay with an obliging relative if that is possible."

"You intend that we should watch the house tonight." I concluded.

"I do, and several subsequent nights, should that prove necessary. I do not expect that it will be so however, since today's events reveal that these people have become desperate, but it would be unwise to ignore the possibility."

"Yes, I see that," she agreed. "But who is the instigator of this, Mr Holmes? Is it my husband? Is it anyone of my acquaintance?"

"You will know all, very soon," he assured her. "But for now, I have certain arrangements to make."

Recognising her dismissal, our client rose at once.

"Thank you, gentlemen. Good day to you."

She smiled faintly and turned away, but it was not until she had almost reached the door that Holmes replied.

"Good day, Mrs Cooper," he answered before I could speak. "Incidentally, I found it not without interest, investigating on behalf of the former Miss Ellen Braithwaite."

With her hand on the door-knob, she became very still. "You knew, then?"

"I did." He returned her gaze expressionlessly. "From the moment I first set eyes upon you."

"Yet you accepted the case I brought to you."

"Only because, as I remarked at the time, it appeared to be interesting."

She regarded us somewhat resignedly, nodded and closed the door quietly after her.

"Holmes, will you be so kind as to explain this to me?" I asked with some irritation as we heard her descend to the street. "I feel you have kept me in the dark, for far too long."

We had settled ourselves in our chairs, before he replied. "I suppose I do owe you an explanation, old fellow, but as you are aware, it is my custom not to share such information until the problem is solved. However, it has not escaped my notice that you have been less than pleased with my treatment of Mrs Cooper. Perhaps the reason will become clear when I explain that she is a member of one of the most notorious criminal families ever to terrorise the East End of London. Doubtlessly she allowed herself to believe that I would be deceived by her married name. The files of Scotland Yard record her numerous arrests for pick-pocketing, and one of suspected murder. This was never proven, but I have long since satisfied myself that her guilt was the most likely explanation for the outcome of the situation at the time. You will see then, that my fear was that her true intention was to involve myself, and possibly you also, in some sort of lawless enterprise, perhaps to provide an alibi. Fortunately, although I have guarded against this throughout our investigation, no suggestion of such a hidden intention has appeared."

"But she stated that her brother is a prominent businessman," I objected. "Surely he could never have obtained her release, were it otherwise."

"Jordan Braithwaite?" Holmes smiled, I suspected at my perceived innocence of the matter. "He is the not the first criminal to live beneath a veneer of respectability, and therefore to wield a degree of influence."

As I paused to consider this, vibration caused our half-open window to rattle. A brewer's dray, badly loaded and driven too fast, passed along Baker Street.

When all was quiet once more, I asked: "But what of Doctor Pressingham? I had assumed, from our previous enquiries, that he was responsible for this affair."

"Never assume anything, Watson," Holmes advised. "All deduction must be based on established fact. One of the informants that I consulted last night referred me to a former confidante of the Doctor who, after some inducement, revealed that Pressingham is being blackmailed. Apparently there was a scandal, years ago when he worked as a surgeon in Leeds. He was accused of drunkenness while operating. The patient died, and the family caused considerable uproar in the press. The Doctor's only chance to save his career was to change both his name and his residence, therefore he moved his practice to the capital. His troubles did not end there however, for his secret was known to another. A certain Mr Elihu Sanderson somehow came by this knowledge, and it was the Doctor's ill-fortune that this man was part of a criminal enterprise that rivalled that of the Braithwaites."

"He then, is the blackmailer?"

"Indeed." Holmes began to fill his clay pipe. "He has used his hold upon Doctor Pressingham to force his co-operation in the persecution of Mrs Cooper. I am quite certain that it is he who was the coachman who drove her to the place of her torment, as I am that there is something in that house that he desperately wishes to acquire."

"Since this man also is connected to a family or organisation of wrong doers, is he not known to Scotland Yard?"

"Lestrade had indicated many times how pleased he would be to get his hands on Elihu Sanderson. Two years ago, Sanderson was being sought for his part in the Tailors and Weavers Bank robbery, in which both a member of the staff and a constable were killed. He has not been seen since, and it is suspected that his family concealed him until it was thought safe to arrange a passage abroad."

"With such a risk, is it certain that he has returned?"

"One of my informants is prepared to swear that he has seen Sanderson visit Doctor Pressingham, several times."

"It's the hangman then, if he is caught?"

"Undoubtedly."

"Will you advise Scotland Yard of your conclusions?"

Holmes nodded his assent. "I have to leave briefly this morning, to ensure that certain arrangements have been made, and I will certainly telegraph Lestrade before I return. By all means spend the time reading or otherwise amusing yourself, old fellow, but after luncheon we should both ensure that our revolvers are well-oiled and serviceable. As soon as darkness falls we will set out for Mrs Cooper's residence, where we will lie in wait. As our adversaries have no means of knowing the extent of her absence, I expect them to appear tonight or very soon after."

The remainder of the day passed surprisingly quickly. Holmes' absence from our lodgings was as brief as he had promised, and we spent time servicing our weapons as he had recommended.

Mrs Hudson served roast pork for dinner, and I was continually aware of the darkening sky as we ate. By the time our coffee pot was empty all light had gone, and my friend wasted no time in springing to his feet and retrieving his hat and coat.

"It will be advisable to be there early," he said, "since our adversaries could arrive at any time."

A carriage awaited us, doubtlessly one of the 'arrangements' that Holmes had mentioned earlier. The driver was as before, a shrewd-faced man who was evidently no stranger to either the detective or his requirements.

There were few exchanges between us during the journey through the gas-lit streets. Holmes sat with his head upon his chest, while I watched the dramas that played in and out of the shadows. Beggars, urchins, women shouting at their husbands as they left them for an evening in the taverns and, now and then, watchful constables, all appeared briefly. Then our conveyance came to a halt, for we had arrived. As my friend had instructed, the driver reigned in the horse some little distance away. With weapons drawn, we alighted and moved stealthily towards our destination. A light mist had appeared, and Holmes paused momentarily to listen for what we could not see.

"There is another carriage, or at least a horse, at the other end of the street," he whispered. "I could hear the beast stamping its hooves. Take care, Watson, for they may already be here."

As we neared Mrs Cooper's house, I saw a light shine briefly.

"Did you see that, Holmes? You were right, our adversaries are already at work."

He held up a hand as a sign that he had heard, as we approached the door. Very slowly he turned the knob and we stepped into a hall that was dark save for the faint light from the sitting-room. We waited and watched shadows flitter across the ceiling as the lamp was moved from place to place, with no effort by the searchers to maintain a silence. I could not tell if there were one or more of them, but a wrenching groan of tortured wood suggested that floorboards were being removed.

Then, an exclamation told me that a discovery had been made. I turned to look at Holmes in the baleful illumination, and in doing so inadvertently stumbled against the door that confronted us. Immediately all activity and noise ceased, and I realised that my clumsiness may have betrayed our presence. Holmes clearly had no intention of waiting any longer regardless, for he threw open the sitting-room door and entered with a flourish.

"Good evening, Doctor Pressingham," he said lightly. "I trust you have found whatever it was that you were seeking. I am surprised to find you alone here, for I was certain that you would be accompanied by Mr Elihu Sanderson."

"You were correct, Mr Holmes," said a voice from the shadows. A tall clean-shaven man, extremely thin, stepped into view. "I am holding a 12-bore shotgun, with a most sensitive trigger. One tiny movement would discharge it, cutting both of you gentlemen down. Kindly drop your weapons to the floor, or I will be compelled to fire."

Holmes glanced at me and nodded, and we both complied.

"What were you searching for?" He asked.

"Something that will be of great benefit to my family and myself," was the reply. "It will allow us to clear the Braithwaites from the East End, once and for all."

"Tell them no more," pleaded Doctor Pressingham. "The less they know, the less will be the evidence against us."

Sanderson smiled grimly. "That does not concern me Doctor. As Mr Holmes can probably tell you, I have nothing to lose. Now, however, we are faced with an additional problem: where do we conceal two bodies, so that they will not be discovered until I am well clear of here?"

"No!" cried the physician, "Not murder!"

"But I am already wanted for murder," Sanderson shrugged. "They can hang a man but once."

He stopped suddenly and became very still. I could hear heavy footfalls outside, approaching the door. Two men, I estimated, constables from their angry commands to open the door in the name of the law. When there was no response, they began to beat on it with their fists.

"It seems that your difficulties have doubled," Holmes observed. "If you choose to begin shooting, the result will be four bodies in need of disposal."

Sanderson moved to the window. Watching us every second, he displaced the curtain slightly and glanced out. It was done so quickly that neither Holmes or I had the slightest chance to act. Indecision crept into Sanderson's face.

"If I croak these two, we might have a chance of getting away through the garden," he told the Doctor. "Go and make sure that the back door is unlocked. If not, break it open with anything you can find."

Doctor Pressingham remained still. Probably paralysed by fear, I thought.

Sanderson seemed surprised that his order had not been obeyed.

"Go!", he shouted with sufficient force for the cry to echo around the chamber.

Because of the poor light I had managed no more than an approximation of the size of the room. The door near the rear window led to the back entrance I presumed, and it was just possible to make out the narrow staircase that provided access to an upper floor. It was from this direction that a command rang out from a new, but familiar voice.

"Stay exactly where you are, Doctor. As for you, Sanderson, I have a heavy-gauge pistol aimed at your head. I am quite sure that I can fire before you can raise your weapon."

"Halloa, Lestrade!" cried Holmes. "I wondered how long it would be, before you made an appearance."

The little detective raised his eyebrows. "You knew, Mr Holmes? You were aware that I had concealed myself and was listening?"

"There were occasional creaks from the floor above. In an old house such as this, they are usually caused by movement. I therefore deduced that someone wished to remain undetected by Sanderson and Doctor Pressingham, and when the constables arrived unaccompanied by an inspector, no doubt to effect a distraction, I knew that you had responded to my message."

"I arrived early, since I had no way of knowing at what time either yourself or these two would put in an appearance."

Holmes nodded. "I trust that, prior to our arrival, their conversation was informative?"

"Indeed." A grim smile appeared briefly on Lestrade's bulldog-like face. "Sanderson is already for the hangman, but I was able to acquaint myself with the present situation also. It won't be long before we close this file, at the Yard." He raised his pistol further.. "No, Sanderson, do not attempt it. Place your shotgun on the floor slowly, before moving away from the door. Doctor Watson, I would be obliged if you would collect his weapon then lift the latch and allow my men to enter. We'll have these two in irons in no time, and I'll decide on Doctor Pressingham's part in this in my office."

I complied, and had hardly stepped back before the constables rushed past me. At Lestrade's direction the two prisoners were handcuffed and removed, by means of a police coach which appeared out of the mist.

"I must congratulate you, Inspector, said Holmes, "not only on your flawless arrangements, but also on saving Watson and myself from a possibly dangerous predicament."

Lestrade smiled broadly, an expression that appeared out of place on his normally serious face. "We do get it right sometimes you know, down at the Yard. I don't understand though, what those two were searching for. Sanderson said that it was something that would benefit his family. That can only mean that it would assist their criminal activities."

"We shall see," my friend replied, as we approached the other end of the room where the floorboards had been removed. I reached into the void and felt nothing, until my hand touched a thick notebook. I extracted it and handed it to Holmes.

He opened it and began to turn the pages. After a moment he gave it to Lestrade, with the comment: "I think you will count this as a good night's work, Inspector."

The Inspector examined it briefly, before taking on the air of someone who has discovered something precious.

"Why, this is a record, possibly a complete one, of all the crimes organised by the Braithwaite family for at least the past five years. All those involved are listed, as are the amounts they were paid for their misdeeds." He lowered the book. "Gentlemen, we have been after them for a long time, at the Yard, but have succeeded in prosecutions for only minor incidents."

"It therefore becomes clear, as they wished the ruination of the Braithwaites and to take over their enterprises, why Sanderson and his family placed such importance on gaining possession of this document," Holmes concluded.

"But why was it hidden here?" I asked.

"That we cannot tell with any certainty, as yet. I would speculate that Jordan Braithwaite concealed it within his sister's house for safekeeping without her knowledge, since she was genuinely puzzled as to what her tormentors sought there. Also, and I would remind you of your disapproval of my attitude towards her, Watson, the book reveals some recent instances of crimes carried out by Mrs Cooper herself. That, together with Dr Pressingham's fate, is for your consideration, Inspector."

The official detective nodded. "Thank you, Mister Holmes. I wonder how the Sandersons learned of this."

"Again, I can only speculate. Every now and then, each gang loses some of its men to the other. Usually the bodies are discovered floating in the Thames, after much ill-treatment. Might it not be that one of the Braithwaites, or a gang member in their confidence, disclosed such information during interrogation intended to reveal something different? This may or may not be true, but it is a possibility."

"And a likely one I would say, Mr Holmes." Lestrade placed the notebook in his pocket. "But I must get this to the Yard. I can hardly wait to see Gregson's face, when I tell him about it."

"Good evening to you then, Inspector," said my friend, before turning to me. "But as for us, Watson, I think we will now return to Baker Street. I have a particularly fine bottle of porter, which I think we will sample before retiring."

www.ingramcontent.com/pod-product-compliance
Lightning Source LLC
Chambersburg PA
CBHW051242260626
47162CB00002B/568